THE ASHLAND
PUBLIC LIBRARY

ASHLAND KENTUCKY

Max Brand's Best Stories

Frederick Faust (Max Brand) and his daughter Judy watch the horse races at Santa Anita, California.

Max Brand's
3 BEST STORIES

Edited by
ROBERT EASTON

DODD, MEAD & COMPANY · NEW YORK

Library of Congress Catalog Card Number: 67-14307

Printed in the United States of America
by Vail-Ballou Press, Inc., Binghamton, N.Y.

ACKNOWLEDGMENTS

THANKS are due Kenneth Millar for critical comments; Carol Brandt for advice and guidance; Darrell C. Richardson for use of information contained in his book, *Max Brand, The Man and His Work*, and in his *Faust Fanzine* magazines; and to William F. Nolan for information concerning Faust films.

Contents

Max Brand and Frederick Faust

MAX BRAND was the best-known pen name of Frederick Faust, creator of Dr. Kildare, Destry, and many other fictional characters who have won favor with readers and viewers the world over. Faust wrote under twenty pen names and his output exceeded thirty million words, the equivalent of five hundred and thirty ordinary books. Motion pictures and radio and television shows based on his work have been presented continually for many years. Few writers have reached more people.

Faust not only had a keen sense of what people wanted, he produced it at a rate that may seem unbelievable. Twenty pages, six thousand words, approximately one tenth of a book, was his daily stint. He seldom revised or rewrote. The script went straight to the printer. He literally talked in print. And the results were published almost everywhere, in *Harper's Magazine* or *Dime Detective, Saturday Evening Post* or *Photoplay, This Week* or *Esquire, McCall's, Good Housekeeping,* or *Western Story,* or in the world's book market into which he reached —perhaps flooded is a better term—in fifteen languages besides English.

This gigantic production covered practically every subject that prose fiction can deal with: fantasy, mystery, spy stories, adventure, the Arctic, the South Seas, westerns, war, historical romance, airplanes, sailing ships, spaceships, science fiction, animal stories, underworld, fashionable society, big business, and big medicine. For good measure he wrote plays and lyric and epic poetry on classical themes.

Nor was Faust's versatility confined to magazine and book production. More than three dozen motion pictures were based on his work. They included *The Untamed*, filmed three times, with Tom Mix originally in the leading role, and *Trailin'*, starring Douglas Fairbanks. *Destry Rides Again* has also been filmed three times, starring in succession Mix, James Stewart and Marlene Dietrich, and finally Audie Murphy. *Destry* was made into a successful musical comedy featuring Andy Griffith and Dolores Grey. *Dr. Kildare* has of course become a household term the world over, thanks to a dozen films and to radio and television shows as well as original novels and stories.

In Hollywood in the glamorous days of the late thirties and early forties when he was creating his Kildare character and many others, Faust was known as a prestidigitator who worked in white magic. He got ideas so fast, produced screen stories so rapidly, that the rumor spread that he was not one man but a front for a corporation. Actually he wrote every word himself on an old Underwood upright typewriter, using the traditional newspaperman's hunt and peck method.

Faust had been a globetrotting reporter in his time,

and it was in the role of reporter that he ultimately met his death. His life was filled with so many adventures and fascinating contrasts that his friends considered it a better story than any he ever wrote.

He was born in Seattle in 1892 and grew up in bitter poverty in the rural San Joaquin Valley of California. From childhood he was driven by bad health and family indigence to rely on his own inner resources, especially reading and thinking. An orphan at thirteen, he—as at least one of the following stories will show—worked on farms and ranches for a living. After attending the University of California at Berkeley, where he became a campus leader and outstanding literary figure, he became in succession a reporter, a sailor, a soldier, a ditch digger, a Bowery bum, and suddenly—all in one fabulous moment in 1917—a successful poet and prose-fiction writer.

Following his first successes came a period of extreme illness. He nearly succumbed to heart trouble, but fought his way back to health. Then he realized a dream by moving with his wife and children to Florence to live in a villa. Concealed behind his pen names and six acres of Italian olive trees and grapevines, Faust wrote poetry in the mornings and in the afternoons and evenings dashed off prose fiction of unparalleled quantity and variety.

Interspersed with cruises to the Greek islands and motor trips through most of Europe (during which he regularly carried his typewriter and typing stand in a trunk at the back of his Rolls-Royce or Isotta-Fraschini and regularly pounded out the twenty breadwinning pages every morning before continuing his trip) were periodic returns to the United States to confer with his literary agent, Carl Brandt, about markets.

"Our problem this year as usual is how to distribute your output of seventeen hundred thousand words," reads Brandt's record of one of these meetings.

Seventeen hundred thousand words a year. This equals twenty-five ordinary length books. And sometimes his annual output exceeded this remarkable figure. And notice that Brandt says *distribute,* not *sell.* There was always a market for Faust's work. He sold 99 per cent of everything he wrote. He goes on selling.

As he grew into a sort of one-man literary movement behind his aliases of Max Brand, Evan Evans, George Owen Baxter, Peter Henry Morland, David Manning, George Challis, et al.—names which not only concealed his identity but gave outlet to his versatility and greater coverage to his market—he was in keeping with the spirit of a fabulous time.

Sometimes a magazine, such as *The American* or *Western Story,* would have two or three stories or novels by him in a single issue, but under different pen names, of course. As many as five United States publishing houses besides several more in Europe and elsewhere were engaged in keeping his output moving.

But Faust was much more than a mass producer or a virtuoso with words. His statement is basically the statement of the affirmative possibilities of life. His king-size heroes and queen-size heroines are evidence of what he thought men and women can be—and do. It is worth noting that he wrote about spaceships as well as sailing ships and believed in the importance of myth long before it became fashionable. He often presented his convictions in terms of myth. He brought forward out of the past the timeless figures, Odysseus, Hector, Achilles, Penelope, Andromache, Briseis, and clothed them in chaps and blue jeans, or whipcords and tweeds, or gold lamé, established them in the United States West, or New York, or Timbuktu, and let them spell out the age-old lessons of courage, love, strength, wealth, or of cowardice, hatred, weakness, and poverty. Intolerance was foreign to him, as the following stories will show. His vision was one of generosity and good will. He is a supremely democratic writer and his essential message is that human resources have almost no limits.

High goals, giant achievements, obsessed him. He was even a big man physically, standing six feet four inches and weighing two hundred and twenty pounds, with gigantic appetites for life, for eating, drinking, loving, working, friendship. His literary masters were the giants Homer, Shakespeare, Chaucer, Rabelais. His personal heroes included King Arthur and the Duke of Marlborough, two that he shared with John F. Kennedy. Yet he belittled his massive prose effort and preferred to think of himself as a poet writing in the tradition of the ancient Greeks. His life was a series of giant contrasts, from poverty and obscurity to wealth and fame, to death on the battlefield in the final struggle against Hitlerism.

A grandfather nearly fifty-two years old, he had gone to Italy to write the story of the United States combat infantry in action. Instead he wrote the last chapter of his own story—that night of May 10, 1944—attacking uphill in the dark with the inexperienced G.I.'s against Field Marshal Kesselring's heavily entrenched, veteran German Army. He carried no weapon except the branch of an olive tree which the G.I.'s had cut and shaped for him when, as a war correspondent, he refused to go armed. He agreed to carry it as a kind of joke that might be good for morale.

Carrying the olive branch of peace, telling stories of mythological heroes of old who had gone into battle carrying clubs, he ended his fabulous career.

Ended? One of his several publishers announced that it had enough Max Brand material on hand to continue issuing Max Brand books for at least a hundred years.

From the Himalayan mass of literature that he left behind, certain stories stand out. Some of these he himself chose as his best. Others have been selected as representative.

As a comment on his versatility it is no more than fair to say that F. Scott Fitzgerald might have written "The King," Jack London "The Wolf Pack and the Kill," Dashiell Hammett "The Silent Witness," but only Faust could have written them all plus the others.

It seems to me that what these stories say is that Faust was not a first-rank "literary" figure but was a master storyteller and a tremendous personality. They tell of an imagination that had its own reality and poetic quality and was second to none in popular appeal. Faust put dreams in print. He composed prose ballads. His importance as a popular mythmaker, particularly in his westerns, is fundamental. As James Fenimore Cooper wrote the myth of the perfectible man in the American West, so Faust wrote the myth of the timeless man, the myth man.

To enter into these stories is easy because he made it so. He knew that the first principle of a writer's craft is to entertain, but underlying the entertainment is a stronger note of power and conviction, of affirmative possibilities that lie beyond defeat, and of a dream made real.

ROBERT EASTON

Santa Barbara, California

The King

One or more films were produced from Faust's work for each of the twenty-seven years of his writing life. He was as legendary in Hollywood as Etherton is in this sensitive and fast-moving short short which was found among Faust's papers after his death. It was first published in *This Week.*

I T WAS a big day when Rudy Zandor consented to dine with me at Chasen's because those were the years when he was astonishing Hollywood with a series of super productions. He was another Sampson whose strength lay not in his long hair but in his perfect self-confidence.

The country he loved, the flag followed, the God he worshiped was Rudy Zandor. So I put in the whole day working on my plot and reached the restaurant rather full of hope.

Zandor was hardly an hour later, which seemed a good sign, and then he came in with a yes man named Gregg and Jimmy Jones, whose real name is Jonascsky. Zandor raised quite a buzz with his entrance because he always dressed for public appearances. This time he wore corduroy trousers, a riding coat buttoned high around the throat, and four days' whiskers. His friends were in dinner jackets for contrast.

Rudy was almost at my table when another murmur started. All eyes left him, and in came Raymond Vincent Etherton in his black coat and white stock like an eighteenth century ghost. It was rather hard on Zandor to have his entrance messed up like that, for he was completely forgotten as the old man went by, looking straight ahead and failing to see the people who spoke to him. He went to his usual corner, waited for his coffee and cognac, and contemplated the dignity of space.

When Dave Chasen in person brought the brandy, Etherton became gently and kindly aware of him, for he was really abstracted, not merely high-hat. Thirty years before, when he consented to be King Arthur for D. W. Griffith, he must have been a glorious man.

Some of the glory hung about him as Henri Quatre in "Ivry" or as Richard the Lion-Hearted in "The Talisman." He never was cast except as a king and he moved through his parts without the slightest acting, merely lending his presence, as it were. The whisper had it that there *was* a dash of real royalty in his blood but no one even in Hollywood dared to suggest the bar-sinister to Etherton.

Even Hollywood was surprised by the appearance of such a man on the screen. He was more a rare legend than a fact. That was why Chasen's buzzed so this evening.

Zandor, in eclipse, looked pretty sour.

"That man," he said, pointing at Etherton. "Who is he?"

Jimmy Jones winked at me. It was the yes-man who gave the answer. A celebrity in Hollywood can't help accumulating them as the northside of a tree gathers moss.

"That's Raymond Vincent Etherton," said Gregg.

"I want him. He has a hungry look. I want him to play Shylock," said Zandor.

"The 'Merchant of Venice' after the big western?" I asked.

"Before," said Zandor. "I'm not doing the western."

My hopes went crash; and at the same moment I heard Gregg ordering caviar.

Jimmy said: "You can't buy an Etherton, Rudy. He doesn't need money, but he acts now and then to raise the level of the screen and show the world what royalty should be."

Zandor waved his hand at Jones. "You bother me," he said. "Go away."

Jimmy Jones went away.

"Now get Etherton. Offer him seventy-five thousand," directed Zandor.

His Number Two boy went over to Etherton and I felt a little sick about Zandor and about myself for being with him.

Etherton was sipping his brandy when the yes-man leaned over his table and started talking. The old fellow showed no sign that he heard a syllable. Presently he laid a bill on the table, stood up, and walked through the Number Two boy as though the fellow were a thin mist. He passed out of Chasen's and Gregg came back to Zandor, astonished.

"Nothing could stop him—not even *your* name, Rudy," he said.

"Why didn't you raise the bid?" asked Zandor, furious. "I don't care what sort of blood he has in him; _nobody_ walks out on me. Why didn't you offer him one hundred thousand?"

"But I didn't have the authority," said the yes-man.

Zandor looked him over from his chin to the sleek of his hair and turned his shoulder; it was plain that there was one parasite less in his life.

It was a rotten dinner. I tried to be bright for a while but gave it up after Zandor had snarled a few times. The great man was preoccupied. In the middle of his chicken _cacciatore_ he jumped up and left the tableware jingling.

"Show me where this Etherton lives," he commanded.

I paid the bill and took him to Etherton's house—small, sedate, withdrawn from the vulgar world behind a formal Italian garden. The California moon, for we have a special variety out here, was laying cool silver over everything and the fountain statue left a perfect shadow on the pool.

The door of the house was open. I don't know why this shocked me so much. It was like seeing the great Etherton with his mouth agape. Zandor leaned on the bell. It made a thin chime of music far inside and we had no other answer. Zandor went in.

"You'd better not do that," I protested. "The old man won't stand intrusions."

"Look!" said Zandor. "I knew it . . . hungry!"

I followed him a step and saw him pointing to the living room; there was enough slanting moonshine to show that it was empty. The waxed floor shone like water, but there was not a stick of furniture. Zandor strode through the open door beyond and into the kitchen. There was a rusted gas stove. Something scurried away on a shelf and I saw a bit of nibbled cheese rind and cracker crumbs. But Zandor was moving on through a naked dining room and into a bed chamber that was furnished with box springs on the floor, a pier glass, and a big, gilded chair in front of the mirror. In the chair sat Etherton wrapped in a black cloak with his white head thrown back and his right hand at his breast, supported by something.

He looked at us with deeply veiled eyes of contempt and seemed about to make a gesture of silent dismissal. It needed another glance to see that all his gesturing had ended, for what supported his hand was the hilt of the little medieval dagger he had driven through his heart.

I looked away from him to the three big photographs which hung on the walls and showed me Etherton as the Lion-Hearted in heavy chain mail, as Henri Quatre with the famous white plume in his helmet, as King Arthur bearded like a saint.

Understanding grew in me. Those rare appearances of Etherton on the screen had not been a casual amusement but the nerve center of his whole life. His parts never had been large but they had made him a king, and with a child's pitiful sincerity he had enclosed himself within a dream. Rather than step outside it, he had starved. I could imagine with what care he dressed himself this evening, borrowed the last possible dollar from a pawnbroker and went out for the final time to see if Hollywood once more would give him a shadowy throne. Instead, it preferred to see in him the wicked moneylender, so he came home and erased himself from the page.

Zandor was triumphant.

"You see? You see?" he roared at me. "I was right. I *did* spot the hunger in him. He's been on a throne for thirty years but when he got the Shylock offer, he knew that I'd seen the starvation in his face. The seventy-five thousand scared him. He was tempted and he almost fell. The hundred thousand would have bought him, lock, stock and barrel. But that fool of a Gregg didn't know how to bargain."

I got out into the garden. It was a warm June night, but I was shivering. Zandor followed me. The bigness of his voice made the fountain pool tremble.

"He wanted to be a king or nothing, you see?" roared Zandor.

"So he came home and ended his reign. You get it? It's big stuff. It's new. It's a picture. And it's mine."

Honor Bright

There were three men in her life. The lover with fifty million. The criminal who knew her as just dirt. And the one old enough to be her father but wasn't. This story is published by permission of the editors of *Cosmopolitan*. Here Faust writes with the popular touch that reached millions of readers and viewers.

ADRIENNE STEPPED into the library through the French window—her family's garden adjoins mine—and sat down in the red tapestry chair near the fire. My Adrienne—your Adrienne, every man's Adrienne—selected that chair because it made a perfect background for her black velvet evening wrap, and she wanted to be near the fire so that the bright blaze of it would throw up little golden lights into her hair. I got up and poured her favorite drink, which is a bit of plain water without ice, just stained with Scotch.

"This is very pretty, Adrienne," I said. "With your profile just so and your head leaning a little, you look like a child."

"When you know the truth, does it matter how I look?" she said. "How is your poor back, Uncle Oliver?"

I had been moving some great heavy pots of hydrangeas

a few days before on the terrace and had given myself a wrench, but it was not sympathy that caused Adrienne to ask that question; something in my speech had annoyed her, and she wished to remind me, in her sweetly poisonous way, that the first sign of age is weakness in the small of the back.

"I'm perfectly well," I said.

"I'm very glad, *darling*," said my Adrienne, "but don't insist on being so strong and manly just now, dear."

I looked up from filling my pipe and waited.

"You know you prefer cigarettes," she explained.

I put the pipe aside without a word and picked up a cigarette.

Adrienne rose and came, rustling, to stand over me with her fragrance while she held the lighter. "Isn't that the wrong end, dear?" she suggested.

I reversed the infernal cigarette, and she lighted it. These near approaches or forays of Adrienne's often make me nervous, and of this truth she is exquisitely aware.

"Are you angry?" she asked.

"Just enough to give you my full attention," I told her. "It's your usual system."

"But I don't come here to annoy you, *do* I, Uncle Oliver?" she wanted to know. "You don't really feel that I come here to annoy you, Uncle Oliver?" she said sadly.

"You come here to think out loud, because I'm so old and safe," I answered.

"Oh no; not really so *safe*," she said.

"Well, well! Who is it this time?" I asked.

"Something terrible happened," she told me.

"What's his name?" I asked cannily. "And who is he?"

"It's not so much a 'who' as a 'what,'" decided Adrienne. "Will you help me, *dear* Uncle Oliver?"

"I suppose so," I said.

She went back to her chair and held out one hand to be gilded by the firelight, yet I felt that only part of her attention was being given to the composition of this picture and that she was in real trouble. I was astonished and touched.

"I have an appointment for eight o'clock," she said. "You won't let me be late? It's frightfully important."

"Very well," I answered. "I won't let you be late. But now let's get on with your problem. What's his name?"

"Gilbert Ware," she said.

I felt a shock of loss and regret. For years I had realized that my Adrienne was growing up, but still it had remained easy for me to think of her in short skirts and with her hair in braids. A child belongs to every man; a woman belongs to one only; and so my heart shrank at the name of Gilbert Ware. He filled both the imagination and the eye. If he was not one of the richest ten men in the country, he was not far behind them. On his mother's side he went back to the best of Massachusetts, and by his father he was Old Virginia; placed in the diplomatic corps by the Ware dynasty, he had tasted the best the world offers by the time he was thirty; and finally he had the beauty, together with the raised eyebrows, of one of the Founding Fathers. I daresay that he was the catch of the whole country. Such a man did not waste his time on children, which meant that my Adrienne was now a woman.

She explained, "He gave a week-end party at his house in

the country, and I was there."

"At his country house?" I said. "Why, Adrienne, you really are getting on."

She did not answer but continued to look sidelong thoughts, so that I understood she was about to tell her story. I took my drink in hand, comforted my sight with her, and prepared to listen. Of course, "uncle" is merely a title that she chose for me, but I have watched Adrienne and listened carefully for several years without coming to the end of her. She is strangely combined of warmth and aloofness. Not even her school friends could nickname her "Addie," and no one fails to put the accent on the last syllable of "Adrienne" because she seems, if not a Latin, at least very different. Actually, her blood is mostly of the far north—Norwegian, I think—and those people of the endless nights have gifts of deep brooding and long, long dreams.

Adrienne is continually in and out of love like a trout in sun and shadow, but the net never seems to take her. When I thought of the name and place of Gilbert Ware in the world, I wondered if this might not be the time. I wondered also how much truth might be mingled in this story with the fictions of Adrienne, for, though I hope she is not a deliberate teller of untruths, she is at least a weaver who loves to have many colors in her web. With the question there came to me a sudden surety that tonight, at least, I should hear nothing but the truth. Also I knew, for no proper reason, that she was to speak of a great event. At this point in my thoughts she began to talk in that voice so light and musical that more than once, it surprises me to say, she has talked me to sleep.

She was quite excited, she said, when the invitation came, for she had seen Gilbert Ware only a few times and, though she had done her very best, she had not been sure that he noticed her. Now she put her mind thoroughly upon the future, as she laid out the things for her maid to pack. She hesitated particularly over the jewels for, if she took none, she might seem dull, and too many might be pretentious. At last she hit on a diamond bracelet—a mere thread of light—and a little ruby pendant of the finest pigeon's blood. The two together might be worth some thirty-five hundred or four-thousand dollars. (Adrienne is very good at figures.)

Long before her packing was finished or her thoughts arranged, young Harry Strode stopped by to drive her down to the country. She permitted this service from him, but not with pleasure. She had been quite fond of Strode at one time and, during an extremely dull evening, she had permitted herself to tell him so. But, since Adrienne cannot endure sulky men with long memories, her liking afterwards had turned the other way.

Once in the car, she was as pleasant as possible. However, this was a dark afternoon with such a roar and rushing of rain that conversation meant straining the voice. She had intended to be kind to Harry, but not in the face of such difficulties. Adrienne, who has more than one of the talents of a cat, found herself, while considering the next subject for talk, so comfortable that presently she was asleep.

She roused when Harry paused to take a hitchhiker in

out of the downpour. He was a pale man of about my age, she said, with his head thrust forward at the end of a long neck like a caricature of all the bookkeepers in the world. A certain restless hunger in his eyes intrigued her for a moment, but then, in spite of the best intentions, she was asleep again; and the fellow sat quietly in the back seat.

At the entrance to Ware's driveway, Strode let out his extra passenger—the lights of a town were only a short distance down the road—and Adrienne remembers how the poor fellow stood in the rain with his hat in his hand, thanking them and waiting for the car to pass on. This roused her so that she was wide awake when they entered the house.

The place was quite a disappointment to her for it combined two faults: it was both baronial and new. Yet she could understand that a man like Ware might simply pick the best of architects and say to him, "Here is the land. Select a proper site and build me an appropriate country house. Suppose you take a year to do it, gardens and all." But the moment she went into the living room she was warmed by the realization that Ware was giving the party entirely for her. Every one of the dozen or more house guests had been chosen from among her younger friends. It was only a pity, said Adrienne, that he had not included some of the older ones. Saying this, she smiled at me.

In the great living room, huge as a Tudor hall, tea was being served in delicate porcelain with faint chimings of silver; and there was Gilbert Ware, as ingratiating and observant a host as though he were by no means the catch of a continent. Adrienne made up her mind to have him. Her tactics were to strike at once and to keep on striking.

When Ware asked her about the trip down, she said, "I don't want to think about it."

"Why not?"

"No—please! It was only a hitchhiker we picked up, and I simply started imagining things about him."

"Something is bothering you," said Gilbert Ware, "so let's have it out." He had a doctor's air, attentive for humane reasons even to foolish stories.

"It was like something you're afraid of seeing by night," said Adrienne.

The storm jumped suddenly at the house and set the tall windows trembling. Since it was only twilight, the curtains had not been drawn, and she looked out over a shimmer of lawn into the green gloom.

"Harry had his eyes glued to the road," she said. "He's such a careful driver, but it seemed to me that he *must* have known what I was seeing as I sat there, pretending to be asleep. In the mirror I could see the man's face; I think I'll always see it."

"The hitchhiker's?"

"It was so pale," said Adrienne. "It was so long and dead and white. . . . Please don't make me remember."

"Don't talk about it; you look sick," said Ware.

"I'll be all right. It was only a dream. There wasn't any reality about it. Nothing so evil *could* be real. You know, the sort of horror that smiles at you in the dark?"

Ware was listening to her but with plenty of reservation in those raised eighteenth-century eyebrows. She realized then that, if she married him, she might find herself playing a part forever. The thought excited her as she went on with the embroideries of her little story. Actually there *had* been something strange about the hitchhiker. Now she enlarged upon him.

She said she had seen the devil wake up in the eyes of the man when, as she raised her hand to her hat, her sleeve fell back and showed the diamond bracelet; she had seen the beast of prey in him appear like some grisly shape that floats up under water, never clearly seen. It wasn't the thought of mere robbery and loss that troubled her but that brooding sense of a monstrous presence.

Gradually the man leaned forward in his seat, preparing to act. She was trying desperately to convey a warning to Harry Strode. If it were too overt, the signal would bring the attack on them instantly. She tried to signal with her eyes, with her hand. She slipped her foot over and touched Strode's. But he remained impervious, simply fixing his eyes on the road and singing a song, said Adrienne, which declared that for alma mater he would stand like a wall and never, never fall; also, when he took the field, he would never yield.

When she talked about the college hymn, something melted in Ware's eyes. A barrier fell, admitting her, and whether or not he believed all the tale, plainly he enjoyed the art of it.

She made a quick ending. A police car, she said, suddenly came up behind them, used its siren, and went by. This was enough to make the hitchhiker change his mind. Perhaps the sight of the uniforms recalled to him certain unforgettable years of punishment. He relaxed in his seat, and a moment later they were letting him out at the entrance to the Ware place. She never would forget him standing in the rain with that faint white mockery of a smile, thanking them for the ride. She had reached the house still half sick, but what saved the day for her was a desire to laugh, because Harry Strode had gone through it all aware of nothing but a desire to rally around a banner and, with a heart so true, die for the red and blue.

Ware chuckled at this. Then he said that the guest rooms of his place were cottages scattered through the grounds but, if she were nervous after her experience, she should have a place in the main building.

"No, no!" said Adrienne. "I've talked it all out now, and I won't think of it again. You were *so* right to make me tell you everything. I didn't want to say anything about it before the rest of them; there's something so ugly about that kind of a story, don't you think?"

Ware's eyes dwelt on her for a moment before he agreed; then he let the general conversation flow in upon them, and Adrienne found the eyes of the other girls fixed on her a little grimly. They took it for granted that she merely had succeeded in putting herself on trial, but her resolution was hardening every instant. She would take this man, to have and to hold; she would take him—if for no other reason—because he was hard to get.

Everyone went to change, and Adrienne was shown to her cottage. There were a number of these cabins, each tucked into a special environment: one by a pool, another drenched in vines, one lost in towering woods, and a fourth sunning itself on a little green hilltop, though there was only rain streaming down when Adrienne was taken to it. It was built snug and tight as a ship's cabin, but it was a complete job even to a sunken pool in the bathroom.

When she had dressed—in black, she said, with only her ruby pendant—she put on overshoes and a featherweight cellophane slicker which were provided and went back to the house with a flashlight. There was only a misting rain, by this time, but the trees still looked a little wild from the storm

A few moments after her return to the house, dinner was announced. When they went in, she found herself at the right hand of Ware and felt that the game was half won. Yet he made no particular effort at the table; he preferred to watch her and smile.

She was surprised when suddenly he asked her what she thought of the house.

"Doesn't it need something?"

"Does it? What would you say? More color?"

"No, but more time."

This seemed to please him. For an instant he came out of the distance and sat within touch of her, his eyes clear and keen, but after that she felt that he had drawn away again. She did not feel that she had failed but that he needed more leisure to make up his mind. She determined to give it to him, so she pleaded a frightful headache and went off to bed early.

By this time the storm had slid away down the sky and out of sight, but a few clouds were flying. The moon hit one of them and dashed the whole weight of it into a shining spray like a bow wave. Adrienne enjoyed these things.

She knew that she was on trial—for fifty million, so to speak—but her eye was turned confidently to the future.

She decided, as she lay stretched on her bed in the cottage, looking at the apple-green ceiling, that Gilbert Ware probably wanted a restful creature for a wife. He was an unhurried sight-seer in life, determined to take nothing but the best. She, with her imaginings and her acting, had amused him for a time. She should have adopted an entirely different role and made herself, like him, a quiet observer, a little tired by the game. Adrienne decided that in the morning she would show him a change of pace.

The moment she reached this intelligent conclusion she grew sleepy, but as she yawned, her arms wide open to welcome the aching drowsiness, she heard a slight sound and observed that the knob of her door was turning. She had locked the door, but a thrill of horror froze her heart. Not since she was a child and ghosts had haunted her in dark corridors had she felt such a thoroughly sufficient chill. She reached for the telephone and turned the dial. The bell in the main house began to buzz with a deep, soft voice. The buzzing continued, a far-away sound on the wire and a hollow echoing in Adrienne. Then not a servant but Ware himself spoke.

"It's Adrienne Lester," she whispered. "Someone is trying to get into my cottage!"

He said, with his eternal calm, "Someone with a long, white, evil face, no doubt?" He laughed and rang off.

She could not believe it, but there it was. Her play-acting had been perfectly patent to him.

The doorknob no longer was turning. Instead, there was

a very discreet sound of metal scratching on metal. She remembered now not the sins of her past but the old fable about the little boy who had called "Wolf! Wolf!" once too often. For an instant she thought of being merely beautiful and helpless; instead, she got up and seized the heavy poker which stood in the brass bucket beside the fire. At the same time the door opened.

A gust of night air came in along with her hitchhiker who looked "like a caricature of all the bookkeepers in the world." He closed the door with his foot and pushed his hands into his coat pockets. He was very wet. When he moved, his feet made squashy sounds in his shoes. The rim of his hat, which he did not remove, hung down around his long, pallid face. A thin purple dye, which soaked out of his coat, had streaked the white of his shirt and, since the coat collar was turned up, had left a mark like a cut across his throat. He looked at Adrienne and at the poker she held, then turned his back on her and went to the bedside table where her jewels were lying. He dropped them into a coat pocket.

He was quite hunched and so thin that she could almost count the vertebrae through his coat, but in spite of his apparent weakness she put the poker back into the brass bucket. She was young, swift, strong, but only as a woman. And, though he was by no means a big man, she knew that he could pluck the weapon out of her hands with ease. The knowledge sickened her a little; for the first time she was insufficient in an emergency. My Adrienne slipped quietly toward the door.

"No," said the hitchhiker, and shook his head at her.

She turned for an instant toward the blackness of the outer night, but she dared not flee because of the nightmare that might pursue her. She went back to the fire.

A small pool was collecting around the man's feet; she watched the growth of it on the Chinese rug across the tongue and lower jaw of a little dragon.

"How do you feel?" he asked.

"I'm all right," said Adrienne.

"You're not afraid?"

"I was, terribly. But it's better now that you're talking," she said.

She thought that it was a pleasant remark, and she made it with a smile, but all the time the sickness of the fear was deepening in her, thickening like a new taste, because the hitchhiker was aware of her from head to foot and from foot to head. It was only for a moment that his eyes touched her in this fashion, but the screaming muscles began to tremble in her throat.

He kept nodding his head up and down in understanding. He ran the tip of his tongue over his lips. "It always makes me kind of laugh," he said, "the way you people get scared. Once I got into a place and in the first bedroom, where I didn't expect it, there was a young fellow lying reading. He'd heard something. He knew I was inside the room, but he didn't dare to turn his head. I stood there and watched. The magazine was resting on his chest, and his heart was thumping so hard that it made the pages keep stirring like leaves in a wind. He was young, and he was twice as big as me; but nothing is as big as the things that come out of the night."

"What happened, then? What did you do?" asked Adrienne.

"Don't scream or nothing," said the thief. "I'm gonna turn out the light."

He turned out the light so that there was only the fire to send his shadow and hers up the wall and over the ceiling in waves and tremblings.

Adrienne picked up the poker again.

"Yeah, you'd fight, wouldn't you?" he said, and laughed a little. "Got anything to drink in here?"

"No," said Adrienne.

"What's over here?" and he pulled open a small door set into the wall.

Two flasks of cut glass glimmered inside the niche. He sniffed at them.

"Brandy and Scotch. Funny how you people never know that bourbon is better than Scotch . . . Have some?"

"No," said Adrienne.

"Here's down the hatch!"

"Don't drink it!" cried Adrienne.

"Why not?"

"Please don't drink it!" she begged.

"Ah, that's what you think, is it? Well, here's down the hatch!"

He took a good swallow, and while his head was back, his eyes half closed, she freshened her grip on the poker, but still she could not act. She put the poker back in place for the second time, because it came to her that all the danger she dreaded was, in fact, closed in the room with her and that she would have to meet it with a different kind of force.

He wiped his mouth on the back of his hand, which made a smear across his face, and then he sat down beside the fire. Adrienne sank into the opposite chair.

"They spent some money on *you* all right," he said. "I remember hearing a rich feller say, once . . . I used to be a plumber, and plumbers hear what people say, but a length of cast-iron pipe rolled on me, and it gave me a kind of a twist in the back, so I wasn't any good, after that. I had to use the old bean, so I used it . . ." He seemed to have lost his place in the conversation. "Where was I at?" He took another drink.

"You were about to say how much money is spent on us."

"This feller was saying that his girl cost ten thousand a year from twelve years up. Travel, governess, maid, school —he said ten thousand wouldn't cover it. Ten thousand for ten years. That's a hundred grand. How many languages you got?"

"French and Italian, a little. And a bit of German."

"You don't look like you would know any German."

"They sent me to Vienna for a year. To study singing."

"I guess you can do that pretty good."

"Not very."

"Sing 'Home on the Range,' dead soft."

She sang "Home on the Range" softly. He finished the flask of Scotch while he listened. He hummed the last part of it in unison with her.

"I never was West," he said, "but I like that song. It's kind of American. It reminds me how big we are . . . I've heard plenty sing it better than you."

"Of course you have." She managed to smile again.

He stared hard watching for the end of the smile, but she kept it, after a fashion, in the corners of her mouth and in her eyes.

"There ain't hardly a good swallow in one of these flasks. Go fetch me the other one, will you?"

"Certainly," said my Adrienne.

She rose and went to the little cupboard. As she turned with the flask of brandy in her hand, she saw that the plumber sat a little higher in his chair, and then she was aware that his body was rigid as she came up behind him. He was waiting, tense and set, for whatever she might attempt to do, but he would not turn his head an inch toward her. She went slowly by him and gave him the flask— and her smile.

He relaxed in his chair. "You feel better, don't you?"

"A lot better," she said.

"I guess you been scrubbed clean every day of your life. I guess you never wear anything but silk?"

"Oh, yes. Oh, lots of other things," she said.

"You don't mind me now if I drink this?"

"I don't mind at all."

"Look," he said.

"Yes," said my Adrienne.

"Maybe there's better singers, but I never heard nobody talk so good. You bet I never heard anybody talk so good." He stood up. "You been pretty all right, and I sort of hate taking your stuff. You know?"

For the first time, in a way that was strange to Adrienne,

he opened his eyes and looked at her with an appeal for understanding. He was apparently about to go, and she would not have to keep on smiling. She felt she had done enough acting in those few minutes to last her the rest of her life.

"It's all right," she said to him." We all have to get along somehow."

"Thanks. I believe you're on the square, but I'll fix this first." He pulled the telephone wire from the wall socket. Then he lifted a finger at her. "You won't budge out of here for ten minutes?"

"I won't budge."

"Ten whole minutes? Honor bright?"

"Honor bright," said Adrienne, and crossed herself automatically.

"Well, I guess that's all right then. Good night to you." He went out of the cottage.

There was a little clock above the fireplace. She noted the hands at five past eleven and resolved to wait for the ten whole minutes, honor bright; but all at once, said Adrienne, she thought of what a scene there would be when she rushed into the big house and told them, how everyone would be roused, and there would be calls for the police, and Gilbert Ware looking frightfully mortified and, for once, thoroughly alert. She thought of these things and ran from the cottage, but before she had taken three steps, the man moved out from behind the corner of the little building. He came straight toward her, slowly, with his hands in his coat pockets, and his black shadow slid silently over the ground beside him, like a man and his

ghost or a man and the black devil, said Adrienne. I wonder why she did not use those quick feet of hers to fly away
to the big house, but all she could do was to creep away
from him through the open door of the cottage. She
backed up until the wall stopped her. Her knees gave way.
My Adrienne crouched with her eyes closed, because she
dared not look for another instant at the long, white,
deadly face of the hitchhiker. But she could feel his shadow
falling over her, cold on her face and breast, she said.

"Well, so there isn't any honor bright," he said. "I
thought maybe you were one of the things for the country
to be proud of. But you ain't. You ain't all right at all.
You're dirt. You're just dirt."

It seemed to Adrienne that the chill of his shadow still
was falling on her, but when she looked up, after a long
time—after a long time when the breath seemed to be stop-
ping in her body—she saw that he was gone, and she was
able to get to the chair by the fire and drop into it.

Only a moment later Gilbert Ware came in. He looked
at the black, wet footprints on the floor, and then dropped
on one knee beside her chair. She was reminded dimly of
other young men who had taken the same position—my
Adrienne always is reminded of someone else, no matter
what a man does.

"I've been a fool—I've been a goddamned fool!" said
Ware, in just as trembling a passion of regret as any other
man. "What happened? What has he done?"

My Adrienne said nothing, not because she was incap-
able of speech, nor because she was remembering the theft
and her fear, but because she was thinking of a loss far

more vital, for which she could not find a name. So she kept on thinking until her thoughts went jogging all the way back to childhood, which was the last time "honor bright" had troubled her soul. She was holding out her hands to the fire which, against all nature, gave her no comfort.

Gilbert Ware took those hands and turned her suddenly toward him so that she had to see his face, all savage with resolution. There was no trace now of that astute and critical spirit which had looked so carefully through her. "When did he go? Has he hurt you? Tell me. Do you hear me, dear Adrienne? What has he done?"

There was one word in this speech which could not help partially reviving such a practical girl as my Adrienne, and yet she still was half lost in that unhappy dream as she answered, "He took the bracelet and pendant. I don't know when he left. The hitchhiker . . ."

"Was it *that* fellow? And I thought it was only a story!" cried Ware.

He jumped for the phone, found it was disconnected, sprang back to her.

"Let him go!" she said. "I don't want ever to see him again. Don't make me see him again, Gilbert."

Gilbert Ware threw a blanket around her and lifted her to her feet. He helped her along the path to the main house.

"You won't have to see him. Of course you won't have to see him. Don't talk, my sweet girl, my Adrienne. You've had a frightful shock. Will you be able to forgive me?"

Miserable as she was, she could not help thinking how

easy it might be to forgive fifty million and Gilbert Ware.

The party at the house had not broken up, and everyone hurried to be of help. Faces leaned over Adrienne as she lay on the couch wrapped in the blanket. Someone chafed her feet. Her fingers were around a mug of hot toddy that warmed her hands and her lips and her throat but could not melt the ice around her heart.

She was conscious of much telephoning back and forth, but she was not prepared for the return of her philosophical hitchhiker, flanked by a pair of proud policemen. In that frame he was a wretchedly starved picture of a man. He had left the muddy country lanes for a highway, and the police had picked him up at once. Ware, bending close beside Adrienne, was saying, "There's only one word for you to speak, and then it's all over. Simply identify the jewels and the man. The law takes on after that. Don't move, Adrienne. Don't sit up."

She did sit up, however, because it was mortally necessary for her to face again those eyes which had looked into her so shamefully far. But the inquiring mind was gone from the thief. All that had been free and dangerous and of the night now was faded into a dim creature who had suffered before and was prepared once more to endure.

"I guess this is the stuff, Miss?" said one of the policemen, holding out the jewels in the palm of his hand. "You just identify it, and he'll take a trip."

She kept trying to catch the glance of the thief, but he stared straight forward at the years of labor, of silence and of shame. His wet hat, now a shapeless sponge, was crushed in one hand, and it was upon this hand that Adrienne was forced, most unwillingly, to focus her attention. There was something abnormal, misshapen and oversized about it. By contrast, Gilbert Ware had such slender fingers, such a rounded but inadequate wrist, that one wondered how he could swing a polo mallet. The thumb of the hitchhiker, for instance, was broadened, thickened and fleshed on the inside to a surprising degree. Across his wrist lay two forking veins as big as her little finger, and all at once she penetrated the mystery. It was simply that the thief had been a laborer. By swinging sledge hammers, by tugging with all his might at powerful wrenches, he had deformed and desensitized his hands until they were merely gross tools, vaguely prehensile.

". . . just a matter of identification," a policeman was saying.

"They aren't mine," she said.

The smiles of the policemen persisted a moment, wavered and went out like lanterns in a sudden wind.

"But wait—but, Adrienne!" said Gilbert Ware.

She shook her head. "Not mine."

"But this is the very fellow you were talking about!" cried Ware.

"I never saw him before."

"My dear Adrienne," said Ware, looking hard at her, "if you're doing this out of charity, please remember that the law has a rightful place in this affair."

She lost track of his voice, watching comprehension break up the calm of the plumber, but even as the hope entered him, and he saw that after all she seemed to be giving him some chance of escape, the manhood seemed to go out of him. Something of his spirit came leering, groveling at her feet.

Ware asked everyone to leave the room. Then he sat down beside Adrienne. "Now what's it all about?" he asked, and he looked at her as a dealer might look at a picture of uncertain authentication.

"I don't know."

"I'm sure you always think your way through before you do anything."

"I try to," she admitted, and she kept searching her mind only to discover that the deeper she went, the more unknown was this new Adrienne.

He was waiting.

"I don't know what the whole truth about this is," she said, "but I have a horrible, naked feeling that I'm going to tell it."

After all, he had lived a bit. He showed it now by saying nothing.

"Did you see his hands?" she asked. "They were real, don't you think?"

"Real?"

"He's worked like an honest man, and he's been a thief. He's been in prison, too, and that's real enough. He could see that I'm all make-believe. I'm not even honestly looking for a husband. I'm just as honest as a cat that wants kittens. I try to be clever, but I'm only silly and young. I've never even made a beginning. I hate it. Oh, you don't know how I hate it.'

"There's something pretty final about this," he said. "I

think you're writing me down as one of the people who never have made a beginning."

And now, in this interval, Adrienne found that she could not tell a pleasant lie. She knew that every second of the silence was saying good-by to fifty million dollars but, instead of speaking, she could only remember the voice of the thief saying, "You're dirt! You're just dirt!"

After a while Ware stood up slowly, still with something between anger and entreaty in his eyes, but when that frightful silence continued, he said, "I'll tell them the hitchhiker isn't the man."

He left the room.

A fortune vanished with him, but with a very convinced longing Adrienne wanted to be out of that house. That was what she told the doctor, when he came a few minutes later.

He said, "You've had a shock, my girl."

"Have I? I'm going to be better, though, now."

"You'd better stay in bed for two or three days."

"Oh, no; I won't need to do that. There's someone I have to see."

"You'd better do as I say, though," he advised.

"But I know me so well," said my Adrienne.

Here she finished her drink, and I knew that her story was finished also; her timing is so perfect.

I blew some smoke upward and watched it vanish. "Fifty million dollars all gone?" I said, but then I saw that there was a shadow on Adrienne, a strange dimness.

"Now tell me about everything," she said, looking at the place where the smoke had vanished.

"Why, it's not difficult, my dear," I told her. "You're unhappy about it because you don't understand the big, quick movement of your own heart; when you saw Ware bearing down with all the dogs of the law on that poor, hunted devil—"

"Oh, nonsense," said Adrienne. "Just as poor and hunted as a wolf. You don't *know*. I mean, a wolf that's perfectly at home in the woods, snow or shine. Don't you see? What am I looking for? Why, I'm looking for a *man,* and that evening I thought I'd found him. But I hadn't. I'd only found a sort of beautiful social legend, or something. The hitchhiker was more of a man."

"Well, yes. Well . . . of course," I said, and gave myself a twist that hurt my back. "I hadn't thought of that. But—just to return a bit—who was it you wanted to see in the pinch? You remember you spoke to the doctor about him."

"Oh, an old, old friend," said Adrienne. "His voice was with me all through it. He's the one I'm to see tonight."

"Better be on your way, then," I told her. "It's ten to eight now."

"Really? Is it as late as that? Then may I ring for Jericho?"

She was pressing the button as I said, "What the devil do you want with *him?*"

Jericho came in. He is made of white hair, yellow parchment, and heavenly spirit.

"Jericho dear," said Adrienne, "is there any cold, cold champagne?"

"There is one just barely turnin' to ice," said Jericho.

"Then we'll have that for an aperitif," she told him.

"And is that pheasant big enough for two?"

"Just perfect, Miss Adrienne."

"Then serve it that way, please," said Adrienne.

"Do you mean that *I'm* the appointment?" I asked, when Jericho left.

"You're the only person who knows enough to tell me what's wrong with me," she said desolately. "But I don't need the telling actually. I know already. Say something or I'm going to cry," said Adrienne, who now was sitting on the arm of my chair.

Jericho brought in the champagne and paid no attention to Adrienne as he began opening the bottle.

"Well, I'll tell you a fact that's better than a story," I said.

"I hate facts," said Adrienne.

"When the Arab mare comes out of the tent in the morning—because the Arabs value their mares most, you know . . ."

"What silly people!"

"They're not silly at all."

"Oh, aren't they?"

"No, they're not. But when the mare comes out of the tent, she looks away off beyond the tribe and over the heads of the family that owns her, and across the desert to the edge of the horizon. She has her tail arched and her head raised, and there's a tremendous expectation in her eyes that makes her master sad."

"But why?"

"Because he knows she's saying to herself: 'When will the real master come!' "

"How rather lovely," said Adrienne.

Jericho had placed in my hand a glass in which the bubbles broke with a crisping sound. "Here's to the real master, my dear," I said.

"Will you find him for me?"

"This is just nonsense, Adrienne," I told her with severity.

"But I'm tired—oh, I'm tired to death!" she said. "I want my life to start."

"Come, come! Let's have this drink."

"Not until you promise me."

"But what?"

"Either find me a husband—I'll ask no questions—or marry me yourself."

"Adrienne!"

"Are you really so shocked?"

"But I'm old enough to be—"

"You *are* old enough, you see. Shall we drink to it!"

"I *shall* find you somebody," said I.

"Of course you will," said Adrienne, raising her glass slowly as though waiting for permission.

I lifted mine in turn and, looking up, saw her all shining and golden through the color of the wine.

Wine on the Desert

Best-known and most widely anthologized of all his western stories, "Wine on the Desert" shows Faust's narrative gift. It first appeared in *This Week* for June 7, 1936.

THERE WAS no hurry, except for the thirst, like clotted salt, in the back of his throat, and Durante rode on slowly, rather enjoying the last moments of dryness before he reached the cold water in Tony's house. There was really no hurry at all. He had almost twenty-four hours' head start, for they would not find his dead man until this morning. After that, there would be perhaps several hours of delay before the sheriff gathered a sufficient posse and started on his trail. Or perhaps the sheriff would be fool enough to come alone.

Durante had been able to see the wheel and fan of Tony's windmill for more than an hour, but he could not make out the ten acres of the vineyard until he had topped the last rise, for the vines had been planted in a hollow. The lowness of the ground, Tony used to say, accounted for the water that gathered in the well during the wet season. The rains sank through the desert sand, through the gravels beneath, and gathered in a bowl of clay hardpan far below.

In the middle of the rainless season the well ran dry but, long before that, Tony had every drop of the water pumped up into a score of tanks made of cheap corrugated iron. Slender pipe lines carried the water from the tanks to the vines and from time to time let them sip enough life to keep them until the winter darkened overhead suddenly, one November day, and the rain came down, and all the earth made a great hushing sound as it drank. Durante had heard that whisper of drinking when he was here before; but he never had seen the place in the middle of the long drought.

The windmill looked like a sacred emblem to Durante, and the twenty stodgy, tar-painted tanks blessed his eyes; but a heavy sweat broke out at once from his body. For the air of the hollow, unstirred by wind, was hot and still as a bowl of soup. A reddish soup. The vines were powdered with thin red dust, also. They were wretched, dying things to look at, for the grapes had been gathered, the new wine had been made, and now the leaves hung in ragged tatters.

Durante rode up to the squat adobe house and right through the entrance into the patio. A flowering vine clothed three sides on the little court. Durante did not know the name of the plant, but it had large white blossoms with golden hearts that poured sweetness on the air. Durante hated the sweetness. It made him more thirsty.

He threw the reins of his mule and strode into the house. The water cooler stood in the hall outside the kitchen. There were two jars made of a porous stone, very ancient things, and the liquid which distilled through the pores kept the contents cool. The jar on the left held water; that on the right contained wine. There was a big tin dipper hanging on a peg beside each jar. Durante tossed off the cover of the vase on the left and plunged it in until the delicious coolness closed well above his wrist.

"Hey, Tony," he called. Out of his dusty throat the cry was a mere groaning. He drank and called again, clearly, "Tony!"

A voice pealed from the distance.

Durante, pouring down the second dipper of water, smelled the alkali dust which had shaken off his own clothes. It seemed to him that heat was radiating like light from his clothes, from his body, and the cool dimness of the house was soaking it up. He heard the wooden leg of Tony bumping on the ground, and Durante grinned; then Tony came in with that hitch and sideswing with which he accommodated the stiffness of his artificial leg. His brown face shone with sweat as though a special ray of light were focused on it.

"Ah, Dick!" he said. "Good old Dick! . . . How long since you came last! . . . Wouldn't Julia be glad! Wouldn't she be glad!'

"Ain't she here?" asked Durante, jerking his head suddenly away from the dripping dipper.

"She's away at Nogalez," said Tony. "It gets so hot. I said, 'You go up to Nogalez, Julia, where the wind don't forget to blow.' She cried, but I made her go."

"Did she cry?" asked Durante.

"Julia . . . that's a good girl," said Tony.

"Yeah. You bet she's good," said Durante. He put the

dipper quickly to his lips but did not swallow for a moment; he was grinning too widely. Afterward he said: "You wouldn't throw some water into that mule of mine, would you, Tony?"

Tony went out with his wooden leg clumping loud on the wooden floor, softly in the patio dust. Durante found the hammock in the corner of the patio. He lay down in it and watched the color of sunset flush the mists of desert dust that rose to the zenith. The water was soaking through his body; hunger began, and then the rattling of pans in the kitchen and the cheerful cry of Tony's voice:

"What you want, Dick? I got some pork. You don't want pork. I'll make you some good Mexican beans. Hot. Ah ha, I know that old Dick. I have plenty of good wine for you, Dick. Tortillas. Even Julia can't make tortillas like me. . . . And what about a nice young rabbit?"

"All blowed full of buckshot?" growled Durante.

"No, no. I kill them with the rifle."

"You kill rabbits with a rifle?" repeated Durante, with a quick interest.

"It's the only gun I have," said Tony. "If I catch them in the sights, they are dead. . . . A wooden leg cannot walk very far. . . . I must kill them quick. You see? They come close to the house about sunrise and flop their ears. I shoot through the head."

"Yeah? Yeah?" muttered Durante. "Through the head?" He relaxed, scowling. He passed his hand over his face, over his head.

Then Tony began to bring the food out into the patio and lay it on a small wooden table; a lantern hanging against the wall of the house included the table in a dim half circle of light. They sat there and ate. Tony had scrubbed himself for the meal. His hair was soaked in water and sleeked back over his round skull. A man in the desert might be willing to pay five dollars for as much water as went to the soaking of that hair.

Everything was good. Tony knew how to cook, and he knew how to keep the glasses filled with his wine.

"This is old wine. This is my father's wine. Eleven years old," said Tony. "You look at the light through it. You see that brown in the red? That's the soft that time puts in good wine, my father always said."

"What killed your father?" asked Durante.

Tony lifted his hand as though he were listening or as though he were pointing out a thought.

"The desert killed him. I found his mule. It was dead, too. There was a leak in the canteen. My father was only five miles away when the buzzards showed him to me."

"Five miles? Just an hour. . . . Good Lord!" said Durante. He stared with big eyes. "Just dropped down and died?" he asked.

"No," said Tony. "When you die of thirst, you always die just one way. . . . First you tear off your shirt, then your undershirt. That's to be cooler. . . . And the sun comes and cooks your bare skin. . . . And then you think . . . there is water everywhere, if you dig down far enough. You begin to dig. The dust comes up your nose. You start screaming. You break your nails in the sand. You wear the flesh off the tips of your fingers, to the bone." He took a quick swallow of wine.

"Without you seen a man die of thirst, how d'you know they start to screaming?" asked Durante.

"They got a screaming look when you find them," said Tony. "Take some more wine. The desert never can get to you here. My father showed me the way to keep the desert away from the hollow. We live pretty good here? No?"

"Yeah," said Durante, loosening his shirt collar. "Yeah, pretty good."

Afterward he slept well in the hammock until the report of a rifle waked him and he saw the color of dawn in the sky. It was such a great, round bowl that for a moment he felt as though he were above, looking down into it.

He got up and saw Tony coming in holding a rabbit by the ears, the rifle in his other hand.

"You see?" said Tony. "Breakfast came and called on us!" He laughed.

Durante examined the rabbit with care. It was nice and fat and it had been shot through the head. Through the middle of the head. Such a shudder went down the back of Durante that he washed gingerly before breakfast; he felt that his blood was cooled for the entire day.

It was a good breakfast, too, with flapjacks and stewed rabbit with green peppers, and a quart of strong coffee. Before they had finished, the sun struck through the east window and started them sweating.

"Gimme a look at that rifle of yours, Tony, will you?" Durante asked.

"You take a look at my rifle, but don't you steal the luck that's in it," laughed Tony. He brought the fifteen-shot

Winchester.

"Loaded right to the brim?" asked Durante.

"I always load it full the minute I get back home," said Tony.

"Tony, come outside with me," commanded Durante.

They went out from the house. The sun turned the sweat of Durante to hot water and then dried his skin so that his clothes felt transparent.

"Tony, I gotta be damn mean," said Durante. "Stand right there where I can see you. Don't try to get close. . . . Now listen. . . . The sheriff's gunna be along this trail sometime today, looking for me. He'll load up himself and all his gang with water out of your tanks. Then he'll follow my sign across the desert. Get me? He'll follow if he finds water on the place. But he's not gunna find water."

"What you done, poor Dick?" said Tony. "Now look. . . . I could hide you in the old wine cellar where nobody . . ."

"The sheriff's not gunna find any water," said Durante. "It's gunna be like this."

He put the rifle to his shoulder, aimed, fired. The shot struck the base of the nearest tank, ranging down through the bottom. A semicircle of darkness began to stain the soil near the edge of the iron wall.

Tony fell on his knees. "No, no, Dick! Good Dick!" he said. "Look! All the vineyard. It will die. It will turn into old, dead wood. Dick . . ."

"Shut your face," said Durante. "Now I've started, I kinda like the job."

Tony fell on his face and put his hands over his ears.

Durante drilled a bullet hole through the tanks, one after another. Afterward, he leaned on the rifle.

"Take my canteen and go in and fill it with water out of the cooling jar," he said. "Snap into it, Tony!"

Tony got up. He raised the canteen and looked around him, not at the tanks from which the water was pouring so that the noise of the earth drinking was audible, but at the rows of his vineyard. Then he went into the house.

Durante mounted his mule. He shifted the rifle to his left hand and drew out the heavy Colt from its holster. Tony came dragging back to him, his head down. Durante watched Tony with a careful revolver but he gave up the canteen without lifting his eyes.

"The trouble with you, Tony," said Durante, "is you're yellow. I'd of fought a tribe of wildcats with my bare hands before I'd let 'em do what I'm doin' to you. But you sit back and take it."

Tony did not seem to hear. He stretched out his hands to the vines.

"Ah, my God," said Tony. "Will you let them all die?"

Durante shrugged his shoulders. He shook the canteen to make sure that it was full. It was so brimming that there was hardly room for the liquid to make a sloshing sound. Then he turned the mule and kicked it into a dogtrot.

Half a mile from the house of Tony, he threw the empty rifle to the ground. There was no sense packing that useless weight, and Tony with his peg leg would hardly come this far.

Durante looked back, a mile or so later, and saw the little image of Tony picking up the rifle from the dust, then

staring earnestly after his guest. Durante remembered the
neat little hole clipped through the head of the rabbit.
Wherever he went, his trail never could return again to
the vineyard in the desert. But then, commencing to picture to himself the arrival of the sweating sheriff and his
posse at the house of Tony, Durante laughed heartily.

The sheriff's posse could get plenty of wine, of course,
but without water a man could not hope to make the
desert voyage, even with a mule or a horse to help him on
the way. Durante patted the full, rounding side of his canteen. He might even now begin with the first sip but it was
a luxury to postpone pleasure until desire became greater.

He raised his eyes along the trail. Close by, it was merely
dotted with occasional bones, but distance joined the dots
into an unbroken chalk line which wavered with a strange
leisure across the Apache Desert, pointing toward the cool
blue promise of the mountains. The next morning he
would be among them.

A coyote whisked out of a gully and ran like a gray puff
of dust on the wind. His tongue hung out like a little red
rag from the side of his mouth; and suddenly Durante was
dry to the marrow. He uncorked and lifted his canteen. It
had a slightly sour smell; perhaps the sacking which covered it had grown a trifle old. And then he poured a great
mouthful of lukewarm liquid. He had swallowed it before
his senses could give him warning.

It was wine.

He looked first of all toward the mountains. They were
as calmly blue, as distant as when he had started that
morning. Twenty-four hours not on water, but on wine.

"I deserve it," said Durante. "I trusted him to fill the canteen. . . . I deserve it. Curse him!" With a mighty resolution, he quieted the panic in his soul. He would not touch the stuff until noon. Then he would take one discreet sip. He would win through.

Hours went by. He looked at his watch and found it was only ten o'clock. And he had thought that it was on the verge of noon! He uncorked the wine and drank freely and, corking the canteen, felt almost as though he needed a drink of water more than before. He sloshed the contents of the canteen. Already it was horribly light.

Once, he turned the mule and considered the return trip; but he could remember the head of the rabbit too clearly, drilled right through the center. The vineyard, the rows of old twisted, gnarled little trunks with the bark peeling off . . . every vine was to Tony like a human life. And Durante had condemned them all to death.

He faced the blue of the mountains again. His heart raced in his breast with terror. Perhaps it was fear and not the suction of that dry and deadly air that made his tongue cleave to the roof of his mouth.

The day grew old. Nausea began to work in his stomach, nausea alternating with sharp pains. When he looked down, he saw that there was blood on his boots. He had been spurring the mule until the red ran down from its flanks. It went with a curious stagger, like a rocking horse with a broken rocker; and Durante grew aware that he had been keeping the mule at a gallop for a long time. He pulled it to a halt. It stood with wide-braced legs. Its head was down. When he leaned from the saddle, he saw that its mouth was open.

"It's gunna die," said Durante. "It's gunna die . . . what a fool I been . . ."

The mule did not die until after sunset. Durante left everything except his revolver. He packed the weight of that for an hour and discarded it, in turn. His knees were growing weak. When he looked up at the stars, they shone white and clear for a moment only, and then whirled into little racing circles and scrawls of red.

He lay down. He kept his eyes closed and waited for the shaking to go out of his body, but it would not stop. And every breath of darkness was like an inhalation of black dust.

He got up and went on, staggering. Sometimes he found himself running.

Before you die of thirst, you go mad. He kept remembering that. His tongue had swollen big. Before it choked him, if he lanced it with his knife the blood would help him; he would be able to swallow. Then he remembered that the taste of blood is salty.

Once, in his boyhood, he had ridden through a pass with his father and they had looked down on the sapphire of a mountain lake, a hundred thousand million tons of water as cold as snow . .

When he looked up, now, there were no stars; and this frightened him terribly. He never had seen a desert night so dark. His eyes were failing, he was being blinded. When the morning came, he would not be able to see the mountains, and he would walk around and around in a circle until he dropped and died.

No stars, no wind; the air as still as the waters of a stale pool, and he in the dregs at the bottom . . .

He seized his shirt at the throat and tore it away so that it hung in two rags from his hips.

He could see the earth only well enough to stumble on the rocks. But there were no stars in the heavens. He was blind: he had no more hope than a rat in a well. Ah, but Italian devils know how to put poison in wine that steal all the senses or any one of them: and Tony had chosen to blind Durante.

He heard a sound like water. It was the swishing of the soft deep sand through which he was treading; sand so soft that a man could dig it away with his bare hands. . . .

Afterward, after many hours, out of the blind face of that sky the rain began to fall. It made first a whispering and then a delicate murmur like voices conversing, but after that, just at the dawn, it roared like the hoofs of ten thousand charging horses. Even through that thundering confusion the big birds with naked heads and red, raw necks found their way down to one place in the Apache Desert.

Our Daily Bread

Young, in New York, and struggling to become a published writer, Faust lived in a rented room in a three-room apartment occupied by a Jewish rabbi, in the city's underprivileged Lower East Side. From this vantage point stems this story.

Mrs. SIDNEY M. LESTER used to come into the grocery store of Kahn & Seidelman every day in the busy time about five-thirty. She looked things over, from the boxes of red apples to the rich hams and golden-brown chickens under the glass of the delicatessen counter. Those bologna sausages, broadly sliced across, those glittering heaps of potato salad, overstrewn with parsley, and the various new touches which came into the store from the kitchen of Minnie Seidelman. Sometimes, but that was in the early days before Kahn & Seidelman understood, one of them asked Mrs. Lester if she were being served. On those occasions she priced some of the delicacies and learned with undying interest, over and over again, that the little tubes of anchovy paste were sixty-five cents and that the dabs of *pâté* cost seventy-five; and three dollars and a half for one tiny little jar of caviar always caused Mrs. Sidney M. Lester to nod her head and look out of the corner of a speculative eye, as though she were telling herself that she must remember this when she gave her party next week.

But the party never came, and in six months of constant patronage Mrs. Lester never bought five cents' worth of provisions of any kind from the store of Kahn & Seidelman. But every day, at about five-thirty, she stole a loaf of bread and walked with dignity into the street.

It would not be easy for most women to steal a loaf of bread. A loaf is about the clumsiest object in the world to conceal. But Mrs. Sidney M. Lester wore a short cloak of black silk, and when she picked up the loaf, she held it between her hip and the pinch of her left elbow, so that it was very well concealed by the cloak. These loaves, you understand, were not the ordinary blocks, soft, pulpy, cellophane-wrapped articles which you get in most stores. Instead, they were long, brown-crusted French loaves which come out of the oven of Minnie Seidelman's own kitchen. If you know what good bread is, go over there to Lexington Avenue this very day and buy a loaf of Minnie Seidelman's bread. It has a good smack to it, I can tell you; with a bottle of milk and an apple, it will make you a fine meal. And every day, at about five-thirty, when the store was filled with shopping women who had finished their day's work and were getting food for supper, Mrs. Sidney M. Lester stole a loaf of that beautiful bread and took it away.

Bernie Kahn saw it first of all.

Bernie is a good boy. He is in high school now, when a lot of youngsters begin to put on airs; but Bernie has no nonsense about him, and when he comes home from school, he rushes through with his homework and then hurries over to help at the store during the rush hour. His cousin, Abe Seidelman, is following that good example, shamed into it. And of course Ruth Kahn and sweet little Rose Seidelman are always around to help out. It's a wonderful thing, the way the Kahns and Seidelmans work together and in their own families find all the help that they need for everything. By the way, Rose Seidelman is the pretty one with the high color. If you say that the apples are not as red as *her* cheeks, she lifts up a quick hand and touches one of them and looks as surprised as though she never had heard this remark in her life before.

But to go back to Bernie, he was the one who discovered the thefts. He was not one of those headlong young fools who shout out the first guess that comes into the head. The first day he suspected. What did he do? The second day he counted every loaf in the stack just before Mrs. Sidney M. Lester went out past the bread counter. And then he counted them again after she went by and found out, as he suspected, that the store was one loaf shy. Any other boy would have talked then and there, but Bernie is really a boy in a thousand. He waited until the next day, and the next day's theft, and then he trailed Mrs. Sidney M. Lester around the corner to the old place which had been turned into a rooming house. When she went in, he looked at the names under the mail boxes and discovered that she lived on the west side of the top floor. When Bernie was thoroughly equipped with this information, he went back to the store, took his father aside, and told him the news.

The brow of his father darkened, but he said nothing. Bernie did not talk about it to the others. He watched his father and kept his mouth shut.

You never saw a boy like Bernie. Nothing can keep him from getting on in the world.

His father, Jake Kahn, is unlike the physical tradition of his family. Martha Kahn has cooked for her entire family with wonderful success all the days of her married life, but she can't put a pound on Jake. He remains as thin as a thinker, and his shoulders bend forward over a narrowing chest.

That night after supper they all went in, as usual, to sit for a half hour with Grandfather Oscar Kahn in the front room. Grandfather Oscar sits there in a brown leather chair and smokes a long pipe that has a China bowl with a cap of silver filigree. It curves down out of the white beard of Oscar and rests comfortably upon the top fold of his stomach, as upon a shelf.

The half hour almost had ended when Jake Kahn said, "Well, we've got one at last."

Grandfather Oscar opened one eye and lifted the white shag of one eyebrow.

"What have you got, my son?" he asked.

"A shoplifter," said Jake quietly.

The stir in the family circle was immense. Grandfather Oscar opened both eyes wide. Only Bernie, rich in knowledge, sat still and said nothing, but watched. He is that kind of a boy

"An old scoundrel of a woman," said Jake, "who steals a loaf of bread from our store every day of her life!"

His indignation put fire in his sunken eyes.

As for Grandfather Oscar, he sank back in his chair and the mouthpiece of his pipe slipped from his lips and the pipe itself sank down to the second fold of his stomach, where it rested again as upon a shelf.

"*Himmel—Gott!*" said Grandfather Oscar.

"There's a jail for such people!" cried Martha Kahn.

"*Himmel—und Herr Gott!*" said Grandfather Oscar.

"I know that sly old thief—I know the very one!" cried Ruth, inspired by afterthought.

Only Bernie Kahn said nothing. He is really a remarkable boy.

Then Grandfather Oscar groaned again, his voice like a rumbling of distant thunder: "*Heilige Himmel—unter Herr Gott der Vater!* A loaf of bread!"

The last four words were unexpected. They struck the rest of the family to a sudden silence. They were rich in surprising implications. They attacked the whole Kahn family of the younger generations as from the rear.

Grandfather Oscar said, "Every day of her life—to steal—a loaf of bread!"

There was such an accent upon "bread" that a shudder ran through the listeners.

After that, Oscar Kahn closed his eyes, lifted his pipe to the uppermost fold of his stomach, and restored the mouthpiece to his lips.

His family stole quietly from the room.

The next day they were changed people. No one said anything to anybody else; and every one of the Kahns had the same idea.

That very afternoon, Abe Seidelman came running to Jake Kahn shortly after five-thirty and cried out, "That old woman—the one in the black cloak—she's a thief!"

"Yeah?" said Jake. He looked down upon Abe not from a superior height of inches, but from a superiority of mind and soul and time. "What did she steal?"

"She stole a loaf of bread!" said Abe. "I saw her put it up under her cloak as slick as you please!"

"She stole a loaf of bread. And so what?" asked Jake.

Bewildering light dawned upon the brain of Abe.

"Geez!" he said, and laughed a little, embarrassed.

"Yeah, sure," said Abe, and he laughed a little again, very softly.

The Kahns and the Seidelmans have lived and worked together for so many years that their mutual understanding is remarkable. In a flash they now knew what their attitude should be toward Mrs. Sidney M. Lester. And that attitude never faltered.

When she came in, always wearing the same dress of black silk, upon which time had shed a sort of dust, almost impalpable, with a collar of black lace concealing the indignities which the years had worked upon her throat, she was sure to get a cheerful greeting from the Kahns and the Seidelmans—not too much, not so much attention that she might become embarrassed, but just enough to warm the air with a touch of neighborliness. Her pleasure was always asked. She always had a chance to price the caviar or the sliced white chicken, or the lobsters, or the *pâté*. And at the moment when she started from the store again, all the Kahns and all the Seidelmans were suddenly very busy, with their faces turned to the rear of the store. At that moment even a flash of lightning would not have been seen by those good people.

As I was saying, this went on for upward of six months before Mrs. Sidney M. Lester failed to appear at the store. Her absence was noted at once. It was the subject of a telephone conversation between the house of Kahn and the house of Seidelman that evening. On the second day again she was missing. And when the third evening did not bring her between five and five-thirty, Bernie went around to the rooming house and rang the porter's bell. A sour old woman said, "Mrs. Lester must be in because she ain't gone out!"

"She's sick, I guess," said Bernie, when he went back to the store.

The Kahns and the Seidelmans were confused and worried by the thought.

Then Jake Kahn did something about it. Jake is a dry, hard-faced man and he is apt to surprise his entire family by the unexpected workings of his brain.

They were about to close the store; the last clients were gone; and Jake's loud, dry voice said: "Ruthie, get a jar of that caviar out of the icebox, and a couple tubes of anchovy paste, and some of them anchovies, and a jar of *pâté*. Bernie, get a dozen of those Southern California navels. Select. No, maybe you better make it half a dozen. Some of those Spanish olives, Abe . . ."

He went on with additional selections.

The unanimity of the Kahns and Seidlemans never was shown to better advantage. The mind of Jake instantly was

apparent to all the rest, and in ten minutes every Kahn
and Seidelman in the store was walking around the corner
on that cold November day—for it was nearly Thanksgiv-
ing and there was ice in every breath they drew. And every
Kahn and every Seidelman of the lot carried something in
hand to the little rooming house where Mrs. Sidney M.
Lester lived.

The sour-faced woman opened the door again.

"Top floor west," she said. "And help yourself!"

She stood at the bottom of the stairs, sniffing, as the
procession climbed.

When they came to the top floor west, Jake tapped.
There was no response. The smiles died upon the faces of
the Kahns and the Seidelmans.

Then Jake tried the door. It opened at once. He peeked
and the Kahns and the Seidelmans peeked behind him.
They saw a neat little living room with a round table in
the center of it, and the center of the table was crossed by
an embroidered runner; and on the runner stood four or
five books, upheld by bronze book ends; and on the wall
there was a picture of a dignified gentleman in tails, making a gesture as though he were in the midst of a public
address. They knew, instantly, that that was Sidney M.
Lester, and that he was dead

"Good!" said Jake, seeing that the inner door to the
bedroom-kitchenette was closed. "We'll get everything on
the table and surprise her. . . ."

They got into the living room. Their eyes gave warning
to one another to make no sound. When Ruthie dropped
the spoon out of the potato salad and it clattered on the

floor, the whole group looked upon her as upon a mortal sinner, and she was frozen with fright.

But presently they had everything laid out so that it would have done you good to see that caviar, packed in glistening ice, and the silver white of pure chicken breast, sliced by Abe—he really has a perfect touch for carving, Grandfather Oscar says; and there were grapes frosted with cold and sweetness and the fragrant big California oranges, richer than the fabled apples of the Hesperides; and so on, through item after item, almost every article that Mrs. Sidney M. Lester ever had priced in the store was represented by that array upon the table.

Then Jake, after taking a final survey of the table, advanced toward the inner door. The Kahns and Seidelmans, unbidden, ranged themselves in a straight line, beginning with Martha Kahn and ending with Bernie, who is the smallest of the family, though of course he more than makes up for inches with brains.

Jake rapped delicately upon that inner door. He waited. He rapped again. Suddenly he rapped very loudly indeed. Martha Kahn caught her breath.

Martha said, whispering: *"Gott mit uns . . . !"*

And then Jake turned the knob slowly, and slowly pushed the door open. He and all the families behind him could look through the door to the chair where Mrs. Sidney M. Lester sat beside the western window with a time-yellowed old letter in her hand, and her head bent thoughtfully to the side, and her eyes looking askance out the window for all the world as though she had just been pricing the caviar or the *pâté* in the store of Kahn & Seidelman.

Jake Kahn did not speak. He turned slowly, and slowly he closed the door

He crossed the room. He opened the door into the hall. Through it filed the Kahns and the Seidelmans, stepping soundlessly. So perfectly were they of one mind that it did not occur to any of them to take even the perishable caviar away; but all remained as they had brought it and arranged—what was to have been a feast, but became a sacrifice. The caviar with its glistening ice, the rich *pâté*, uncovered, the snow-white slices of chicken which Abe had carved, all stood there in order, and the California oranges, at a dollar and twenty-five cents a dozen, gave into the air an aromatic fragrance purer than the purest incense in a church.

The Kahns and Seidelmans went noiselessly down the stairs with big Martha Kahn weeping silently all the way and Jake comforting her, for he understood the nature of their loss.

The Wolf Pack and the Kill

This is from Faust's partially autobiographical novel, *Harrigan,* into which he incorporated some of the adventures that made his life at times as exciting as the stories he wrote. The scene is the deck of the tramp steamer *Mary Rogers,* bound outward from Honolulu.

THE SMILE of Captain McTee was like the smile of Satan when he watched Adam driven from the Eden.

"Strip to the waist," he said, and turned on the crew.

"You know me, lads. I've tried to break Harrigan, but I've only bent him, and now he's going to stand up to me man to man, and if he wins he's free to do as he likes and never lift a hand till we reach port. Aye, lick your chops, you dogs. There's none of you had the heart to try what Harrigan is going to try. If you had, you'd have got what Harrigan is going to get. Keep back. Give us room. If one of you gets in the way I'll have him flogged for it afterwards."

If they did not actually lick their chops there was hunger in their eyes and a strange wistfulness as they watched Harrigan strip off his shirt, but when they saw the wasted arms, lean, with the muscles defined and corded as if by famine, their faces want blank again. For they glanced in turn at the vast torso of McTee. When he moved his arms his smooth shoulders rippled in significant spots—the spots where the driving muscles lay. But Harrigan saw nothing save the throat of which he had dreamed. It was round and hard. It would be almost impossible for ordinary hands to get a grip on it—but if the red hands of Harrigan found such a grip— His head tilted back and he laughed.

"Aye, he's mad!" muttered a sailor. "His mind's gone."

"Are you ready?" said McTee.

"Ready."

"This is to the finish?"

"Aye."

"And no quarter?"

Harrigan grinned, and slipped out to the middle of the deck. Both of them kicked off their shoes. Even in their bare feet it would be difficult to keep upright, for the *Mary Rogers* was rollicking through a choppy sea, twisting and heaving from time to time like a bucking horse. Harrigan sensed the crew standing in a loose circle with the hunger of the wolf pack in winter stamped in their eyes, but dull and hopeless, like those who have hunted long and tasted no meat.

McTee stood with his feet braced strongly, his knees sagging now and again to the sway of the deck, his shoulders drooping to give effect to a quick blow, his hands poised. But Harrigan stole about him with a gliding, unequal step. He did not seem preparing to strike with his hands, which hung low, but rather like one who would leap at the throat with his teeth. The ship heaved and twisted willfully as McTee's knees sagged. Harrigan sprang and his fists cracked—one, two. He leaped out again under the captain's clubbed hands. Two spots of red glowed on McTee's ribs and the wolf pack moistened their lips and glanced from one to the other.

"Come again, Harrigan, for I've smelled the meat, not tasted it."

"It tastes red—like this."

And feinting at McTee's body, he suddenly straightened and smashed both hands against the captain's mouth. Mc-Tee's head jarred back under the impact. The wolf pack murmured. The captain made a long step, waited until Harrigan had leaped back to the side of the deck to avoid the plunge, and then, as the deck heaved up to give added impetus to his lunge, he rushed. The angle of the deck kept the Irishman from taking advantage of his agility. He could not escape. One pile-driver hand cracked against his forehead—another thudded on his ribs. He leaped through a shower of blows and clinched.

He was dashed about as a dog shakes a rag. He was crushed against the rail. He was shaken by a quick succession of short arm punches. But anything was preferable to another of those long, driving blows. He clung until his head cleared. Then he shook himself loose and dropped, as if dazed, to one knee. As he crouched he saw the Negro giant squatted at one side with his head thrust forward and his upper lip writhen back over the white, fanglike teeth. Then McTee's bellow of triumph filled his ears. The captain bore down on him with outstretched hands to grapple at his throat and beat him into submission against the deck, but at the right instant Harrigan rose and lurched out with stiff arm. The punch drove home to the face with a shock that jarred Harrigan to his feet and jerked McTee back as if drawn by a hand. Before he recovered his balance Harrigan planted half a dozen punches with every ounce of his weight lunging behind them, but though they shook the captain, they did not send him down, and Harrigan groaned.

McTee bellowed again. It was not pain. It was not mere rage. It was a battle cry, and with it he rushed Harrigan. They raged back and forth across the deck, and the wolf pack drew close and sagged farther back, murmuring, cursing beneath their breath. They had looked for a quick end to the struggle, but now they saw that the fighters were mated. The greater strength was McTee's; the greater purpose was Harrigan's. McTee fought to crush and conquer; Harrigan fought to kill.

The blows of the captain flung Harrigan here and there as wind knocks a piece of paper down a street, and yet he came back to meet the attack, slinking with sure, catlike steps. The heel and pitch of the deck sometimes staggered the captain, but Harrigan seemed to know beforehand what would happen, and he leaped in at every opening with blows that cut the skin.

His own flesh was bruised. He bled from mouth and nose, and the current trickled down to a smear across his chest, but what was any other pain compared with the torture of his clenched fists? It made his arms numb to the elbow and sent currents of fire through his veins. His eyes

kept on the thick throat of McTee. Though he was
knocked reeling and half senseless, his stare never changed,
and the wolf pack caught each other by the arms and
shoulders and with their heads jutting forward with eagerness watched, waited. The "Ha!" of McTee rang with the
strength of five throats. The "Wah-h!" of Harrigan purred
like a furious panther's snarl.

Then as the frenzy left Harrigan and the numbness de-
parted from his arms, he knew that he was growing weaker
and weaker. McTee was master; he felt it with a soul-
filling bitterness. His blows fairly bounced from the body
and even the head of the captain; he might as well have
hammered a great chunk of India-rubber. In McTee's eyes
he saw the growing light of victory, the confidence, the
strength of surety. His own wild hunger for blood grew
apace with his desperation. He flung himself forward in a
last effort.

A ponderous fist driven with the speed of a whiplash
thudded against his chest and threw him back, the other
fist cracked home between his eyes, fairly lifting him from
his feet and hurling him against the base of the wheel
house. With the recoil he pitched forward to his face upon
the deck, and the weight of McTee dropped upon him. He
was raised by the shoulders and his face beaten against the
planks. Then a forearm shot under his shoulder and a
hand fastened on the back of his neck in an incomplete
half-Nelson. As McTee applied the pressure, Harrigan felt
his vertebral column give under the tremendous strain. He
struggled furiously but could not break that grip. Far
away, like the storm wind in the forest, he heard the moan

of the wolf pack.

"Give in! Give in!" panted McTee.

"Ah-h!" snarled Harrigan.

He felt the deck swing and jerked his legs high in the air. He could not have broken that grip of his own strength, but the sway of the deck gave his movement a mighty leverage. The hand slipped from his neck, scraping skin away, as if a red-hot iron had been drawn across the flesh. But he was half loosed, and that twist of his body sent them both rolling one over the other to the scuppers of the ship—and it was McTee who crashed against the rail, receiving the blow on the back of his head. His eyes went dull; the red hands of Harrigan fastened in his throat.

"God!" screamed McTee, and gripped Harrigan's wrists, but the Irishman heaved him up and beat his head against the deck.

McTee's jaws fell open, and a bloody froth bubbled to his lips; his eyes thrust out hideously.

"Ah-h!" snarled Harrigan, and shifted his grip lower, his thumbs digging relentlessly into the hollow of the great throat. Where his fingers had lain before remained the red print of their pressure.

McTee beat with clubbed fists at the contorted, grinning face above him; Harrigan twisted his head once more against the deck, and this time the giant limbs of the captain relaxed as if in sleep. Then through the fierce singing in his ears the Irishman heard a yell. He turned his head. The wolf pack saw their prey pulled down at last. They ran now to join the kill, not men, but raging devils, and Harrigan, as they came, seemed to see once more the surging crowd of soldiers in Ivilei which had beaten in vain against the fists of this fallen monster. He loosed his hold; he sprang to his feet, catching up a marlinspike, and whirled it above his head.

"Back!" he shouted.

The rushing circle checked; all save the huge Negro, who kept on, his hands stretching before him like a starved man clutching at bread. The marlinspike clicked on his head with a sound like metal against metal. He spilled forward on the deck, his arms falling loosely about the feet of the Irishman, who bestrode the body of the captain.

"Come, all av ye!" screamed Harrigan. "Ye shtood by an' watched me soul burnin' in hell."

But they shrank back, growling one to the other savagely, irresolute. The Chinaman was making beast noises deep in his throat. There came a moan at Harrigan's feet. He leaned over and lifted the bulk of the captain's inert body. As if through a haze, he saw the chief engineer and the two mates running toward him and caught the glitter of a revolver in the hands of the first officer. The Irishman's battered lips stretched to a shapeless grin.

"Help me to the captain's cabin," he said. "He's afther bein' sick."

Internes Can't Take Money

From Faust's own experiences and those of his close friend, George Winthrop Fish, a New York surgeon, came this first "Kildare story." It started a series that spread from magazines to books and films, and then to radio and television, and made Dr. Kildare a household word (and personality) throughout the United States and much of the world. *Cosmopolitan* published this in March 1936.

JIMMY KILDARE used to get away from the hospital every afternoon and go over to Tom McGuire's saloon on the avenue. He always drank two beers. An interne in the accident room has to have the brains in his fingertips in good order all day long, but two beers don't get very far between a man and himself if he has a bit of head on his shoulders, and Jimmy Kildare had.

McGuire's saloon was comfortable in a dark, dingy way. The sawdust was swept out only once in two days, and the floors were never scrubbed except the evening before Election Day. Just the same, it was a good place. It made Jimmy Kildare think of the barn out on the old farm. The faces of the bums and crooks and yeggs who lined up at the bar were sour, just like the faces of the cows and horses that were lined along the mangers of the barn—long, and all the lines running down except for their arched eyebrows with the fool look of the cows.

When Jimmy Kildare leaned an elbow on the worn varnish of McGuire's saloon, it was always easier for him to think of home. The future to him was a great question mark, and New York was the emptiness inside the loop of the mark. Add a few strokes to the question mark and you get a dollar sign.

Jimmy Kildare used to think about that but he never dared to think very far because, when he began to dream, he always saw himself back on the farm in the frosty stillness of an autumn morning where every fence post and every wet rock said to him, "Jimmy, what are you doing away back here?"

The only times that he escaped entirely from those dreams were when he was working at the operating table, all scrubbed up and masked and draped in white. But even when he was going through the wards and looking into the life or death that brightened or shadowed the eyes of his patients, the old days and the terrible sense that he must return to them used to come over him.

He always wanted more relaxation from his work than those two beers in McGuire's saloon, but he knew that his purse would not stand it. The hospital paid for his laundry. It gave him three meals a day of soggy food. Otherwise, he had to find himself entirely, except for an occasional lift from famous Doctor Henry Fearson. Fearson from his height had noticed Kildare in medical school and had made it possible for him to carry on when home funds ran out.

Perhaps it was pity that moved Fearson to make those loans. Perhaps it was a quiet belief that there was a talent in the youngster. Kildare never could decide what the motive was, but he loved Fearson. During the interneship Fearson's loans became almost negligible, possibly because an absent-minded genius like Fearson forgot that an interne is an unpaid labor slave. A lot of the other lads were the sons of affluent doctors, and they were always going places on days off, but they never took Kildare and he could not afford to take himself. He wasn't a very exciting companion; he wasn't good-looking; he wasn't stylish.

There was only one day at the hospital for him to write down in red, and that was the occasion when he had assisted at a kidney operation. In the blind red murk the scalpel of the operating surgeon made a mistake and a beautiful fountain of blood and life sprang upward. Jimmy Kildare snatched a forceps and grabbed at the source of that explosion. He reached through a horrible boiling red fog and clamped down. The fountain ceased to rise. Afterward the artery was tied off, and a blood transfusion brought the patient back to life.

That day the great Henry Fearson stopped Jimmy in a corridor and gripped him by the shoulder and said, "You've got it, Kildare!"

Jimmy shrugged and hooked a thumb. "That back there? That was just luck," he said.

But Fearson answered: "Surgery is like tennis. There's no luck except bad luck."

Afterward, Jimmy Kildare went to his bare concrete cell

and sat for a long time looking at the wall until the wall opened and showed him a brief glimpse of heaven. Then he said: "Henry Fearson—by God!" and a great promise began to live along his blood stream.

Then the trouble started at McGuire's saloon.

The bartender was named Jeff. He had only one eye. Sometimes he wore a leather patch over it; sometimes he wore a watery glass eye that didn't fit. He was, Kildare gathered, a real force in the precinct because he knew by first name practically every voter in the district. This fellow Jeff never looked at Jimmy Kildare. He always had his one eye fixed on the habitués of the place, for McGuire's saloon had long ago ceased being a money-maker. It was merely a political nerve center vital to McGuire's power in the town.

One day a man in a blue suit and green necktie came into McGuire's saloon when Jimmy Kildare was having his beer. He was a big young man with a blunt, rather fleshy face, like a prize fighter out of training. He said, "H'are ya, Jeff? Give me a drink, will you?"

Then he dropped to the floor, with his arms thrown wide. The sleeve pulled up from the right arm and showed Kildare that the forearm was cut clean across, well above the wrist.

Jeff, the bartender, put a hand on the bar and leaped over it. He dropped on his knees and began to cry out: "Hanlon! Hey, Hanlon!"

Jimmy Kildare got out of the saloon and went back to the hospital. An interne who takes supplies out of the hospital is—well, he is a thousand times worse than a burglar, because he is trusted. But Jimmy Kildare took supplies from the hospital. He kept thinking of that young, rather fleshy face, battered, but somehow honest. Not honest enough, of course, or else he would have taken that gaping wound straight to a doctor.

Yet he might not be a criminal who dreaded having a doctor report his case to the police. There were many stories in the precinct of men who died silently, refusing to name their assailants to the officers of the law, and all of those who died in that manner were not thugs. It merely seemed that in McGuire's following and among his enemies there were men who lived according to a new standard of morality about which Kildare knew nothing. And he determined to put from his mind all thought of the letter of the law, remembering only that great silent oath which dwells in the soul of every good doctor—that promise to relieve the suffering ones of this world.

He took from the hospital retractors, sutures, needles, iodine. He went back to McGuire's and found the door locked.

He banged heavily on that door until Jeff looked out at him and said: "What do you want? Get out of here!"

Kildare said: "Unless those cut tendons are sewed together properly, Hanlon won't have a right arm. The forearm will shorten. The hand will turn in. There won't be any power in it."

"Hell!" said Jeff, looking down at him. Then he said: "All right! All right!" He reached out, grabbed Kildare by the shoulder and dragged him into the family room of the saloon.

Somebody said, "He's dead!"

Hanlon lay on two tables that had been put side by side. His feet hung over the end of one table.

Kildare said, "Get out of my way." A big man barred him, arms spread wide. Kildare kicked him violently in the shins. The fellow howled and hopped away on one foot. Kildare shoved his hand over Hanlon's heart and heard Jeff say: "Cut it out. This is a kind of a doc. They got them over in the hospital like this. Maybe he knows something."

Kildare said: "He's only fainted. Be useful, some of you." He began to unwrap the towel, exposing the instruments.

"He's come and brought the stuff," said Jeff. "Who would of thought!"

Kildare began with iodine. Then he made two men hold Hanlon's right arm. They had put a clumsy tourniquet above the elbow. Kildare got to work on the tendons. He made Jeff and another man hold the retractors that kept the wound gaping for his convenience.

Jeff said, "It makes me kind of sick."

The other man said: "Watch what he's doing, you dumb cluck! The kid's got eyes in his fingers. Watch what they do!"

Kildare put the tendons together one by one, matching the ends with care, and then securing them with mattress stitches, using threads of black silk. You could see the zigzag pattern of the little threads against the cordage of the tendons, all frayed at the cut ends.

Someone said, "Who did it?"

Another man said: "Who do you think, dummy? Dennis Innis, of course."

"He'll get Innis yet," said another.

"He ain't gunna have no gun hand to get Innis," said the first speaker. "There won't be no brains in that right hand of his, even when this slick job is finished. The wits is cut out of it."

Kildare told himself that he must not think of the meaning behind that right hand. He kept on matching the severed ends of the tendons and making the stitches. Then Hanlon wakened from his trance and began to curse and struggle.

Jeff said: "You damn fool, this doc is saving your hand. Shut up, will you!"

Hanlon shut up. Suddenly he extended his limp right arm toward Kildare. "Okay," he said, and kept his muscles flaccid. Only the loudness of his breathing told of his pain.

When the wound was closed and Kildare stepped back from his work, Hanlon sat up. Jeff and another man—he who had worked with the retractors—were rubbing the blood from Kildare's hands with painful care. He surrendered his hands to them like tools of infinite value in the trust of friends. A warmth flowed like strong drink through his brain.

Hanlon stared at Kildare, saying, "Who are you?"

"Oh, go to hell!" said Jeff. "This is Doctor Kildare. He's a right guy. Oh, go to hell, will you!"

Hanlon smiled. "Sure," he said. "Sure I'll go." And he looked down at his right hand, which rested on one knee.

For two days Jimmy Kildare did not return to Mc-Guire's. Then habit picked him up and shoved him through the front door. There were four men standing at the bar and Jeff, the bartender, was singing an Irish melody in a husky voice. Two or three of the others kept him company. Jeff broke off in the middle of the song. He went to the end of the bar where Kildare stood and focused on the doctor the blue-gray light of his one eye, warmer, suddenly, than sunshine.

"I thought you was passing us up lately, Doc," said Jeff. "What you having? The same?"

"The same," said Kildare.

The four faces turned and stared.

Jeff was filling the tall glass with beer. He said, to the beer: "Yeah. Okay. It's him."

Nobody looked at Kildare any more. They looked, instead, at his image in the mirror behind the bar. Kildare felt their eyes more than ever.

"Go hop on the phone," said Jeff.

Someone left the room. There was silence as Jeff brought the beer to Kildare.

Kildare tasted it. "This seems better than usual, Jeff," he said. He never had used Jeff's name before.

"Yeah, and why the hell wouldn't it be better?" said Jeff. "Beer comes that way. Good and bad. You know, Doc."

One of the men sauntered toward Kildare and said: "I'd like to meet you, Doc. I'm—"

"You back up," said Jeff. "Who d'you wanta meet, anyway?"

The man stopped short and turned away, unoffended. He said: "Okay! Okay!" and went back to his place.

When Kildare had finished his glass of beer, he put the

money for it on the bar. "Well, so long," he said. "So long, Jeff."

Jeff shoved the money back toward Kildare. "What's that for?" he demanded, with a fierce light in his one eye. "Now listen, will you? Quit it, will you? . . . And where's your second beer, anyway?"

Kildare felt giddy. "Why, yes, a second one, please," he said.

The glass was filled for him. Jeff was scowling bitterly. He shoved the second beer onto the bar with a savage shortness of gesture, disdaining the money with a touch of his hand. But Kildare let the silver lie there.

The door creaked open behind him. "Hello, Jeff," said the newcomer, behind Kildare's back.

Jeff, in place of answering, wagged his head toward Kildare.

A big red-faced man with a whisky pungency about him stood beside Kildare at the bar. He wheezed a little as he spoke. His voice was husky but warm.

"I'm McGuire," he said. "Pleased to know you, Doctor Kildare. Damn pleased. Like to know more of you out of the same keg. What're you having, Doctor? Don't mean to say you stick to beer, do you?"

"He's gotta work. You know," said Jeff.

"Yeah, sure. Sure," said McGuire. "This is a pleasure, Doctor Kildare. By the way, a friend of yours asked me to give you a letter. He wants you to open it when you get back home. . . . Make mine small, Jeff. Make it right but make it small. Boys, have something with me!"

The envelope was stuffy and soft and fat. Jimmy Kildare

went back to his concrete cell in the hospital and opened it in private. He counted twenty fifty-dollar bills.

He sat down on the edge of his bed. A man doesn't have to space out and span out a thousand dollars. It does for itself. And it meant release from prison to Kildare.

For two days Kildare fought himself with all the appetites of his years closing his throat. Then he went back to McGuire's saloon.

Jeff looked at him with brotherly fondness and served him two beers. Kildare put his money on the bar, and Jeff took it, saying: "You don't need to do that, Doc. But thanks, anyhow."

Then Kildare pushed the envelope across the table. It was resealed, but rumpled and finger-soiled. "This is for Mr. McGuire," he said, and went out.

Afterward, he felt empty but he felt stronger, too. Like a man in training for a fight, fasting before the encounter.

He went right back to McGuire's saloon the next day, and there he found McGuire himself at the bar in a brilliant checked suit. He looked at Kildare with trouble in his eye.

"Now, listen, kid—Doc, I mean," said McGuire, without prelude. "What the hell? I mean, I got the double of that in my pocket."

Kildare blushed as he answered: "You see, I'm an interne. Internes can't take anything for their work. It's against the rules. If an interne could take anything, people in the wards would bribe him to get the extra attention."

"Wards? Who's talking about wards?" demanded Mc-

Guire. "Hell, I'm talking about a job in my saloon."

"I've never done any jobs outside the hospital," said Kildare, getting redder than ever. "It's not allowed."

"You never did a job in this saloon?" demanded McGuire, with anger.

"No," said Kildare. "I never did anything here."

"My God!" said McGuire. He added, "Gimme a drink, Jeff."

But Jeff remained frozen for a long moment. Only by degrees was he able to thaw out and get into action. Kildare finished his beer and hurried back to the concrete cell, the smell of carbolic acid and the empty loop of the question mark which embraced his future.

If you work very hard, one day rubs out the other. Kildare worked very hard and for a long time gave up beer and McGuire's, until a telephone call summoned him, weeks later. He went over to McGuire's place and found Pat Hanlon at the bar.

"All right, you two," said Jeff, spreading his hands on the bar like a benevolent father. Hanlon went to Kildare and took his hand. He held it for a long time, while his eyes went over Kildare.

"They certainly take it out of you guys at the hospital," said Hanlon.

"That's just the game," said Kildare.

"Who wants to play a game where he's always 'it'?" asked Hanlon. "Listen, Doc. Have a drink with me, will you?"

Jeff whispered, leaning across the bar: "What's it going

to be, Doc?"

Kildare said shortly, "I pay for my own, in here."

"Come on. Aw, quit it," said Jeff.

Hanlon said, "You'll have something with me, brother."

"I don't drink," said Kildare, "unless I can pay for it." A blind anger took hold of him. He was staring at the perfection of Hanlon's clothes.

"Aw, quit it!" said Jeff. "Listen, Hanlon, the kid don't mean it. He don't mean anything; he just don't know."

"The hell he don't!" said Hanlon, and turned his back suddenly on Kildare. He took three steps.

"Are you gunna be a damn fool, Hanlon?" asked Jeff, perspiring with anxiety.

"No," answered Hanlon. He turned to Kildare again. "Why be so damn mean?" he asked. "Look!"

He held out his right hand. He worked the fingers back and forth.

"It's okay, see?" he said. "I been to see a doc. He said what you done was a masterpiece. He said nobody could of done better. Look—there ain't any scar even, hardly. Now, why be high-hat with me? You could have my guts."

Jeff interpreted across the bar: "You hear, Doc? You could have everything he's got. Say something to him."

Kildare said: "I can't have anything to do with you. That goes for the whole bunch. I like you all right. When I can help out any of you, I want to do it as long as you don't ask me to take care of a crook."

"Hanlon ain't a crook!" cried Jeff. "He's the right-hand man of McGuire, Doc. Hanlon's all right."

"I'm glad he is," said Kildare. "But over there at the

hospital they watch us all the time. I'm only an interne. I like you all fine. I can't know you!"

Hanlon's eyes dwelt on the middle section of Kildare's body. "All right," he said.

Jeff again leaned over the bar. "Does that go for me, kid?" he asked.

"Ah—I don't know. I'm going back to the hospital," said Kildare.

"Am I a thug?" asked Hanlon.

"I don't know," said Kildare.

"Hanlon!" shouted Jeff.

Hanlon straightened with a quick jerk. "All right," he said, still making that cold survey of Kildare's anatomy.

Kildare got to the door before Jeff said, "Doc, for God's sake!"

Kildare paused. He could feel Hanlon like a leveled gun behind him.

"Listen, Doc," said Jeff. "Hanlon has a wife."

"That's all out," said Hanlon. "Quit it."

"Oh, shut your face, will you, Pat?" demanded Jeff. "His wife's going to have a baby soon, and there's no doc he can get. Income tax. Hanlon's all right. But income tax. They want him. And they've got the girl watched. They're waiting for him to go back to her. Understand? He's gotta get her a doctor he can trust. Listen, Doc, will you take care of her?"

Kildare said, "Well, Hanlon, why didn't you tell me?"

So Kildare went. It was a nice little apartment all done up in French-gray. Everything was simple. A new Pat Hanlon entered the world.

Kildare remained by the bed until the effects of the ether wore away from the mother. She kept saying, "Is it a boy, Doctor?"

"Yes," he would answer, and her eyes would shine at him, only to grow dim again from the effect of the drug.

Then the baby began to cry, and the sound drew the girl back to full consciousness. She held the baby in the hollow of her arm and crooned over it.

Kildare went back to McGuire's, where Pat Hanlon sat in the back room with his head bowed into his hands. He lifted his head and glared at Kildare.

"It's all right," said Kildare. "Your wife is a sweetheart, Hanlon. And now she's got a fine son to keep her company."

Said Hanlon, "And how's my girl, Doc?"

Kildare gripped his two hands hard together. He said, "She's the happiest soul in New York, right now. She wants me to tell you that she loves you."

Hanlon flung a sheaf of bills on the table. "Will you for God's sake take some of it?" he pleaded.

"No," said Kildare.

"Do you despise me that much, Doc?"

Kildare patted the big shoulder. "I don't hate you, Hanlon," he said. "But I'm an interne. I can't take money."

But Kildare's nerves were still shaking when he got back to the hospital, for perhaps the world did not need any more Pat Hanlons. He sat on his bed after he had made his rounds and looked at the tremor of his hands.

Doctor Henry Fearson had passed Kildare in a corridor, and he had stopped to greet his idol. "How's everything,

Doctor Fearson?"

"Everything? Things never are right except in patches," said Fearson, and went on.

But the dark of the underworld still clung to Kildare as he sat there. His roommate came in and said: "Only three months before we get out of this lousy hole. Where do you hitch up after that?"

Kildare lifted his head. "Fearson says he wants me in his office," he remarked.

"Fearson? That's a hell of an out for you, brother. Don't you know that?"

Kildare said deliberately, "He's the finest man and the best doctor I know."

"Oh, yeah, oh, yeah! We all know that. But he owes money that he shouldn't."

"What do you mean?"

"I don't know, but they've got him."

"Why?"

"Something about money. We all know Fearson is a saint, but even saints can be framed. Fearson is framed. They're going to cut his head off. He can go work on a farm in about a month!"

And Kildare thought again of the farm on the autumn morning. He thought of the lofty intellectual brow of Fearson, and that gaunt boy in overalls. He kept on thinking, and the next afternoon he needed his beer.

When he got to McGuire's, Hanlon drew him straight into the back room.

Hanlon said, as they sat down to beer: "Now listen, Doc. McGuire wants to talk to you. He says you could vote the precinct."

"I could what?" asked Kildare.

"You don't know what people around here think of you. When you go down the street, does anybody speak? The bums along the pavement, I mean?"

"Yes," said Kildare. "They come over to the accident room, too, and ask for me. Yes, they all seem to know me."

"You been a coupla years around here. You've taken care of a hundred dirty bums, and they've talked about you. You wouldn't take money. You could vote the precinct," said Hanlon. "They all know you're a guy that's done something for nothing. McGuire says: 'Chuck the regular line. Throw in with him.' He can get you five thousand the first year, besides gravy. And then eight thousand, ten thousand and right on up. And twice as much on the side."

"I'm only an interne," said Kildare.

"What are you thinking of, with that dreamy look?" asked Hanlon.

"I'm thinking of an apartment all done in French-gray," said Kildare.

"Aw, hell!" laughed Hanlon. "You could have ten like that. I mean, McGuire wants to cut you in on something rich. By the way, why don't you come see us? My wife gives me a temperature talking about you."

"I'd like to see you both," said Kildare, "but tell McGuire I'm not a politician. I'm an interne."

"You want the stuff but you're afraid to take it. Is that right?" asked Hanlon.

"Maybe," said Kildare.

"What are you afraid of?"

"I'm afraid of dirt that soap and water won't wash off."

"McGuire's got to talk to you himself," said Hanlon. "You certainly are tough. Well, all that's left to me is my own personal angle. I mean, the old girl down there holding the kid and asking what have I done for the doc. Now listen, Doc. Don't be a damn fool. I've got twenty-five hundred dollars—"

"I don't want your money," said Kildare.

"Meaning it's dirty? Meaning I'm dirty, too?" shouted Hanlon.

"You take it any way you please."

Hanlon's fist started. But it was only the flat of his hand that struck heavily across Kildare's face.

Kildare came off his chair swinging. Hanlon caught his arms.

"You sap, I gotta mind to wring your neck—I gotta mind to do you in!" shouted Hanlon. "Get out!"

Kildare got out.

His nose was numb half an hour later, but his hand was steady enough in the operating room.

He was washing up afterward, when he said to his roommate, "Any more about Fearson?"

"Aw, he's sunk."

"How do you know?" Kildare asked.

"My old man's on the inside. He told me. They're going to make a goat of Fearson," said Vincent. "Money. He's got to pay off, and what the hell money has he got to pay off with when he's cleaned to the gills in the market?"

Afterward, Kildare went to see Fearson in his office.

"Are you in bad shape?" asked Kildare.

Fearson looked at him.

"You mean more to me than anybody in the world," said Kildare. "I'd give blood for you. Are they doing you in because you need money?"

"Who's been talking to you?" asked Fearson.

"Somebody. I hope it's a lie. I hope I'm simply making a damned fool of myself."

"You haven't made a damned fool of yourself. It's true," said Fearson. "I played once in my life with crooks. Now they've got me."

"What are you going to do?"

"I'm going to wait for the knife, that's all," said Fearson.

"I've got five hundred dollars," said Kildare. "I can get my hands on that."

"I need four thousand in cold cash by tomorrow night," said Fearson. "Get that for me if you can."

He offered no thanks. Kildare went back to his room. He needed no supper. He needed no sleep. He sat at the window and let the light from the next street lamp show him the dingy world of house fronts across the way. Toward morning, he lay down and slept for an hour. His head was ringing all morning as he went about his work. Noon came and he swallowed a few morsels, but the thought of Fearson choked him.

That afternoon he swallowed his pride and made himself go to McGuire's saloon. Only Jeff was there, reading a paper.

"Where's Hanlon?" asked Kildare.

Jeff said, beneath a scowl, "Hanlon hit you yesterday?"

"That doesn't matter," said Kildare. "There's a friend of mine in trouble."

"Who is he?" asked Jeff.

After a time Kildare murmured: "You don't know him. Fearson is his name."

"Fearson? Why, he . . . Sure I know him," said Jeff. "Is he a friend of yours?"

"Friend?" said Kildare. "He's the only friend I have." Then he added, smiling, "Outside of you, Jeff."

"Yeah, I know what you think of me," said Jeff. "I know what you think of all of us. Fearson, eh?"

"Where can I find Hanlon? I've got to see him."

"Hanlon's on the booze again," said Jeff. "I don't know where he is. When the news got out what Hanlon done to you, his wife had hysterics. That drove him out of his house. He came here, and McGuire gave him hell. I don't know where Hanlon is. He's been going straight ever since his son was born, but now he's on the loose."

"You don't think I could find him?"

"Nobody could find him. Even McGuire can't find him."

Kildare went back to the hospital.

Doctor Reichmann came up to him after surgery. "What the devil's the matter with you, Kildare?" he asked. "You were all thumbs today!'

"What the hell of it?" said Kildare.

"Are you saying that to me?" demanded Reichmann. "You confounded—"

Kildare walked away. A thing like that was enough to smash a young doctor's career, he knew. The oldsters will take anything rather than impertinence. He was very tired. Nothing mattered.

He got back to his room. Someone announced a telephone call.

He went to the telephone. A deep voice said over the line, in a guarded tone, "Is this Doctor Kildare?"

"Yes."

"There's a man lying here with a bullet through his lungs. Can any doctor in God's world do anything about it?"

"No," said Kildare.

And then he remembered the new work in chest surgery. There was a doctor who had saved the lives of policemen shot down by thugs in line of duty. In the old days they used to give morphine to men shot through the chest. Morphine, and let them die. But the new doctor had showed another way. Kildare knew about it.

"Nothing?" the voice was saying.

"Yes. Maybe," said Kildare. "Why?"

"That's all," said the voice.

Fifteen minutes later, Kildare was called out to the reception room. There were two fellows neatly dressed in brown suits, both wearing bow ties, both with the same hard, casual look.

"You telephoned to me fifteen minutes ago," said Kildare.

"That's right. Will you come try your hand on our friend?"

"Have you reported that *accident* to the police?" asked Kildare.

The pair looked steadily at him.

"Will you come?" said the first man.

"And compound a felony?" asked Kildare. "And smash my reputation?"

"There's money in it, Doc," said one.

And then Kildare remembered. There was no one in the world from whom he could get money except Pat Hanlon. And Hanlon had disappeared.

"Wait a minute," said Kildare.

He went to Fearson's office. It was late but Fearson opened the door. "All right. Come in!" he said.

"What's the deadline?" asked Kildare.

"Deadline for what?" asked Fearson.

"That four thousand," said Kildare.

"Oh that?" said Fearson. He smiled, his mouth twisting. "They *do* give me a deadline, like the villains in a book. I have till midnight, Kildare. Now, you go to bed and for-get—"

"I've been in jail here for a long time," said Kildare. "You're the only right man I've met among the lot. You've been hope to me, Fearson. And that means life, too. *You* keep on hoping till midnight comes, will you?"

He went back to the two in brown and said briefly, "I want four thousand dollars for the job."

"Yeah? That ain't what we heard about you. But I know strangers are different," said one of them, and he laughed. "Want to see the money now?"

"No," said Kildare.

They put him into a fast car and shot across town to an obscure side street.

They unlocked the door of a house with a tall, narrow front and ran up the stairs inside ahead of Kildare. He followed them into a bedroom with a single electric globe glaring from the ceiling.

On the bed lay a man with a bloody bandage about his chest. He was thirty, say, and big and lean. His face was evil, and Kildare thought, "If I help this man, I'm sold to the crooks forever."

Where the bandage did not bind the man, the lean of his big arching ribs was visible. He was naked to the waist. He had on trousers and black shoes that no one had thought to take off his feet.

A man rose from beside the bed. "He's passing out," he said. "It's no good. I knew it. Anywhere between the belly and the shoulders, and nothing helps them but morphine to make it easy."

"You talk like a fool, and I don't want fools around me," said Kildare. "Get out of here and heat some water. Somebody, take his shoes off."

He slit the bandage across. The hole was right in the lungs. It wasn't one of those lucky glancing bullets. It had ripped right through the middle.

The hole in front was quite a small puncture, rimmed with dark purple. The hole in the back was bigger. There wasn't much blood. That was the hell of it. The bleeding would be inward.

Kildare, leaning over the bed, began to listen and tap with a steady, hammerlike finger. He tapped all around and located the place where the hemorrhage was forming. When the blood clot had formed a complete stoppage, then the heart would move across to the other side of the body, and after that, only God could keep the victim from dying.

There was no hope—except what that new doctor had indicated. Kildare happened to know about it because Fearson had pointed out the new work to him.

Here the door to the room pushed open. Kildare looked over his shoulder and saw on the threshold Pat Hanlon and Jeff, with guns in their hands.

One of the fellows in brown had gone into the kitchen. The other two men stood quietly against the wall. One of them said: "Here's Hanlon. Shooting Dennis Innis here wasn't enough for him. He wants us all. Watch yourself, boy!"

Hanlon said: "You guys keep your shirts on. Innis had it coming to him, and you know it. Doc, how come you to play with this bunch of louses? Get out!"

Kildare stood up from the bed. He said: "I want two dishes boiled in water. I want plenty of hot water. Listen to me, Hanlon. If Innis dies, you'll burn. You're going to throw in with these fellows and help me. If you do that, I can pull Innis through, I think."

"You can't. He's got it through the lungs," said Hanlon. "The only right thing I ever done. I'm gunna get you out of this dump. Come on, Doc."

Kildare cried out in a voice that was strange to his own ears: "You murdering lot of childish half-wits, give me your guns! . . . Here, you, come out of the kitchen. There's not going to be any shooting. Hanlon, if we don't fix Innis, it's the electric chair for you."

The man came slowly out of the kitchen, his hands above his head, an automatic dangling from one of them. "I guess I hear it straight," he said.

"On that chair!" shouted Kildare, pointing. "All of 'em."

Five men piled seven guns in a glistening heap.

"It's a new kind of game," mumbled Hanlon. "Only the doc knows the rules."

"Get that hot water in here," said Kildare.

Three of them hurried to the kitchen. Kildare began to swab iodine, and he took a big syringe the moment the dishes and the water were brought to him.

"Look at him," whispered Hanlon. "Stabbing him through the heart."

Kildare was shoving the needle right into the lung, two inches, three inches. That was the start of the new idea.

Jeff grunted: "Back up, you birds. This doc is the only Christian in the world."

Then above the operation leaned hard-breathing shadows, closely grouped, a weight on Kildare's soul. He could feel the cold of sweat on his upper lip. He drew out the plunger of the syringe, and the red of the blood followed and filled the glass cylinder. He squirted it out into the warm dish, with the citrate to prevent clotting. He found a vein in the left arm with the second syringe, and injected the blood back into the arm.

Hanlon said: "I get it! Look, you dummies! He pulls the blood out of the lung so's Innis can't suffocate. Then he shoves the same blood back into his body. A regular blood transfusion. What he loses one place he gets another, and the old lungs don't fill up. Oh, does this doc know damn near everything!"

"Be quiet," said Kildare and went on working.

Jeff said: "When you think what the kid can do! Look, Hanlon! Color is coming back into Innis' face already. Why'd you go and sock lead into this bum, anyway? Even if he knifed you, you could let it go at that, couldn't you?"

"I thought he was too thick with my wife," said Hanlon. "Hell, I see how dumb I was. Quit talking, Jeff, will you?"

"Yeah. All I say is it's a damn good thing you got a buddy like me to keep you in with the brainy birds like the doc here," said Jeff. "You took and socked him the other day, didn't you?"

"All right! All right!" said Hanlon.

Then it was an hour later, and Kildare was saying: "Innis, stop talking. If you talk, you'll kill yourself. Lie still. I've given you morphine to make you sleep, and you'll sleep. Just lie still, will you?"

Innis whispered, with eyes closed, smiling: "Hanlon always was a damn fool. I never could get near the gal." Then he stopped talking.

"Is it gunna be all right, Doc?" asked Hanlon.

"He has nine chances out of ten," said Kildare. "That's all I can tell you."

"Nine of your chances is better than ninety of the next dirty mug," said Hanlon. "Doc, I wish you would stand up and take a couple of good swipes at me! I'd thank you for it, while you was paying yourself back."

Kildare leaned back in the chair. One of the men brought a cold glass and put it in his hand. It was a stiff Scotch-and-soda. He drank it like beer.

The neatness was gone from Innis' friends. Their brown suits were bunched around the shoulders. They looked at Kildare as one might stare at a being from the other world.

"This'll make you feel better, Doc," said one of them, pulling out a wallet and counting bills from it. "Here's the four thousand. We make it five for luck."

Kildare leaned forward. And then Jeff stepped between him and the money.

"Buddy," Jeff said, "if you make a mug of all of us by trying to bribe the doc, I'm gunna sock you myself."

"Back up, Jeff," the man said. "He asked for it, didn't he?"

"He was kidding you, you big stiff," said Jeff. "Listen. He's an interne. He can't take anything. He won't take anything. He's too clean for that. He's the only honest man I ever seen. Now, get him out of here, Hanlon."

The money had disappeared while Kildare's hand was still reaching for it. He thought of Fearson and started to protest. But he was helpless when Jeff and Hanlon put hands on him.

They got him quickly down the stairs. Behind them, the man with the money called: "If Innis gets well, we can all the old stuff. We're friends, Hanlon."

Out on the street Jeff said: "Thank God we got the tip and followed you. Don't ever trust yourself with yeggs like that."

"I've got to get back!" cried Kildare. "I've got to get that money."

Hanlon said: "'Doc, did you want that dirty money?"

"Fearson—" blurted out Kildare.

Jeff growled: "Quit it, Doc. Fearson is safe. Nobody ain't gonna worry him. Not after the chief knew he was your friend. You know who he owed the money to? McGuire. The dummy of a doctor had tried some gambling, was all."

Kildare stopped short. "You mean it's all fixed?" he asked.

"Listen, McGuire would fix *hell* if you said the word," declared Hanlon. "Come on, Jeff. The doc needs a drink."

They rushed across town in Hanlon's car to McGuire's saloon. It was shut and empty. Jeff opened it up.

"Whisky?" he said.

"Yes," said Kildare.

Jeff clinked out three glasses on the bar. He brought out a squat bottle and filled the glasses from it.

"Will you have this on me, Doc?" asked Hanlon.

Kildare turned and saw Hanlon's eyes wide open, almost frightened.

Hanlon said, "I'd like to be able to tell the wife that you'd been having a drink with me—"

"Leave him alone, dummy," interrupted Jeff. "He's never taken anything from us yet, has he?"

"Will you have it on me?" pleaded Hanlon. "Or would you like to smash in my dirty face first?"

Kildare, looking through the dim plate-glass window, saw the glare of the night lights over the top of the elevated. "What time is it?" he asked.

"It's eleven-forty-five," said Pat Hanlon, still waiting.

"I've got time for this one," said Kildare, "and there's nobody I'd rather drink it with. Here's to you, Pat."

The Claws of the Tigress

Faust claimed to care little for prose fiction and less for research, but he spent much of his time doing both. What he liked perhaps best of anything was Italy. Here prose and research and Italy are brought together in a characteristic historical novelette. "The Claws of the Tigress" first appeared in *Argosy* under the pen name, George Challis. It later made part of a novel, *The Bait and the Trap*, which was issued in hardcover by Harper and in paperback by Ace Books. Faust wrote this tale in Villa Negli Ulivi, his villa among the olive trees, in Florence.

CATERINA, Countess Sforza-Riario, high lady and mistress of the rich, strong town of Forli, was tall, well made, slenderly strong, and as beautiful as she was wise. She used to say that there was only one gift that God had specially denied her, and that was a pair of hands that had the strength of a man in them. But if she had not a man's strength, she had a man's will to power, and more than a man's headlong courage.

She was not quite as cruel as Cesare Borgia, her neighbor to the north who now was overrunning the Romagna with his troops of Swiss and French and trained peasants, but she was cruel enough to be famous for her outbursts of rage and vengeance. That sternness showed in the strength of her jaw and in the imperial arch of her nose, but usually she covered the iron in her nature with a smiling pleasantry.

Three husbands had not been able to age her; she looked ten years younger than the truth. And this morning she looked younger than ever because her peregrine falcon had three times outfooted the birds of the rest of the hawking party and swooped to victory from the dizzy height of the blue sky. The entire troop had been galloping hard over hill and dale, sweeping through the soft soil of vineyards and orchards; crashing over the golden stand of ripe wheat; soaring again over the rolling pasture lands until the horses were half exhausted and the riders nearly spent. Even the troop of twoscore men-at-arms who followed the hunt, always pursuing short cuts, taking straight lines to save distance, were fairly well tired, though their life was in the saddle.

They kept now at a little distance—picked men, every one, all covered with the finest steel plate armor that could be manufactured in Milan. Most of them were armed with sword and spear, but there were a few who carried the heavy arquebuses which were becoming more fashionable in war since the matchlock was invented, with the little swiveled arm which turned the flame over the touch-hole of the gun, with its priming.

Forty strong men-at-arms—to guard a hawking party. But at any moment danger might pour out at them through a gap in the hills. Danger might thrust down at them from the ravaging bands of the Borgia's conquering troops; or danger might lift at them from Imola; or danger might come across the mountains from the treacherous Florentines, insatiable of business and territory. Therefore even a hawking party must be guarded, for the countess would prove a rich prize.

The danger was real, and that was why she enjoyed her outing with such a vital pleasure. And now, as she sat on her horse and stroked the hooded peregrine that was perched on her wrist, she looked down the steep pitch of the cliff at whose edge she was halting and surveyed the long, rich sweep of territory which was hers, and still hers until the brown mountains of the Apennines began, and rolled back into blueness and distance.

Her glance lowered. Two men and a woman were riding along the road which climbed and sank, and curved, and rose again through the broken country at the base of the cliff. They were so far away that she could take all three into the palm of her hand. Yet her eyes were good enough to see the wind snatch the hat from the lady's head and float it away across a hedge.

Before that cap had ever landed, the rider of the white horse flashed with his mount over the hedge, caught the hat out of the air, and returned it to the lady.

The countess laughed with high pleasure.

"A gentleman and a gentle man," she said. "Here, Gregorio! Do you see those three riding down there? Bring them up to me. Send two of the men-at-arms to invite them, and if they won't come, bring them by force. I want to see that white horse; I want to see the man who rides it."

Gregorio bowed to cover his smile. He admired his lady only less than he feared her. And it was a month or two since any man had caught her eye. He picked out two of the best men-at-arms—Emilio, a sergeant in the troop, and Elia, an old and tried veteran of the wars which never ended in Italy as the sixteenth century commenced. This pair, dispatched down a short cut, were quickly in the road ahead of the three travelers, who had stopped to admire a view across the valley.

The lady countess and her companions, gathered along the edge of the cliff, could see everything and yet remain screened from view by the heavy fringe of shrubbery that grew about them.

What they saw was a pretty little picture in action. The two men-at-arms, their lances raised, the bright pennons fluttering near the needle-gleam of the spearheads, accosted the three, talked briefly, turned their horses, took a little distance, and suddenly couched their spears in the rests, leaned far forward, and rushed straight down the road at the strangers.

"Rough—a little rough," said the Countess Sforza-Riario. "Those two fellows are unarmed, it seems to me. That Emilio must be told that there is something more courteous in the use of strangers than a leveled lance."

But here something extremely odd happened, almost in the midst of the calm remark of the lady. For the two men who were assaulted, unarmored as they were, instead of fleeing for their lives or attempting to flee, rode right in at the spearmen.

One drew a long sword, the other a mere glitter of a

blade. Each parried or swerved from the lance thrust. He of the long sword banged his weapon down so hard on the helmet of Emilio that the man-at-arms toppled from the saddle, rolled headlong on the ground, and reached to the feet of the horse of the lady.

She was on the ground instantly, with a little flash of a knife held at the visor of the fallen soldier.

"Good!" said the countess. "Oh, excellently good!"

She began to clap her hands softly.

The second rider—he on the white horse—had grappled with hardy Elia. Both of them were whirled from the saddle, but the man-at-arms fell prone, helpless with the weight of his plates of steel, and the other perched like a cat on top of him. His hat had fallen. The gleam of his hair in the bright sunlight was flame-red.

"And all in a moment!" said the countess, laughing. "Two good lances gone in a trice. Roderigo, you should have better men than that in your command."

The captain, scowling, and biting an end of his short mustache, swore that there had been witchcraft in it.

"Aye," said the countess. "The witchcraft of sure eyes and quick, strong hands. . . . Did you see the lady leap from her horse like a tigress and hold her poniard above the helmet of your friend? Look, now! They are stripping the two of their armor. The big fellow is putting on that of Emilio; the redhead takes that of Elia. Roderigo, take three of your best lances. Down to them again, and let me see them fight against odds, now that they are armed like knights. . . . Ah, what a glorious day—to go hawking for birds and end by stooping out of the sky at men!"

The four men-at-arms were quickly in the saddle and sweeping down the short, steep road; but here the countess found herself too far from the crash and dust of the battle. To gain a nearer view, she galloped after the four leaders, and the armed men, the courtiers, followed in a stream.

Those loud tramplings hardly could fail to be heard by the men in the roadway beneath; in fact, when her ladyship turned the shoulder of the cliff and could look at the scene, she found her four warriors already charging, heads down, lances well in rest, straight in on the pair. And these, in their borrowed armor, with their borrowed lances, galloped to meet the fresh shock.

Six metal monsters, flaming in the sun, they crashed together. The big fellow had lifted one of the men-at-arms right out of the saddle, but the counter-shock knocked his own horse to its knees; and at that instant the rearmost of the four men-at-arms caught the stranger with a well-centered spear that bowled him in his turn out of the saddle and into the dust.

He whose red head was now covered by steel had a different fortune. Riding straight, confident, at the last instant he dropped suddenly to the side, which caused one spear to miss him utterly, while the second glanced off his shoulder. But his own spear caught fairly on a man-at-arms, knocking him over like a ninepin.

"This is jousting!" cried the countess. "Glorious God, *these* are men."

He of the white horse, his spear shattered to the butt by the shock of the encounter, whirled his white horse about and went hurling against the only one of the men-at-arms who remained mounted. In his hand he swung not a sword but the old battle-ax which the veteran Elia had kept at the bow of his saddle.

In the hand of the rider of the white horse it became both a sword to parry with and a club to strike; a side sweep turned the driving spear of the soldier away, and a shortened hammer-blow delivered with the back of the ax rolled the other fellow on the road. All was a flying mist of dust, through which the countess heard the voice of a girl crying:

"Well done, Tizzo! Oh, bravely done!"

She had ridden to the spot where the larger of the two strangers had fallen, and leaning far down, she helped him, stunned as he was, to his feet. And now, springing instantly into an empty saddle, he unsheathed his sword and prepared for whatever might be before them.

There was plenty of work ahead.

The men-at-arms of the countess, swiftly surrounding the cyclone of dust, were now ranged on every side in a dense semicircle which could not be broken through. And as Tizzo saw this, he began to rein his white horse back and forth, whirling the ax in a dexterous hand as he shouted in a passion of enthusiasm:

"Ah, gentlemen! We only begin the dance. Before the blood gets cold, take my hand again. Step forward. Join me, gallants!"

One of the men-at-arms, infuriated by these taunts, rushed horse and spear suddenly on Tizzo; but a side twist of the ax turned the thrust of the spear aside, and a terrible downstroke shore straight through the conical crest of the helmet, through the coil of strong mail beneath, and stopped just short of the skull. The stricken fighter toppled from the saddle and seemed to break his neck in his fall.

Tizzo, still reining his horse back and forth, continued to shout his invitation, but a calm voice said: "Bring up an arquebus and knock this bird out of the air."

Not until this point did the lady call out: "Stay from him. My friend, you have fought very well. . . . Pick up the fallen, lads. . . . Will you let me see your face?"

Tizzo instantly raised his visor.

"Madame," he said, "I should have saluted you before, but the thick weather prevented me."

The countess looked at his red hair and the flame-blue of his eyes.

"What are you?" she asked.

Some of her men-at-arms were lifting the fallen to their feet and opening their helmets to give them air; by good fortune, not a one of them was very seriously hurt. The huge, heavy rounds of the plate armor had secured them from hurt as, oftentimes, it would do during the course of an entire day's fighting.

Defensive armor had outdistanced aggressive weapons. Gunpowder was still in its infancy. The greatest danger that a knight ordinarily endured was from the weight of his armor, which might stifle him when he was thrown from his horse in the midst of a hot battle.

And Tizzo was answering the countess, with the utmost courtesy: "I am under the command of an older and more important man, my lady."

He turned to his companion, who pushed up his visor and showed a battered, grizzled face in which the strength of youth was a little softened into folds, but with greater knowledge in his brow to make him more dangerous.

"I am going to take the short cut, Tizzo," said the other. "The trust is a two-edged knife that hurts the fellow who uses it, very often, I know, but here's for it. Madame, I am the Baron Henry of Melrose; this is the noble Lady Beatrice Baglione, sister of Giovanpaolo Baglione; this is my son Tizzo. We are on the road from near Faenza, where we've just escaped from the hands of Cesare Borgia, after a breath of poisoned air almost killed me. We are bound back towards Perugia. There is our story."

The countess rode straight to Beatrice and took her by the hands. "My dear," she said, "I'm happy that you escaped from that gross beast of a Borgia. How could I guess that such distinguished strangers were passing through my territory? Come with me into Forli. You shall rest there, and then go forward under a safe-conduct. My Lord of Melrose—those were tremendous blows you gave with that sword; Sir Tizzo, you made the ax gleam in your hand like your name. I thought it was a firebrand flashing! Will you come on with me? Some of the rest of you ride forward to the castle. Have them prepare a welcome. . . . Ah, that Borgia! The black dog has put his teeth in the heart of the Romagna, but he'll fight for my blood before he has it!"

The countess, talking cheerfully in this manner, put the little procession under way again, and they streamed up the winding road toward the top of the cliff. But all her courtesy was not enough to cover the eyes of Beatrice.

Caterina of Sforza-Riario headed the riders, naturally, and Tizzo was at her right hand, more or less by seeming accident. A little back of the two came Beatrice at the side of Henry of Melrose. And the girl was saying: "Do you see how she eyes Tizzo? She is making herself sweet as honey, but I know her. She's a famous virago. . . . How can Tizzo be such a fool as to be taken in by her? I don't think she's so very handsome, do you?"

The baron looked at her with a rather grim smile for her jealousy. "She is not worth one glance of your eyes, Beatrice," he declared. "But Tizzo would be a greater fool still if he failed to give her smile for smile. She has three birds in her claws, and if she's angered, she's likely to swallow all of us. She never was so deeply in love that could not wash her hands and her memory of the lover clean in blood. Be cheerful, Beatrice, or you may spoil everything. Smile and seem to enjoy the good weather. Because I have an idea that after the gates of Forli Castle close behind us it will be a long day before we come out again."

They passed over the green uplands and sank down into the road toward the walled town of Forli. The city itself was a place of considerable strength, but within it uprose the "Rocca"—or castle on the rock—which was the citadel and the stronghold of the town. No one could be real master of Forli until he had mastered the castle on the rock as well. And young Tizzo, riding beside the countess, making his compliments, smiling on the world, took quiet note of the mouths of the cannons in the embrasures of the walls.

The drawbridge had already been lowered. They crossed

it, with the hollow echoes booming beneath them along the moat. They passed under the leaning forehead of the towers of the defense; they passed through the narrows of the crooked entrance way; they climbed up into the enclosed court of the powerful fortress.

Tizzo was the first on the ground to offer his hand to hold the stirrup of the countess. But she, laughing, avoided him, and sprang like a man to the ground. Like a man she was tall—almost the very inches of Tizzo; like a man her eye was bold and clear; and like a man she had power in her hand and speed in her foot. She looked to Tizzo like an Amazon; he could not help glancing past her to the more slender beauty of Beatrice and wondering what the outcome of this strange adventure would be.

II

The courtesy of the countess might be perfect, but it was noticeable that she assigned to the three strangers three rooms in quite different parts of the castle.

The Countess Riario, stepping up and down in her room, said to her maid: "You, Alicia—you have seen him —what do you think?"

"Of whom, madame?" asked the maid.

"Of the man, you fool," said the countess.

"Of which man, madame?" asked the maid.

"Blockhead, there was only one."

There was a beautiful Venetian stand near by, of jet inlaid with ivory; and the capable hand of the countess gripped the stand now. The maid had saved herself from a

fractured skull more than once before this by the speed of
her foot in dodging. But she knew a danger when she saw
it, and her brain was stimulated.

"There was the noble young gentleman who rode with
you into the court, madame. There was he, of course. And
when he took off his helmet and I saw the gold of his
hair—"

"Red—silly chattering idiot—red hair. Would I waste
my time looking at golden hair? Insipid nonsense—gold—
in the purse and flame in the head—that's what I prefer!"

"When I saw the flame of his hair, madame, and the
blue of his eyes, I understood that he was a very proper
man, though not exactly a giant—"

"Judge a dog by the depth of his bite, not by the length
of his muzzle," said the countess. "I saw that slenderly
made fellow carve the helmet of that Giulio almost down
to the skull—the helmet and the coif of mail beneath it!"

"Jesu!" cried the maid.

"And with a stroke as light and easy as the flick of a
hand, the white hand of an empty girl. He *is* a man, Alicia.
I want to send him a gift of some sort. What shall it be?
. . . Wait—there is a belt of gold with amethyst studs—
have that carried to him at once, and give him my wish
that he may rest comfortably after his hard journey and
the work of the fighting—ah ha—if you had seen him
battling, Alicia! If you had seen him rushing among my
men and tumbling them over as though they were so many
dummies that had not been tied in place. The ring of the
ax strokes is still in my ears. He tossed the spears aside as
though they had been headless straws. It was a picture to

fill the heart, Alicia . . . Why are you standing there like
a lackbrain? Why don't you take the belt to him instantly?"

"I beg the pardon of madame . . . You forget that you
already have given it to Giovanni degli Azurri."

"Ah—ah—that Giovanni? Is he still in the castle? Is he
still in the Rocco?"

"Madame, you had supper with him last night; and dinner before it; and breakfast in the morning—"

"Did I? That was yesterday. He has a dark skin. I hate a
man with a greasy skin. Besides, he talks too much! Here!
Take this lute to the noble Tizzo. Tell him it is from my
hand, and then we'll see if he has wit enough to sing a song
with it; and through the singing, he may be able to discover that his room is not very far from mine—not very far
—hurry, Alicia! Wait—give something to the others. To
the baron—let me see—there was a man, Alicia. Ten years
younger, and I would not have changed a dozen Tizzos for
one such big-shouldered fighter. He jousts like a champion
and handles a sword like a Frenchman. Have a good warm
cloak of English wool carried to him. And then the girl—I
hate silly faces, Alicia. I hate silly, young, witless, thought-
less faces. Do you think that young Tizzo has an eye for
her?"

"One would call her pretty enough to take a young
man's eye," said the girl.

"Pretty enough? Silly enough, you mean to say. Take
her a dish of sweet meats with my compliments. Pretty
enough? Look at me, Alicia. Tell me how I appear, now
that I'm no longer a girl, in the eyes of a man."

Alicia, directly challenged in this manner, fell into a trembling so that her knees hardly would bear her up. Her glance wandered wildly out the window toward the brown and blue Apennines. If she did not tell the truth, she would be beaten; if she did not convey some sort of a compliment, she would be cast out of her sinecure which brought her a better income than any two knights in Forli possessed. The Apennines brought no suggestions into the mind of Alicia. She looked out the opposite window over the plains as far as the distant blue stream of the Adriatic.

"Madame," she said, "the truth is a thing that ought to be told."

The countess, at her mirror, viewed herself from a different angle.

"Go on, Alicia, tell me the truth," she commanded.

"The fact is, madame, that when men see you in the morning they are filled with delight; in the full light of the noonday—a time for which madame the countess doesn't care a whit anyway—a man would think you a very handsome good friend; and in the evening light, madame is always adored."

"At noon the wrinkles show, eh?" asked the countess.

"No, madame, but—"

The countess turned her head slowly, like a lioness, so that the strength of her chin and the powerful arch of her nose stood in relief against those same blue Apennines beyond the window.

"Well—" she said. "Well, run about your business. And don't forget to take the lute."

It was ten minutes later when Alicia, out of breath, tapped at a door in a certain way; and it was opened almost at once by a tall, powerfully built man in early middle age, his beard and mustaches close-cropped to permit the wearing of a helmet, his complexion swarthy, his eye easily lighted, like a coal of fire when a draught of air blows upon it.

He glanced down the hall above the head of the girl to make sure that she was alone, took her by the elbows, kissed her, and drew her into the room.

"Now, Alicia, what's the news?" he asked.

She paused for a moment to recover her breath and begin her smiling. She was a pretty girl, with pale tawny hair and only a touch of shrewish sharpness about the tip of the nose and the forward thrust of the chin. By twenty-five or so she already would begin to look like a hag.

"Trouble for you, Giovanni," she said. "In that lot of people whom the countess picked up while she was hawking, there was a red-headed and blue-eyed young fellow who has caught her eye. She sent me to him with that enameled lute as a present."

"The one which I gave to *her?*" exclaimed Giovanni.

"The very same one. She never can remember who has given her things," the girl said.

"I had better find a way to call the man into a quarrel," said Giovanni. "The countess will always forgive what a sword-stroke accomplishes honestly."

"Yes, of course," said Alicia. "And if the stranger should happen to cut your throat, she would bury you today and forget you tomorrow. This Tizzo of Melrose—have you heard about him?"

"No."

"Well, there is a rumor running about the castle now. One of the men-at-arms was at the taking of Perugia, when Giovanpaolo Baglione returned to the town, and this is the Tizzo who rode beside him. He does strange things with an ax. There is a story that he shore through the chains that blocked the streets of Perugia against the horsemen of the Baglioni."

"Cut through the street-chains? With an ax? Impossible!" said Giovanni.

"Just now, when the fighting men of the countess attacked him, he knocked them about, and whacked them off their horses. He is not big, but he strikes terribly close to the life every time he swings his ax; and a sword is like a magic flame in his hands. It burns through armor like the sting of a wasp through the skin of the hand."

"Ah?" said Giovanni. "That sounds like enchantment."

"It does. And the countess saw the fighting and is enchanted. Giovanni, have a good care—"

"Hush!" said he. "Listen!"

He held up his hand and began to make soft steps toward the single casement that opened out of his room upon one of the castle courts. Alicia followed him, nodding, for the trembling music of a lute had commenced, and than a man's voice began to sing, not overloudly, one of those old Italian songs which have originated no one knows when or where. Roughly translated, it runs something like this:

"What shall I do with this weariness of light?
The day is like the eye of a prying fool
And the thought of a lover is burdened by it.
Only the stars and the moon have wisdom.
Of all the birds there is only a single one,
Of all the birds one who knows that night is the time for song.
And I of all men understand how to wait for darkness.
Oh, my beloved, are you, also, patient?"

From the casement, leaning into the deep of it, Giovanni saw a crimson scarf of silk, with a knot tied into the center of it, drop from a window, and as it passed a casement immediately below, a swift hand darted out and caught it. There was only a glimpse of a young fellow with flame-red hair, and gleaming eyes, and laughter. Then he and the scarf he had caught disappeared.

"Did you see?" said Giovanni, drawing back darkly.

"I saw. And I had warned you, Giovanni. Something ought to be done."

"Yes, and before night. But if the devil is so apt with weapons—well, there is wine and poison for it, Alicia."

"There is," agreed the girl simply. But still she was held in thought.

"What was in that scarf?" asked Giovanni.

"A ring—or an unset jewel, with the fragrance of her favorite perfume drenching it. Giovanni, you must send him away."

"Aye, but how?"

"Well, you have a brain and I have a brain. Between the two of us we must devise something. Sit there—sit there still as a stone, and I'll sit here without moving until we've devised something. The air of Italy cannot be breathed without bringing thoughts."

III

Tizzo of Melrose, as the day turned into the night, whistled through his teeth and did a dance along a crack in the timber floor of his room. His feet fell with no noise, and always, as he bounded forward and backward, they alighted exactly on the line. It was a mere jongleur's trick, but Tizzo, when the humor seized upon him, was merely a jongleur. And one day he wanted to do that same dance high in the air on a tightly stretched rope.

A soft tap at the door stopped the dance. He stood with his balancing arms outstretched for a moment, listening, and heard a soft rustle go whispering down the outer hall and vanish from hearing. After that he opened the door and found on the threshold a little folded missive.

He opened it, and inside found the writing which most quickly made his heart leap. It was the hand of Beatrice—a little more roughly and largely flowing than the writing of that high lady, perhaps, but still so exactly like it that Tizzo did not pause to consider the differences. He kissed the letter twice before he closed the door and then read it. It said:

Tizzo:
There is frightful danger for all of us in the Rocca. But we have found an unexpected friend. Your father and I already have been smuggled out of the castle. We are waiting for you outside the town.

When you receive this letter, go straight down to the eastern court. There you will see a horse covered by a large blanket. It will be your own Falcone. The man leading it will unlock the postern for you. Go quietly through the town, keeping your face covered with your mantle and the blanket on the horse so that you will not be known. On the main road to Imola, beyond Forli, you will reach a farmhouse with a ruined stable beside it. The house will seem to be unoccupied, but go straight in through the front door and call. Your father and I are waiting.

God bless you and keep you. The countess is a devil incarnate. Come quickly.

BEATRICE

Tizzo went quickly.

He clapped on his head his hat with the strong steel lining, belted his sword about him, and was instantly in the corridor. He walked with a free and careless swing. There was nothing about him to indicate that he moved with fear of danger in his mind except the silence of his step, graceful, and padding like the footfall of a cat.

He passed through a great lower hall with the hood of his cloak pulled forward so that his face was shadowed. A door opened. Somewhere music was beginning, the musicians scraping at their instruments as they tuned them. In a very few minutes the countess would be expecting to receive her guests for the great banquet.

But Beatrice was no rattle-brained girl. And if Henry of Melrose had consented to flee from the castle like a thief, then it was certain that the Countess Riario was a mortal danger to them, all three.

That was the thought of Tizzo as he passed out into the

eastern court, where he saw not a living soul. He looked up at the windows, most of them dark, a few faintly illumined by the steady glow of lamps in the lower rooms, and of flickering torches above. Then, in a farther corner, something stirred. A man leading a draped horse stepped out into the pallid starlight and Tizzo went straight to him. When he was closer, the blanketed horse lifted head and whinnied, a mere whisper of sound. But it told Tizzo louder than trumpets that this was Falcone.

The fellow who led the stallion gave the strap instantly into Tizzo's hand. Not a word was spoken. The man, who was a tall figure wrapped up to the brightness of his eyes in a great mantle, fitted a key into the small postern gate. The lock turned with a dull, rusty grating; the door opened; over the narrow of the causeway Tizzo led the horse.

"Whom do I thank?" he murmured as he went through the gate.

But the postern was shut quickly, silently behind him.

An odd touch of suspicion came up in the heart of Tizzo; and at this moment he heard the whining music of strings come from a distant casement with such a sense of warmth and hospitality and brightness about it that he could not help doubting the truth of the letter of Beatrice.

This hesitation did not endure a second. He was on the back of Falcone again, his sword was at his side, his dagger was in his belt, and if only he could have in his grasp, once more, that woodsman's ax with its head of the blue Damascus steel, he would have felt himself once more a man free and armed against the perils of the world. However, the thought of Beatrice and of his father expanded before him pleasantly.

He jogged the stallion through bystreets. They were dark. Once a door opened and a tumult of voices, a flare of torches poured out into the street, brawling and laughter together; but Falcone galloped softly away from this scene and carried his master safely out of the town onto the broad surface of the famous road which slants across the entire north of Italy.

A moon came up and helped him to see, presently, a ruined farmhouse fifty steps from the edge of the pavement; the roof of the stable beside the house had fallen in through two-thirds of its length. The house itself had settled crookedly toward the ground. The windows were unshuttered. The door lay on the ground, rotted almost to dust.

Tizzo dismounted at this point and walked forward a little gingerly. The long black of his shadow wavered before him with each step he made over the grass-grown path; and that shadow like a ghost lay on the broken floor of the old house, slanting into it as Tizzo stood at the threshold.

"Beatrice!" he called.

The sound of his voice traveled swiftly through the place, came emptily back to him in an echo.

He stepped a few strides forward. Through the door, through two windows, the moon streamed into the interior. He could make out a pile of rubbish that had fallen from the wreck of half the ceiling; a huge oil jar stood in a corner; he could make out, dimly, the outlines of the fireplace.

"Beatrice!" he called again.

"Here!" shouted a man behind him. And at once: "At him, lads, before his sword's out—in on him from every side—"

Three men were rushing through the doorway full upon him, the moon flashed on their morions, on their breast-plates and the rest of their half-armor such as foot soldiers usually were equipped with. They came in eagerly with shields and swords, the sort of equipment which the Spanish infantry were making famous again in Europe.

Tizzo whipped out his sword so that it whistled from the sheath. If he could get through them to the door, Falcone was outside, but only a ruse would take him that far. He ran at them with his sword held above his head, shouting a desperate cry, as though with his unarmored body he would strive to crush straight through them. And they, all as anxious to drive their weapons into him, thrust out with one accord.

He was under the flash of their swords, hurling himself headlong at their feet. Once before he had saved his life by that device. Now he was kicked with terrible force in the stomach and ribs.

The fellow who had tripped over him fell headlong, crashing. Another had been staggered and Tizzo, as he gained his knees, thrust upward at the back of the man's body. A scream answered that stroke. A scream that had no ending as the man leaped about the room in a frightful agony.

And Tizzo, gasping, breathless, rose to face the attack of the third soldier.

The strokes of the short sword might be parried; but the shield gave the man a terrible advantage and he used it well, keeping himself faultlessly covered as he drove in, calling at the same time: "Up, Tomaso! Up! Up! Alfredo, stop screeching and strike one blow, you dog. Take him behind! Have you forgot the money that's waiting for us? Are fifty ducats thrown into our laps every day?"

Alfredo had stopped his dance, but now he lay writhing on the floor; and still that horrible screeching cut through the ears, through the brain of Tizzo.

He saw Tomaso lurching up from the floor. His sword and shield would put a quick end to this battle of moon-light and shadow, this obscure murder.

Tizzo with his light blade feinted for the head of the third soldier; the shield jerked up to catch the stroke which turned suddenly down and the point drove into the leg of the fellow above the knee. He cursed; but instinct made him lower his shield toward the wound and in that moment the sword of Tizzo was in the hollow of his throat.

He fell heavily forward, not dead, fighting death away with one hand and striving to hold the life inside his torn throat with the other. Tizzo snatched up the fallen shield and faced Tomaso, who had been maneuvering toward the rear of the enemy to make a decisive attack.

"Mother of Heaven!" groaned Tomaso. "What? Both down?"

The screeching of Alfredo turned into frightful, long-drawn groaning, sounds that came with every long, in-drawn breath. Tomaso fell on his knees.

"Noble master! Mercy!" he said.

He held up sword and shield.

"By the blood of God," said Tizzo, "I should put you with the other two. But I was born a weak-hearted fool. Drop your sword and shield and I may give you your life if you tell the truth."

The sword and buckler instantly clattered on the floor.

"I swear—the pure truth—purer than the honor of—"

"Keep good names out of your swine's mouth," said Tizzo. "Stand up."

The soldier arose and Tizzo, stepping back, leaned on his sword to take breath. He saw the man who had been stabbed in the throat now rise from the floor, make a staggering stride, and fall headlong. He who lay groaning turned, lay on his face, and began to make bubbling noises.

"Do you hear me, Tomaso?" asked Tizzo.

"With my soul—with my heart!" said Tomaso.

"Who was to pay you the fifty ducats?"

"Giovanni degli Azurri."

"Ah?" said Tizzo. He looked back in his mind to the dark face and the bright eyes of the man who had appeared at the table of the countess for the midday meal. In what manner had he offended Giovanni degli Azurri? Undoubtedly the fellow was acting on the orders of the countess.

"Tell me, Tomaso," he asked, "what is the position of Giovanni degli Azurri in the castle of the countess?"

"How can I tell, lord? He is one of the great ones. That is all that I know, and he showed us fifty ducats of new money."

"Fifty ducats is a large price for the cutting of a throat."

"Highness, if I had known what a great heart and a noble—"

"Be silent," said Tizzo, freshening his grip on the handle of his sword.

He had to pause a moment, breathing hard, to get the disgust and the anger from his heart.

"This Giovanni degli Azurri," he said, "is one of the great ones of the castle, and a close adviser of the countess?"

"He is, *signore*."

The thing grew clear in the mind of Tizzo. The countess already knew that he and his father had parted from the Borgia with sword in hand. Would it not be a part of her policy to conciliate the terrible Cesare Borgia, therefore, by wiping an enemy out of his path? But she would do it secretly, away from the castle. Otherwise, the thing might come to the ears of the High and Mighty Baglioni of Perugia, who would be apt to avenge with terrible thoroughness the murder of their friend.

And Henry of Melrose? Beatrice Baglione? What would come to them?

It was a far, far cry to Perugia. Help nearer at hand must be found to split open the Rocca and bring out the captives alive.

He began to remember how, to please the fair countess, he had accepted the lute from her and sung her the love song. And a black bitterness swelled in his heart; a taste of gall was in his throat.

IV

His name was Luigi Costabili; his height was six feet two; his weight was two hundred; the horse that carried

him was proud of the burden. Luigi Costabili wore a
jacket quartered with the yellow and red colors of Cesare
Borgia, with "Cesare" written across the front and across
the back. His belt was formed like a snake. He wore a helmet on his head and a stout shirt of mail.

His weapons were his sword, his dagger, and the pike
which infantry used to defy cavalry charges. It was not
quite the weight or the balance to serve as the lance of a
knight, but still it could offer a formidable stroke or two in
practiced hands—and the hands of Luigi Costabili were
very practiced. Among the enrolled bands of the Romagnol peasantry who followed the Borgia there was not a
finer specimen than Costabili. He knew his own worth
even better than he knew his master's. Therefore he paid
little heed to a slender man who rode out onto the Faenza
highway on a white stallion. But when the stranger came
straight on toward him, Luigi Costabili lifted his pike
from his foot and stared, then lowered the weapon to the
ready.

The stranger had red hair and bright, pale blue eyes,
like the blue one sees in a flame. When he was close to
Luigi, he called out, in the most cheerful and calm voice
imaginable: "Defend yourself!" and drew a sword.

"Defend myself? I'll split you like a partridge!" said
Luigi.

And he let drive with his pike. He had practised a
maneuver which the master of arms said was infallible. It
consisted of a double feint for the head, followed with a
hard drive straight for the body. Luigi used that double
feint and thrust with perfect adroitness and facility, but

the sword did a magic dance in the hand of the other; the pike was slipped aside, and the white horse, as though it was thinking on behalf of its master, sprang right in to the attack. He was far lighter than the charger Luigi bestrode, but he drove his shoulder against the side of Luigi's big brown gelding with such force that man and rider were staggered.

Luigi dropped the pike, caught for the reins, snatched out his dagger, and then had his right arm numbed by a hard stroke that fell on it below the shoulder.

If that blow had been delivered with the edge, Luigi would have been a man without a right arm and hand during the rest of his days; but the whack was delivered with the flat of the blade only and the result was merely that the dagger dropped from the benumbed fingers of the big soldier.

He looked down the leveled blade of the red-headed man and felt that he was blinded. Helplessness rushed over him. Bewilderment paralyzed him as effectively as though he had been stung by a great wasp. So he sat without attempting resistance and allowed a noosed cord to be tossed over him and his arms cinched up close against his sides.

A turn of the cord about the pommel of the saddle secured him as efficiently as though he were a truss of hay.

"What is you name?" asked the stranger.

"Luigi Costabili," said the peasant, "—and God forgive me!"

"God *will* forgive you for being Luigi," said the other. "Do you know me?"

"I know the trick you have with your sword," said

Costabili.

"I am Tizzo of Melrose," said the stranger.

Costabili closed his eyes. "Then I am a dead man," he groaned.

"Luigi, how do you come to ride such an excellent horse?"

"It was given to me by the Duke of Valentinois himself, because I won the prize at the pike drill of the whole army."

"He is going to give you a greater gift than that," said Tizzo, "if you will carry safely and quickly to him a letter that I'll put in your hands."

"I shall carry it as safely as a pigeon, highness," said poor Luigi. "But you—pardon me—you are not Tizzo. He is half a foot taller than you."

"I am Tizzo," was the answer, accompanied by a singular little smile and a glint of the eye that made Luigi stare.

"Yes, highness," he said. "You are whatever you say, and I am your faithful messenger."

"Luigi, if I set you honorably free and let you have your weapons, will you do as you promise and ride straight to the duke?"

"Straight, my lord! Straight as an arrow flies or as a horse can run . . . Tizzo . . . the captain himself!"

The last words were murmured.

In the Rocca of the town of Forli, Caterina Sforza strode up and down a tower room with the step of a man. Anger made her eyes glorious, her color was high. She looked what she was—the most formidable woman that ever gripped a knife or handled thoughts of a sword. Her passion had risen high but still it was rising.

Most of the time she glared out the casements toward the sea on one side and toward the mountains on the other; only occasionally did she sweep her eyes over the figures of the two who were before her, their hands and their feet weighted down with irons. Henry of Melrose carried his gray head high and serenely. But his jaw was set hard and his eyes followed the sweeping steps of the virago. The Lady Beatrice, on the other hand, looked calmly out the window toward the mountains and seemed unconscious of the weight of the manacles that bound her. She maintained a slight smile.

"Treachery," said the Lady of Forli, panting out the words. "Treachery and treason!"

The men-at-arms who remained in a solid cluster just inside the door of the room stirred as they listened, and their armor clashed softly. Giovanni delgi Azurri, their leader, actually gripped his sword and looked at the big Englishman as though he were ready to rush at him with a naked weapon.

"One of you or both of you know where the sneaking, hypocritical, lying thief has gone and how he managed to get out of the castle," cried Caterina Sforza.

"If my son is a thief," said the Baron of Melrose, "will you tell us what he stole?"

"My smallest jewel case with my finest jewels in it!" declared the countess.

Here the eyes of Giovanni degli Azurri glanced down and aside suddenly. And the corners of his mouth twitched slightly.

"A great emerald, two rubies, and a handful of diamonds!" said the countess. "Gone—robbed from me—stolen—by a half-breed dog! A half-breed dog!"

She stopped and stamped, and glared at the Englishman. His color did not alter as he answered without heat: "You have tied up my hands with iron, madame. But even if you had not, in my country a man cannot resent a woman's insult."

"A scoundrel!" cried the countess. "I could see it in his face. A sneaking, light-footed, quick-handed thief! Ah, God, when I remember the red heart of fire in the biggest of my rubies . . . and gone . . . gone to an adventuring, smiling, singing, damned mongrel. But I'll tear it out of you! The executioner knows how to tear conversation out of the flesh of men. Stronger men than Henry of Melrose have howled out their confessions, and I've stood by and listened with my own ears—and laughed—and listened—and laughed. Do you hear me?"

"I hear you, madame," said the big Englishman.

He looked steadily, gravely, toward the sinister grin on the face of Giovanni degli Azurri.

"Will you tell me now," demanded the countess, "where Tizzo has gone? Or must the rack stretch you first? Will you tell me what poisonous treason enabled him to get out of my castle without permisson?"

"Could no one else have let him go?" asked Melrose.

"Giovanni degli Azurri," said the countess. She turned

and fixed a blazing eye on the face of her favorite.

But Giovanni smiled and shook his head. "Is it likely that I'd steal the jewels of your highness and give them to that redhead?" he asked. "Had I any special reason for loving him?"

"No," declared the countess, convinced suddenly and entirely. "No, you had no reason. But treachery was somewhere in this castle. Treachery is still here, so complete that it is trusted in. So complete that one of them sneaks away with his theft and two of the others remain behind— confident that they can flee away when they please—God— I stifle when I think of it! I am made a child—a child—"

She strode across the room and buried her grip in the bright hair of Beatrice. A jerk of her hand forced the head of the girl back, but it did not alter her expression, which remained calm, half-smiling.

"If the Englishman has the strength to hold out in the torture-room," said the countess, "how long will *your* courage last, eh? How long before you will be squealing and squawking and yelping out everything you know?"

"Try me, then," said the Lady Beatrice. "Take me down, quickly. Heat the pincers. Oil the wheels of your rack."

The countess relaxed her grip and stepped back. She began to stare with narrowed eyes into the face of the girl.

"There's as much as this in you, is there?" she asked.

"I am the sister of Giovanpaolo Baglione," said the girl. "And I shall be the wife of Tizzo. And what can you rats of the Romagna do to the old Perugian blood?"

The countess struck with a powerful hand, twice. The

blows knocked the head of Beatrice from side to side. Her hair loosened and rushed down, streaming over her shoulders; but her eye was undimmed.

"What a fool you are!" she said to Caterina Sforza. "Do you think that you can break me with your own hands? Take me to the wheel. Stand by and watch the rack stretch me. Then use the bar and break me, while I laugh in your face—and sing—and laugh!"

"Take her! Now! Take her! Giovanni, drag her by the hair of the head down to the dungeon rooms."

Giovanni degli Azurri made two or three eager steps across the room before the sudden thunder of the voice of Melrose shocked him to a pause.

"Do you forget the Baglioni?" Melose shouted. "Do you know that Perugian banners will be flying all around your town of Forli within a month? Do you know that when the walls of the Rocca are breached a river of blood will run out of the gap? I say, for the two blows that have struck her face, two hundred of your men will die, madame!"

The countess stared curiously at Melrose, half her passion almost instantly gone.

"Take the girl—but not by the hair of the head," she said to Giovanni degli Azurri. "And now away with you. Let me stay here a moment with the baron, alone."

The girl walked uncompelled toward the stairs. From the head of them she smiled back over her shoulder toward Melrose.

"We'll find each other again," she said.

"We shall, by the grace of God," said the Baron.

"I'd put a quicker trust in Tizzo," said Beatrice, and

then the crowd of mailed fighting men formed about her and their descending steps passed down the stairs. Giovanni degli Azurri, going down last, called out: "Are you safe with him, alone?"

The countess pulled from her girdle a dagger with a seven-inch blade, the light dripping from its keenness like water from a melting icicle. "This is enough company for me," she said. "See the girl safely locked up before you come back."

When Giovanni was gone, she turned to Melrose again. The last of her passion was falling away from her, though she still breathed deep.

"My lord," she said to Melrose, "what was the mother of Tizzo?"

"An angel out of the bluest part of heaven," he answered.

"Is the thief's blood in you, then?"

"He would no more steal from a woman than he would lie to the face of the Almighty."

"But the jewels are gone, and he has gone with them—and behind him he leaves in my grip his father and his lady. You, my lord, are a brave man; but your son is a dog. I prove it to you by the things he has done. Can you make an answer?"

The face of the baron grew very pale. He said: "Madame, what you say seems to be true. He was here—and now he is gone. I tell you my answer. You see my right hand. Well, this hand is not such a true servant to me, or so close to my blood, as my son is. That is all I can say."

"So? Well—perhaps you are right. Perhaps you are right. But your face is a little too white, my lord. I think that strange things are happening in the Rocca and that you know something about them. And the executioner will ask you questions on the rack. I am sorry to say it. You have an old head and a young eye. I am very sorry for you. But— your blood in your own son condemns you . . . If I could put hands on him, I would eat his heart—raw! And I shall have my hands on him. You've heard me shouting and raging like a fool. But I can be quiet, also. You will see that I keep to my promise, letter by letter."

"Madame," said Melrose, "I am young enough to be afraid of you; but I am old enough not to be afraid of death."

She looked at him with a smile that was almost pleasant.

"I like that. There's something neat in what you say. Will you speak as well when you're on the rack?"

"I hope so."

"Go before me down the stairs, then," said the lady. "For once be discourteous to a lady and walk before her. Thank you. I'm sorry that the irons make your step so short . . . Take care, my lord, and don't let yourself fall on the stairway. What a pity if such a wise and elderly gentleman should be hurt by a fall, in my house!"

She began to laugh, and the sweet echoes of her laughter ran before them down the steep stairs and came softly back from below.

V

Cesare Borgia lay on his back in the sun with a mask over the slightly swollen deformity of his upper face, his eyes closed, his attention fixed on nothing but the stir of the wind in the grass about him, and the clean fragrance of moist earth and flowers, and the weight of the sun's heat pressing down upon him, soaking through his clothes, through his body.

Beside him, always standing erect, was Alessandro Bonfadini, the pallor of whose face would never be altered by all the sunshine that pours out oceans of gold over Italy every summer. Men said that his body was so filled with the poisons which he took as preventatives in the service of his dangerous master that neither sun nor air could work upon him as it worked upon other men. It was even said that, when he sat in a perfectly dark room, a dim halo was visible creeping out of his skin—a thin, phosphorescent glimmering which could be just noted. So that he seemed, in the darkness, like a ghost of a ghost.

And even in the broad daylight, one could not look at his cadaverous face without thinking of death.

The door to the walled garden of the tavern opened. An armored soldier called: "Bonfadini! Bonfadini!"

Bonfadini turned and waved a hand to command silence. But the soldier persisted: "A message from Captain Tizzo . . ."

The Borgia leaped suddenly to his feet.

"From Captain Tizzo?" he exclaimed. "Bring the man to me instantly."

He went striding off with great steps, a huge man, startlingly powerful the moment he was in motion. Through the silk of his hose, the big calf muscle slipped or bulged like a fist being flexed and relaxed.

Before him, voices called orders that were repeated far away. And Bonfadini ran to keep close to his master.

They were halfway through the garden before Luigi Costabili appeared, with the dust of his hurried ride still white on his uniform. He was busily trying to dust off that white when he saw the duke and fell on his knees.

"Get up and don't be a fool," said the Borgia. "Soldiers kneel to their king or their God; but in the Romagna my men in armor kneel to nothing but a bullet or a sword stroke. Stand up, and remember that you are a man. Have you seen Captain Tizzo?"

"I have here a letter from him. I met him on the high road."

"Why didn't you arrest the traitor and bring him here?" asked the Borgia.

His voice was not angry, but the peasant turned a greenish white.

"My lord, I tried to arrest him—but I was prevented—"

"You had bad luck with him and his sword," said the Borgia. "Well, other people have had bad luck with that will-o'-the-wisp. Bonfadini, read the letter to me. Was Captain Tizzo alone? On the white horse, Falcone? Was he well?"

"Alone, my lord—there was no one with him—he seemed—I don't know, my lord. He doesn't seem like other men."

"He is *not* like other men," agreed the Borgia. "Because you brought me a letter from him, here is five ducats . . ."

"My lord, I thank you from my heart; you are very kind."

". . . and because you failed to bring the man himself —holla! Lieutenant! Catch this fellow and give him a sound flogging!"

Luigi was led off.

"Read! Read!" said the Borgia, and began to walk up and down in a great excitement.

The white face of Bonfadini, unalterable as stone, slowly pronounced the words of the letter: " 'My noble lord: I left you the other night in such a hurry that I hardly had time to tell you why I was going. And certainly I did not know where. The only thing that was obvious was that my father was fighting for his life, and then running for his life. Since then, I've heard something about a moonlight night, a dead cat, and poison in the air. It seems that my father, not knowing as I do the excellent heart of your highness, grew a little excited . . .' "

"Good!" said the Borgia. "Not knowing as he does, eh? Ah, Bonfadini, there is a red devil on the head and in the heart of that Tizzo that pleases me. I wish I might have him back with me again."

"Would it be wise, my lord, since he knows that his own father was almost poisoned in your house?"

"But not by my orders, perhaps. Who can tell?"

"Yes," said Alessandro Bonfadini, "who can tell?"

"Continue the reading."

Bonfadini went on: " 'First he warned Lady Beatrice to leave the tavern. His mind was half bewildered by the effects of the poison. He looked for me, failed to find me, and then went on with the next part of his program, blindly. You, my lord, were to die. He went straight to your room, broke into it, and, at the moment when I heard you call out for help, was about to cut the head of your serene highness from your noble neck. You may recall the moment when I got to the spot. It was one thing to realize . . .' "

"True!" said the duke. "Very true, Alessandro. When he ran in, I was on one knee, desperate. The big Englishman fenced like a fiend. But then Tizzo flashed in between us, and took up the fight. Even Tizzo could not win quickly, however. Have I showed you how they leaped at one another? Until by the flashing of their own swords, I suppose, they recognized one another—otherwise it would have been a sweet bit of family murder in my room that night."

The duke began to laugh.

"Shall I continue, my lord?" asked the cold voice of the poisoner.

"Get on! Get on!" said the Borgia. "It warms my heart even to think of that cat-footed, wild-headed, fire-brained Tizzo. Was there ever a name so apt? The spark—the spark of fire—the spark that sets a world on fire—that's what he is!"

The poisoner read: " 'However, the three of us managed, as you know, to escape from the hands of your men; we rode like the devil across country and found ourselves in the morning of the next day surrounded by the men-at-arms of the Lady of Forli. You know her, of course. She's a big creature, handsome, with a good, swinging step, and a hearty laugh and an eye that brightens wherever it touches. But a twist of strange circumstances made her decide that I would be better under ground than above it. Unlike your tactful self, she used three murderers instead of a whiff of poisoned fragrance on a moonlight night. However, the moon helped me. I danced with the three of them till two fell down and the third was willing to talk. He told me a story that leaves my blood cold and my skin crawling.

" 'My lord, I am safely out of Forli. But inside of it remain the two people I love—my father and my lady. To ride to Perugia is a long journey; and it would take them a long time to attack Forli from that distance.

" 'But your highness is within arm's stretch of Forli. You easily can find the will to attack the place. It is just the sort of a morsel that would slip most easily down your throat. The Rocca, if you haven't seen it, is an excellently fortified place, but your cannon will breach its walls. However, what I hope is that a night march, a night attack might sweep all clean. And God will give me the claws of a cat to climb those walls and come to the help of my lady.

" 'Do you need to be persuaded further? Is not my lord's heart already twice its usual size? Is not your mouth watering and your brain on fire?

" 'Well, I can offer nothing of great value, because I have spent my fortune as fast as it was showered on me. I hate to use pockets or hang purses around my neck, and therefore I have no place to carry money.

" 'However, my lord, I have one thing remaining, and it shall be yours. Will you have it? Two hands, two feet, and a heart that will never weaken in your service.

" 'For how long shall I serve you? That, my lord, is a bargaining point. The devil might demand my service for life. But the Borgia, perhaps, will let me off with three months. For three months, my lord, I am at your beck and call, but there are certain slight conditions that I would like to make and certain little Borgian duties which I would avoid as, for instance,

item . . . stabbing in the back

item . . . poison in wine or elsewhere

item . . . midnight murder in the dark

but otherwise, I am completely yours.

" 'If my lord chooses me and my service on these terms, he may ride out of the tavern and take the road toward Forli. I shall be waiting to meet him if he is accompanied by not more than two men-at-arms.

" 'Ever my lord's faithful servant and obedient friend—Tizzo.' "

The Borgia began to laugh again. "Where is the Florentine secretary?" he asked. "Where is Machiavelli? Call him down to me here and let me have his advice on this letter and its writer. This Machiavelli has a young brain but a good one."

Accordingly, a young man dressed all in black entered the garden a moment later. He was of a middle size, and when he took off his hat to the duke, he showed a head of rather small dimensions, covered with glistening black hair. His lips were thin and secret. Perhaps it was they that gave a slight touch of the cat to his face. His eyes were very restless, very bright.

"Niccolò," said the duke, "here is a letter. Read it and tell me what to think of the writer."

Machiavelli read the letter half through, raised his head to give one bright, grave look to the duke, and then continued to the end.

After that he said, without hesitation: "If this is an elderly adventurer, I'd have him put out of the way as soon as possible; if it is a low-born man, have him thoroughly flogged where ten thousand men may hear him howl; but if he is young and well-born, I would attach him to me at any price."

"Good," said the Borgia. "Machiavelli, you have a brain that the world will hear from one day. There is something about you that pleases me beyond expression. Do you notice that he is willing to meet me if I don't bring with me more than two men-at-arms? That's characteristic of this Tizzo. If the odds are only three to one, he feels at home . . . Horses! Horses! Machiavelli, you and Bonfadini alone shall ride out with me to meet this red-headed fellow."

VI

They rode straightaway from the tavern, the duke giving orders for the company of Tizzo's Romagnol infantry to be gathered at once. And with that word, behind, the Borgia rode on between Machiavelli and Alessandro Bonfadini. In his hand, Cesare Borgia carried a naked ax that looked like the common ax of a woodsman, except that the color of the steel was a delicate blue. They had not gone down the road for a mile when something white flashed behind them from a tuft of willows and a rider on a white stallion was in the way to their rear.

The Borgia called out and waved the ax over his head.

"That's Tizzo," he said. "As wary as a cat, and as dangerous as a hungry tiger. I tell you, Machiavelli, that if he thought any great purpose would be served by it, he would ride at us and put his single hand against the three of us."

"He may be a very sharp tool," said Machiavelli, "but he will be in the hand of a very great artisan."

At this, the Borgia smiled. He rode out ahead of the other pair, and Tizzo came to meet him, doffing his hat, then closing to take the hand of the Duke of Valentinois. The duke kept that hand in a great grasp.

"Now, Tizzo," he said, "I have you. I accept your own terms. Three months of service. And this evening I start with my army for Forli. It is, as you suggest, a morsel of exactly the right size to fit my throat. But what if that hardhearted devil of a Caterina Sforza murders her prisoners before we can storm the walls of the castle?"

"Aye," said Tizzo, "I had thought about that, too. What other chance can I take, though?"

"Here is Bonfadini whom you remember well," said the duke.

"My father remembers him better, however," said Tizzo, looking grimly at the stone-white face of the poisoner.

"And here is my friend and adviser, good Niccolò Machiavelli. He has come from Florence to look into our ways."

"He will find many wonderful things," said Tizzo dryly.

But the Borgia merely laughed; for his spirits seemed high from the moment he had read the letter of Tizzo. "Ride on ahead of us," he said to Tizzo. "There are your Romagnol peasants that you were forming into good soldiers. They haven't forgotten you. Go on to them. They're good fellows and they love you."

A swarm of the peasants, bright in the red and yellow quarterings of the Borgia, had poured across the road from the tavern. Tizzo galloped his white horse toward them and was greeted by a loud shouting of: "Duca! Duca!" in honor of the duke, followed by a thundering roar for Tizzo, the captain.

"Now that you've seen him," said the duke to Machiavelli, "what do you think of him?"

The young statesman said: "That is the sort of a sword that I would leave in the scabbard until there was straightforward work to do."

"Perhaps. His men love him. Do you see them swarming and throwing up their hands in his honor? Now they have him off his horse and carry him on their shoulders. . . . He has taught them to shoot straight, fence, and obey orders. They love him because he has made them stronger men. I tell you, Niccolò, the day may come when every Italian will love me because I have made Italy a strong nation."

"The virtues of age," said Machiavelli, "outweigh the sins of youth, always. Today is greater than all the yesterdays."

"They still shout themselves hoarse. I knew they were

fond of him, but this is devotion. Such a man could be a dangerous force in an army, Niccolò."

"When a tool has accomplished its purpose," said Machiavelli, "it should be broken before it is thrown away."

The Borgia glanced aside at him, and then, slowly, smiled. Bonfadini was smiling also.

That blue-headed ax of steel which the Borgia had carried to the meeting on the road by Faenza was once more in the hands of Tizzo. His sword was at his side. The white horse stepped lightly beneath him. He was not cased from head to foot in complete steel, as most mounted soldiers were, but wore merely an open helmet, or steel cap, with a breastplate and shoulder-pieces. Equipped in this light manner, he was a lighter burden for his horse when he rode and, on the ground, those quick-thinking feet of his would be able to dance more swiftly.

The dance itself would not be long in starting.

The dawn had not yet commenced but it would not be long delayed; and Tizzo's peasant soldiery, armed with arquebuses and pikes and short swords, moved behind him with a steady thrumming of feet.

He had been given the vanguard; a mile back of him came the French soldiers with the famous Swiss pikemen behind them; and last of all, at such a distance that the rumbling of its wheels could not be heard, moved the clumsy artillery which might have to batter down the gates of the town if Tizzo could not take them with the first rush.

Another rumbling, a growing thunder, was beginning to come down the road at a walking pace toward Forli, and Tizzo reined back his horse to ask what the noise might be.

"The carts of the farmers bringing in produce for the markets," said one of the peasant soldiers. "They load their carts in the evening, and they start in the darkness so as to get to Forli just before daybreak. The market must be opened at sunrise, you see."

"Carts—sunrise—produce . . . Perhaps those carts will carry something more than vegetables when they get through the gates of Forli. Down in that ditch, every man of you. Do you hear? If one of you stirs, if one of you coughs or sneezes, if one of you allows the head of a single pike to shine in the moonlight, I'll have that man's head on the ground at my feet."

He saw his column sink down out of sight into the ditch. And suddenly he was alone in the road with the brilliant moonlight flooding about him and Forli lifting its gilded shoulders in the distance.

He could see the fort of the Rocca looming above the city.

With a hundred men to surprise such a place? He felt as though he had empty hands.

He passed on a short distance toward the town, then turned his horse and let it jog softly back up the road. The carts were in view, now, a whole score of them trudging along, the owners walking at the heads of the horses, the carts piled high with all sorts of country produce; the squealing of pigs sounded, and now and then the drowsy cackling and cawing of disturbed chickens as the carts rolled over a deeper rut or struck a bump with creaking axles.

Tizzo held up his hand when he came to the first cart. "Halt there, friend!" he commanded.

"Halt yourself and be hanged," said the Romagnol. "We're already late for Forli. What puts *you* on the road so far from a warm bed at this time of the morning?"

Two or three of the other peasants ran up with clubs in their hands to join in any altercation that might follow, but Tizzo knew these hardy Romagnols too well to interfere with them in this fashion. He reined the white horse aside and called out: "Up, lads, and at them!"

The thing was ended in one rush, Tizzo's voice calling: "Hands only! No daggers or swords! Don't hurt them, boys!"

So it was done, in a moment; the tough Romagnols, overwhelmed by numbers, were quickly helpless, and over the brief babbling noises could be heard only the voices of several of the farmers' wives, crowing out their laments as they sat up on the tops of the loaded carts.

Tizzo brought quiet.

He rode up and down the line, saying cheerfully: "Friends, you have been robbed and cheated and taxed by the Countess Sforza-Riario for a good many years.

"Here I am with some of the men of the Duca. If I open the gates of the town with your help, it will belong to Cesare Borgia before midday. Do you hear me?"

A man growled out the short answer: "Why change one robber for another?"

"The Duke of Valentinois and the Romagna does not

rob peasants," said Tizzo.

"All dukes are robbers."

"Of course they are," answered Tizzo, chuckling, "but this one only robs the lords and ladies and lets the peasant alone. For the food that his troops need, he pays hard cash."

The readiness of this reply and the apparent frankness of it brought a laugh from the peasants.

"I leave you your cartloads unharmed," said Tizzo. "I put a ducat in the hand of every man of you. I leave your women behind you on the road, here. I throw a few of my men into each cart, and we roll on through the gates. Do you hear? If we pass the gates unchallenged, all is well. If one of you betrays us, we cut your throats. Is that a bargain?"

And one of the peasants answered with a sudden laugh: "That's a soldier's true bargain. Come on, friends! I'd as soon shout 'Duca!' as yell 'Riario!' Let's take the bargain; because we can't refuse it!"

VII

Caterina, Countess Sforza-Riario, gathered a big woolen peasant's cloak more closely about her and raised the lantern so that she could see better the picture before her. It was the Baron of Melrose, naked except for a cincture, and lashed up by the hands so that his toes barely rested on the floor. In this posture he could support his entire weight only for a few moments on the tips of his toes, after which the burden of his body depended from his wrists.

He had been lashed there long enough to be close to exhaustion and now a continual tremor ran through his body, and the big muscles of his legs twitched up and down, and shudderings pulled at the tendons about his shoulders. But still his gray head was carried straight.

The countess broke off a bit of bread and ate it, and then swallowed a bit of wine which a page offered her on one knee, holding the silver salver high.

"How long before the strength goes out of his legs?" she asked. "How long before he hangs from the wrists like a heavy sack tied up by the two ears?"

A tall, powerful man stepped out of the shadows a little and looked more closely at the prisoner. He reached up and felt the shoulder muscles of Melrose, then the trembling, great muscles of the thighs.

"He'll endure until not long after dawn," said the executioner.

"And how long after that, Adolfo, before the tendons begin to pull and break in his shoulders?"

"He is a heavy man," said the executioner, "but he is well muscled. You see that right arm, particularly?"

"That's the arm of a swordsman," said the countess. "And I hear that he's a famous fellow with a sword."

"After the middle of this morning, he never will be famous again," said Adolfo.

"Will his arms be ruined?"

"Forever," said Adolfo. "Until he dies, he will have to be fed, like a baby."

"Do you hear that, my lord?" asked the countess.

Melrose looked at her, with the sweat of the long agony running down his face. He said nothing.

"There is something Christian in the sight of suffering like this," said the countess. "After watching you, my lord, I'll be able to say my prayers with more feeling, for a long time."

"Of course you will," said the executioner. "I always go to church after I've killed a man in here."

He looked without a smile over his domain, the gibbet-like beams that projected from the wall, here and there, and the iron machines with projecting spokes, the iron boots, also, together with the little wedges which are driven between the metal and the knee, gradually crushing the bone as wedge after wedge is added. And there were other devices such as strong gloves which pulled on easily but were fitted with fishhooks inside; in fact, there were a thousand little devices that helped Adolfo to play on human flesh and nerves like a great musician.

But best of all, the foundation of all the most perfect torments, was the great rack, whose sliding beams could be extended through the pressure exerted by a big wheel which worked against a screw. Here the body could be drawn out to the breaking point—or literally torn in two. But, when the flesh was all taut, the accepted practice was to strike the limbs and the joints one by one with a small iron bar, so breaking the tensed bone with ease. Sometimes the leg and arm on one side would be wrecked forever before the prisoner "confessed." Sometimes both legs went. Sometimes a single stroke of the bar made the screaming victim begin to shriek out whatever he could remember, whatever he could invent—anything to end the torture.

Adolfo, looking over his possessions, had good reason to

smile. He felt like a miser in the midst of his hoard.

"How long will it be before dawn?" asked the countess. "Very often they go to pieces when the gray of the morning commences to strike their faces."

"Another half-running of the hour glass, highness."

"Very well."

"No, it is beginning even now," said the jailer.

"The day is about to commence," said the countess to Melrose. "Will you tell me now, my friend, where I'll be able to find Tizzo, and who it was in my castle that let him go free from it?"

Melrose, staring at her, parted his lips as though to speak, but he merely moistened them and set his jaws hard again. His eyes were commencing to thrust out from his head under the long-continued pressure of the torment.

Here a confusion of tumult broke out in the town.

"What's that?" asked the countess. "Are my silly people starting a fiesta before sunrise?"

Adolfo, running to the casement, leaned into it and listened. He started to cry out: "This is no fiesta, highness, but a trouble of some—"

But here the countess herself cried out: "Do you hear it? They have passed the wall—they have broken into Forli. Oh, the careless, treacherous, hired dogs that are in my army! Do you hear? . . . Ring the alarm bells. Call for—"

The uproar was washing rapidly across the lower level of the town, and the voice of the crowd streamed like a flag across the mind of Melrose. He could hear the shouting grow from confusion into syllables that were understandable: "Duca! Duca! Tizzo! Tizzo! Tizzo!"

It seemed to him that the voices were pouring from his own throat in an ecstasy. And in fact they were. He was shouting involuntarily: "Tizzo! Tizzo! Tizzo!" and he began to laugh.

The countess had jerked a door open and was crying orders to the men-at-arms who waited outside it; Aldolfo leaned, fascinated, at the casement and still was there when the countess slammed the door and hurried back into the torture chamber.

"The red-headed wildcat has come into Forli to claw us all to death!" cried the countess. "Set his father free—quickly, Adolfo! Suppose Tizzo dreamed what had been happening here—he would make the stones of the Rocca melt away and come in at us with all his devils behind him."

Melrose, released from the ropes that held him, leaned feebly against the wall, breathing hard, his head for the first time bowed.

"Have him taken to the Lady Beatrice," said Caterina Sforza. "Guard them both as you would guard the balls of your eyes. Hai! How they yell in the streets! Are the Borgia and Tizzo saints and deliverers to my own people? Ah, if I were only a man—but today I *shall* be a man!"

The day had in fact begun, the green gray of the dawn glowing on the edge of the sky as she ran from the room and down the stairs.

Adolfo was saying: "Noble Signor Melrose, you will never forget that I have done nothing for my own pleasure, but all by command? Lean on me, highness. Step slowly. So! So!"

VIII

It would not be many minutes now, Tizzo knew, before the rioting soldiery of the duca had penetrated into every part of the castle; and somewhere in the Rocca were his father and Beatrice. They must be reached at once.

It was true that the Borgia controlled his men carefully during nearly every emergency, but when a stronghold had been taken by open assault, there was only one sort of a reward that could be offered to the victors—the sacking of the place. And when the wild-headed victors found women—

Tizzo looked grimly over his little group of prisoners. There was one elderly fighting man with a grizzled head, his face now as gray as his hair. Tizzo took him by the arm with a strong hand.

"In the Rocca," he said, "there are two prisoners. One is the Englishman—the big Englishman with gray hair and a red face—the Baron Melrose. And there is a girl—Beatrice of the Baglioni. Do you know where they may be kept, now?"

A dull eye rolled toward the face of Tizzo in utter lack of comprehension. Fear had benumbed the brain of the prisoner. Tizzo used the most powerful stimulant known to the Italian mind. He snatched a handful of silver out of his purse and jangled the ducats in front of the man.

"This money goes to you, if you can tell me where they're apt to be found. If you can lead me to them before some of the raiders reach them—you get this money today and a whole purse of it tomorrow."

The man opened his mouth and eyes as though he were receiving both spiritual and mental food.

"I think I know where they could be found," he said. "Follow me, highness. Quickly, because they may be on the opposite side of the Rocca."

He set off at a run, down the stairs, and then at full speed along a corridor that rose and fell and twisted and angled. Not a single man of Tizzo's company followed. Doors right and left invited them to hunt for plunder.

And the whole castle was turned into a screaming-house. The shouts of the men were nothing. It was the thin screaming of the women that drove like sword strokes through the brain of Tizzo.

They were in one of those endless corridors which most Italian fortresses were apt to have for a rapid means of getting from one part of the place to another.

Groups of plunderers lurched into the runway, here and there, but the shout of Tizzo made them scatter before his coming. He had thrown off his steel cap so that his red hair would make him more readily known.

And wherever he was seen, the men of the Borgia gave him a cheer—and went on about their business which would strip the famous Rocca to the bone long before noon in that day.

The panting voice of Tizzo's companion halted him, led him now through a side door and up another winding stairs into a tower where there was a great noise of trampling and battle.

So he rushed up into a big room with an old, vaulted

ceiling that rested on stout piers. At the head of the stairs a half dozen of the Borgians were fighting against a larger band of the defenders of the Rocca. And yonder in a corner he saw what he had been praying for sight of—Henry of Melrose, unarmored, but with a sword in his hands, heedless of the outcome of the fighting as he held his place in front of a smaller, slenderer figure. That was Beatrice Baglione. It must be she—now he could see the color of her dress—now her face, like a star to a sailor.

"Beatrice!" he shouted, and leaped into the fight, his head unarmored as it was. "Beatrice!" he cried, and "Beatrice!" It was his battle-cry, and with each utterance, he struck with the terrible swift ax, right and left.

He had come at a good time, for the Borgians were having enough of this fierce struggling and were giving up when he sprang into the lead and rallied them.

And he heard a woman's voice coming out of a visored helmet and shouting, shrill and high: "Giovanni degli Azurri! There is your man! There is the one who brought all this ruin down on Forli! There is Tizzo of Melrose! Kill him now, and I swear that this is the happiest day of my life."

The outcry of the countess inspired all her men. They had been on the verge of retreating; now they made a sudden rally. Two of the Borgians were driven back over the edge of the floor and fell into the well of the stairs; Giovanni degli Azurri put his sword with a downright stroke through the throat of a third. The other pair gave back from the side of Tizzo and called on him to give up a hopeless fight. But he could not be drawn away. Down the

length of the room he saw the big form of his father striding; and Beatrice, helplessly unarmed as she was, hurrying
after him.

When he should have retreated, he leaped in suddenly,
springing here and there like an erratic dancer. He used
the light sword in his left hand like a dagger to ward off
blows; the ax in his right hand made lightning circles.

One of these flashing arcs of light glanced against the
helmet of Giovanni degli Azurri and staggered that champion.

The second blow would have killed him outright, but
here Caterina Sforza herself ran forward and struck a good
two-handed blow at the head of Tizzo.

He had not expected actual fighting from the countess.
His hastily reared guard received the blow and turned the
edge of it, but the force of the flat sword was enough to
knock him to his knees.

He heard the scream of Beatrice like a ray of light
gleaming across his mind. The two Borgians, inspired by
the attack he had delivered, had closed in from the sides
and they lustily struck out to protect him. But the decisive
blow came from Henry of Melrose.

He had come in on the rear of the Sforza men on the
run. A long lunge drove the point of his sword through the
gorget rivets at the back of the neck of one man-at-arms.
That fellow was down, never to rise again. And now with a
huge stroke the baron dropped a second man-at-arms.

That second of interval had put Tizzo back on his feet
again. He swerved from the lunging sword of Giovanni
degli Azurri and struck with his ax at the junction be-

tween the helmet and the gorget. The steel split; the ax sank in; and Giovanni degli Azurri, dropping his sword, clasped his throat with both hands and fell sprawling to his knees.

His fall was the end. The other defenders threw up their mailed hands and shouted for quarter. Only the virago, Caterina Sforza, scorning surrender, lifted her sword over her head and rushed in for a final attack. A side-stroke of Tizzo's ax knocked the sword out of her grip and sent it clanging against the wall. He caught her by the hands and held her fast. She groaned with rage like a man and suddenly stopped struggling.

A strange voice called to them from the floor. It was Giovanni degli Azurri, his visor raised so that he could gasp in more air, and the blood-bubbles breaking on his lips. He had risen to his knees, but now he began to sink down again.

"I confess—my God forgive me!— it was your maid who stole the jewels; and I forged a letter in the hand of Lady Beatrice to draw him out of the Rocca; I posted the three men to murder him at the rendezvous beyond the town. And now—now—"

He slipped to his side. Caterina Sforza dropped on her knees and screeched out: "Giovanni, what do you mean? What do you say?"

"Aye—for love of you," muttered Giovanni.

She struck him with her mailed hand across his bleeding face. But he was already past feeling. He fell on his back and died with one groan and one quick updrawing of the knees.

The Countess Riario looked up from his dead face at Tizzo and Beatrice in one another's arms. The girl was wiping the sweat and the blood from the face of her lover with the puffed velvet sleeve of her dress.

They were laughing together; and the baron stood by them leaning on his sword, smiling faintly as he watched their joy.

Except for Tizzo, the Borgians had rushed on to find less fighting and more loot, herding their new prisoners before them.

And now from the wounded and the dead the blood spread across the floor in widening pools that interlinked and made little flowing streams.

The countess walked straight up to Melrose.

"My lord," she said, "I have given you the treatment of a common criminal. Will you reward me for it by giving me good advice?"

"Madame," said the Englishman, "a knight is sworn to serve *all* ladies."

"Tell me what to do, then. Surrender to Cesare Borgia or throw myself from the casement, there?"

"If you were my daughter," said the baron, "I'd hope to see you leap from the wall and die; but since you are the noble Countess Riario, I expect you to take my arm and let me lead you to the Duke of Romagna."

She hesitated, glaring savagely at him. Then, with a shrug of the shoulders and a laugh, she accepted his arm.

All day the riot rang and roared through the streets of Forli and through the courts and rooms of the Rocca; but when night came, joy had exhausted itself. A few drunken voices sang in the town and Niccolò Machiavelli listened to them with a pleased smile as he sat by the side of the duke at the casement. Cesare Borgia rather lay than sat in a great chair, his head flung back.

"A successful day," said Machiavelli. "You have Forli, town and citadel. It has cost you only a few men, and the work has been done by one who has rewarded himself."

"Tizzo?" murmured the duke.

"I see him standing on the rampart with the girl in his arms. They are like one bit of black paper, curiously carved and held up against the moon between thumb and forefinger."

"Fools always find happiness in foolish ways," said the Borgia. "But you see that I know how to use edged tools?"

"This time—yes. But the next time you may cut your hand to the bone."

The Silent Witness

The detective-mystery-spy story field would not at first glance seem one that a writer of westerns, love stories, and historical romances should enter. But Faust did so successfully. This short short is from *Black Mask Detective Magazine* that once published Dashiell Hammett, Raymond Chandler, and most of the best whodunit authors. The noted critic-scholar-editor H. L. Mencken was once an editor of *Black Mask*.

Riddle pressed the Bentley bell and then held the doorknob while he stared through the glass into the downstairs hallway. It had the nakedly expectant look of all entrances to push-button apartment houses. The lock began to click rapidly; it kept on clicking after he had entered the hall and pressed the elevator button.

Everything happened very slowly. He heard the elevator door slam shut above him, a deep-voiced humming began in the throat of the shaft and descended gradually toward him. The lighted elevator slid past the diamond-shaped peephole. It halted. The inner door was pushed clanging back by the ghostly fingers of the machine.

He entered, pressed the button of Number 6, and watched the door slowly roll shut, obeying the electric mind. With a soft lurch the elevator started up the shaft.

At the sixth floor the automatic brake stopped the car softly and the inner door rolled gradually back. This mechanized precision, this mindless deliberation, screwed up Riddle's nerves to a breaking tension. He had to set his lips and his lean jaw and make ready to endure what he knew was ahead of him.

Then the outer door of the elevator was snatched open by Gay Bentley. She leaned against the edge of it with her eyes so big and dark that she looked like a white-faced child. Riddle put his arm around her and closed the door while she clung to him, saying: "Dick. . . . Dick. . . . Dick. . . ."

He took her through the open door into the living-room of her apartment. It was exactly in order, disappointing the horrible expectation with which he had entered. The floor lamps cast two amber circles on the ceiling and two white pools on the floor. The huge litter of a Sunday news-paper lay scattered on the davenport and on the table there was a tall highball glass, almost full.

"Where?" asked Riddle.

She pointed toward the bedroom door. "I'll come with you," she said.

He shook his head. "You sit here. No, lie down."

"I'll go mad if I lie down," said Gay. Her lips began to tremble and her eyes rolled, so he picked her up and laid her on the davenport amid the rustling of the newspaper.

"You be quiet. Will you be quiet? Close your eyes!" commanded Riddle.

She closed her eyes and he crossed the floor with the

sense of her light, firm body still making his hands feel strong. He needed that strength of spirit when he entered the bedroom and saw Tom Bentley lying on the bed, far over against the wall with his right arm stretched out, pointing an automatic at his friend in the doorway. But Bentley's half-open eyes were drowsily considering something on the white of the ceiling instead of Riddle, and a spot of deep purple appeared on his temple with one thin, watery line of blood running down from it.

Riddle went back into the living-room where Gay Bentley already was off the couch and sitting on the piano stool with her face in her hands. She started up to face Riddle. He wandered to the table and picked up the unfinished highball. When he tasted it, he found the whisky good but the drink was tepid; it had come to the room temperature.

"The police?" whispered the girl. "Do we have to call the police?"

He sipped the tepid highball again before he put down the glass.

"I want a drink, Gay," he said.

"Take this. It's mine but I don't want it."

"This? *This* is yours?" he asked, looking suddenly at her.

"Ah, but you like a man's drink," she nodded, unobservant. "I'll make you a fresh one."

She passed him on the way to the pantry, and clung close to him again for an instant.

"Oh, Dick," she whispered, "think what animals we are! When I found him, my mind stopped, and all I could do was to come out here and go through the motions of mixing a drink. . . . Think of that! And then I remembered you. Thank God for you! Thank God for you!"

She went on to the pantry.

"How do you want it?" she called.

"Just like yours," said Riddle. He saw his own pale, thin face in the glass above the fireplace and stared at the gloomy image entranced.

"Just like mine?" she repeated, surprised. "But two lumps of ice, you always take."

"No. Just like yours. One lump. That will do," said Riddle.

She brought the drink back to him, and he sank down into a chair at the table. He put his chin on his fist and stared at nothingness. The girl stood behind him with her hands on his shoulders.

"Poor Tom!" she said. "I know you loved him, Dick, but try not to take it too hard. He *was* unhappy, you know."

"I knew," said Riddle, "and I kept away from him for a month. . . . Was it money, Gay?"

"No," she answered.

"It had to be debts that drove him to it. There was nothing else," insisted Riddle.

"There was something else," she replied.

"What under heaven?" asked Riddle, jerking up his head so that his face almost touched hers.

"Jealousy, Dick," said the girl.

"Jealousy?" cried Riddle. "Jealousy of you, Gay?"

She made a pause, with her face still close to his, before she answered carefully and gently, as though to a child:

"You know we haven't been so very happy together, lately."

"After a few years, the bubble and zip goes out of most marriages," said Riddle.

"Ah, it was more than that," she answered.

"You mean there *was* a definite reason for his jealousy?" demanded Riddle. "You mean that there was another man?"

She was silent again before she answered just above a whisper: "Ah, Dick, you blind, blind fellow!"

Riddle reached up and caught one of her hands from his shoulder. "What the devil do you mean, Gay?" he asked.

"He knew I loved someone else," said the girl.

"Who?" asked Riddle.

She pulled to get free. "I don't want to talk about it. I can't talk about it," she said. "Not to you."

Riddle let her hand go.

"You mean that I'm the man?" he said.

She gave him no answer but walked across the room to the window and stood there looking out. A breeze came in from moment to moment and set her bright hair shimmering over the smooth and soft of her neck. She stood there an eternity of minutes. The silence between them— between her beauty and his friendship with the dead man —that silence sang on for minutes.

He tasted her drink on the table then, quickly, took a small swallow from his own glass. After that he glanced at his watch. The silence drew out in length like a dark thread. . . .

"You know that Tom was my best friend?" he asked.

"I know everything," said the girl. "It was because he cared about you so much that I first began to care—too. . . ."

Her voice broke a little. Riddle went to her and took her by the shoulders. He seated her firmly in a chair.

"That's all to be talked about afterward," he told her. Then, walking up and down the room, he said: "Tell me what you know about it."

She lay back in the chair with her head partly turned away from him and her eyes almost closed and sometimes a smile that was characteristic of her when she talked appeared on her lips. Now, at thirty, wrinkles pinched her eyes a little at the corners but her smile was still very lovely. She talked slowly.

"I went out just before five. I couldn't remember but I thought I had a tea engagement with Martha Gilbert and I couldn't get her on the phone. I didn't find Martha. I ran into Jud Mowbray a little later, and he insisted on cocktails. I didn't want one, but I sort of had to. . . . After a while I left him and got back here at around a quarter to six. And I found Tom—like that; and then I telephoned to you."

Riddle nodded.

"You saw Tom and he was dead—of his own hand. Then you poured yourself this drink and then you telephoned to me."

"What does the drink matter?" she asked, with a sudden curiosity.

"The police always want to know everything," said Riddle. "They eat up every detail. And I'll have to ring them in a moment. You poured yourself this drink about forty-five minutes ago, let's say?"

"Yes. Almost exactly."

He sipped her drink, carefully, and then tried his own. He said nothing—endlessly.

"Then by the time I arrived," he finally said, "your drink hadn't been standing more than twenty minutes, had it?"

"No. Of course not! . . . Dick, what's the matter with you?"

"Nothing," said Riddle, standing up and seeing the white of his face in the glass again. Then he glanced at his wrist. A half hour had come—and gone.

He went to the telephone but paused there for a long moment until she asked: "What's in your mind, Dick?"

"I was thinking of the first days out of college when Tom and I were fighting our way up."

"*You* fought your way up," said Gay Bentley, "and Tom kept sliding back in spite of all his scratching. He was a derelict before the end and the only thing that drew him along was the towline you threw to him, Dick, darling. . . ."

He picked up the receiver and began to dial.

"I want the police," he said.

"Not so soon, Dick!" cried the girl. "I don't want their dreadful, blunt faces near me. I couldn't stand them!"

"This is One Forty-two East Hargreave Street," said Riddle. "On the sixth floor, apartment D, Thomas Bentley is dead. It is murder. . . ." He hung up.

"Murder? Murder?" cried the girl. "Dick, what are you talking about?"

"About a man I loved, and a woman I used to love, too," said Riddle, "and an alibi rotten all the way through."

He sipped from the glasses on the table, one after the other.

"This drink of mine has been standing here for half an hour, but it's still cold," he said. "It still will be cold when the homicide squad arrives and hears me testify that your glass was room temperature when I came in. . . ."

"Dick, what do you mean?" she gasped. "What crazy idea is in your head?"

"My idea," said Riddle, "is that you *were* out of the house to collect your alibi, but you poured your drink, here, before you left, and all the time you were away the highball was going ahead like an automatic machine gathering warmth and registering murder. *You* killed Tom."

She went to pieces, flew at him, beggingly.

"Dick, throw the stuff out of the window! Dick, you wouldn't kill me, would you? Not like a rat; you wouldn't kill me, Dick, would you?" she sobbed to him. "I needed a drink—to do it! But, Dick, because I love you— Oh, throw it away!"

He covered the glass with his hand. He could not look at her but he knew she was shrinking away from him now—toward the door. And then that she had slipped out into the hallway, running.

Now she would be pressing the button of the elevator frantically; but he knew with what an unhurried steadiness it would respond.

A siren screamed out of the distance and turned loose its howling in Hargreave Street. Riddle opened his eyes as he listened, and in the mirror the white image stared back at him in astonishment and horror.

The Kinsale

Faust's mother was Irish and from her he took a love of
Irish lore, whether Americanized or not, and to it added
his own mythology as in "The Kinsale." This story first
appeared in *The Saturday Evening Post*. Readers wrote
for a long time afterward asking where the mythical
Clonmel Valley was located.

Few people know that within a few short hours of
Manhattan there is a valley so truly a part of the Old
Country that when a real Irishman comes to it from over-
seas, he rubs his eyes and blesses himself twice. It is called
Clonmel Valley, and there are plenty of O'Connors and
O'Haras and O'Reillys, O'Mores, O'Tooles, Shaugh-
nesseys, O'Briens, McCarthys, O'Connells, Donoghues,
O'Dwyers, O'Malleys, Flahertys, O'Sullivans, and the like,
in it. They came, bringing with them some of those big,
roomy Irish mares whose heads could fill a clothesbasket
and whose quarters block a barn door. They settled in
Clonmel Valley, of course, because the rolling green country spoke to their hearts. Here there was grass as good as
Kentucky's and water as fine as Vermont's. What did it
matter to an O'Hara, an O'Malley, an O'Connell, or the
like, if the soil was only one plowshare deep and that, after

a few workings, the furrow would have to be tooled along among the rocks? It mattered not at all as soon as they saw the horses smacking their lips on the sweet pasturage; and by the time the first crop of potatoes was well out of the ground, the whole lot of them felt securely at home. In Clonmel Valley, to this day, people farm for food and not for hard cash, so to speak. They still live in the little white houses that the men of the famine built. They still plow their small ragged fields by horse power, and nothing grows greater in the valley except the big stone walls added to from the crops of rocks every year, and the hedges and the Irish hunters that jump them.

It was of the horses that Daniel Kinsale was thinking, when he first read the letter that told him of the death of Uncle William Kinsale. Daniel himself was fifty-five and he had been out of Clonmel Valley since he was a lad, but he still remembered seventeen hands of hell-fire roaring over wall and ditch and hedge. The Clonmel hounds are blown thin by the wind of their own racing and only a Clonmel fox could stay ahead of them for three fields. Kinsale felt the hunting breeze in his eyes before he looked down to the letter again.

> . . . and of course you'll come back to us, Danny darling, and be head of the family, for there's no other Kinsale at all to do it except Kerry Kinsale, and he's only twenty-five, and in love, God pity him, and the girl will have none of him, which is the breaking of his poor heart every day of his life, and Kerry such a bright good upstanding boy. . . .

When Daniel realized that he was The Kinsale, he knew that the time had come for him to close shop and hark

back to the home country; so he spent a week or so selling
Prendergast Steel short, and when he had broken the stock
down to its all-time low, he bought it all in again and let
it soar as it pleased and put another million in his pocket.
So, with a picture of Clonmel horses in his eye and a
thought of Federal surtaxes in his brain, he went back to
the Valley to give things a look.

It warmed his heart like Irish whisky, it did him good as
deep as Black Label itself could reach, to see again men of
the Clonmel build, all with a ton of strength layered
around their shoulders, upheld by legs of whalebone and
steel. It did him good to see the Clonmel girls, too, for in
the whole world there is not their like for clean bone and
lovely heads and eyes of pure blue fire. Everyone knows
that it was with the outcasts of Clonmel, the weeds and seconds, that Mr. Ziegfeld first brightened the American
stage. When Daniel Kinsale looked at those girls again, he
realized why he had never married. He wished that he
were ten years younger; then he wondered if he were indeed too old, for with horses and women it's the knowing
that counts.

When Daniel got off at the station, he was glad that he
had not driven down in the limousine, or in the big blue
two-seater, or in any other of his cars, for he saw that the
age of rubber never had rolled into Clonmel. There was
no polished road metal for it to roll on, but only the same
old rocky carriage lanes and byways. No taxicabs served the
station, and Daniel had himself delivered by the grocery
wagon.

There are nothing but lanes and byways in Clonmel
Valley, no main roads at all, and in place of taxicabs,

which soon wear out on the bumps and rocks, people drive themselves in carts or rattle around in old cars.

The groceryman was an O'Toole. He said: "You wouldn't be a certain Danny Kinsale, would you? I remember blackin' his eyes for him two or three times when we were back in school together."

"Well," said Kinsale, "the last I remember was you spitting out blood and teeth."

O'Toole shook him fondly by the hand.

"I thought there was a wee look of the Valley about you," he said.

When Danny Kinsale was on the driver's seat of the grocery wagon, he said to the delivery boy: "What's new in the Valley?"

"Ah, it's a dull, dead place altogether," said the boy, "and nothing ever happens in it. I'm going to be away from it soon, thank God!"

"What will you do?" asked Kinsale.

"I can't tell, just," said the delivery boy. "Some say that there's room in the Marines for another, but I'm thinking of the ring, maybe."

"How old might you be?" asked Kinsale.

"Fifteen," said the boy, "but fifteen in Clonmel is twenty any other place in the world, thank God! . . . That's where Mike O'Dwyer was killed last year, right there by that bridge."

"What was the killing of him like?"

"Ah, he had a little trouble with Willie O'Malley, was all."

"And Willie killed him?"

"No, the whisky killed him."

"The whisky?"

"The whisky and a new horse he was riding," said the boy.

"It's not all clear to me," said Kinsale, "an O'Malley, and whisky, and a young horse, and a dead O'Dwyer at the end of it."

"Well, it's easy enough," said the boy. "For after O'Dwyer had whipped O'Malley good, he had a few drinks around to tell people the news, and it left him dizzy on the gray colt, and the colt slipped and threw him at the bridge, and that's all the story there is of it."

"I've been long out of the Valley," said Kinsale, nodding.

"One could see that without the telling," said the boy.

"That off horse looks as though it could jump," said Kinsale.

The boy looked at him, and then he spat.

"And you after telling me!" he said. "Jump? Man, he can lep a house! But I'll sell him cheap."

"What's cheap?" asked Kinsale.

"Five hundred, say. A horse that's right up to your weight and would give a man a kind ride."

"Is he sound?"

"Would I offer him if he wasn't sound?"

"There wouldn't be a bit of bog spavin on that near leg, would there?" asked Kinsale gently.

"Ah, well," sighed the boy, "and what's a bog spavin between a horse and man that know one another? . . . Is this your house?"

Kinsale got down with his bags and walked to the house. A redheaded young man was plowing with two horses in the field beside. When he heard Kinsale knocking, he stopped and sat on the plow.

"Go around to the back door!" he bawled.

"The front door is good enough for me," said Kinsale. "Why should I go to the back?"

"Because my aunt is a deaf woman unless she sees your face."

"Who might you be?" shouted Kinsale.

"I'm the man of the place," said the youth.

"Have you got a name to you?" asked Kinsale.

"Kerry Kinsale, and what's it to you?"

"I'm your Uncle Danny and you be damned!" called Kinsale.

Kerry Kinsale rose from the plow. He wore heavy boots and the ground was deep from the working, but he ran lightly to the wall, leaped it in his stride, and arrived on the porch without panting. He shook hands.

"Let go of me!" commanded Kinsale. "You're breaking my bones!"

"I'm that glad to see you!" said Kerry.

He lifted the bags. He took them in one hand by the two grips and pushed open the front door.

"Go in, Uncle Danny, and God give you the comfort of the house," said Kerry.

Kinsale went into a front room that had a carpet on the floor and a family album on the center table; and, under glass along the wall, fading pictures of the dead looked down upon him. Kerry's voice was booming in the back of the house. Anne Kinsale came running into the room. The women of Clonmel do not grow older; they simply become a bit thin and smile somewhat less. Anne Kinsale kissed her younger cousin and then pushed him off to arm's length.

"I'm proud to see you, but your color's not right, Danny," said she. "Why didn't you come to the wake and the funeral?"

"Did you bury him well?" asked Daniel.

"It was a twenty-gallon wake," said Anne Kinsale, "and all of the best."

"I couldn't come myself, but I sent down five cases," Kinsale pointed out.

"We tried it, all around," admitted Anne, "but there wasn't a real taste to it, so we gave it to the young folks."

"It was twenty years old!" said Kinsale. "And it cost—"

"Ah, lad, maybe it was time that weakened it," suggested Anne. . . . "Kerry, isn't there a drop for the happy meeting?"

Kerry brought in a stone jug and glasses. He filled the glasses neatly, holding them in one hand and rolling the jug over the bend of his forearm.

"Here's to you, Uncle Danny, long and deep!" he said.

Kinsale swallowed his own portion and breathed carefully over the aftertaste. He looked down.

"Take it back into the kitchen, Kerry," said Anne. Afterward she murmured, "Wipe your eyes while he's out of the room, Danny, and no one will ever know."

He took out a handkerchief and rapidly wiped his eyes.

"Takes me a little by the throat," he said, "after these years."

"Aye, Danny, you're soft, you're soft, but a bit of Valley life will harden you. . . . Kerry, take his bags into the front bedroom."

Stones rattled down the slope of the hillside. One of them sprang against the side of the house with a heavy thump; and Kinsale saw a girl sliding a horse down the slope with a comet's tail of dust whipped up into the air behind.

"Holy heaven!" said Daniel Kinsale.

"Don't be swearing, Danny," said Anne. "When you were a young loose-mouthed boy, how many times was I telling you that both the angry and the foolish way of swearing are damn bad?"

"There's a gray horse coming down Carrick Hill with a woman or a wildcat on top of it," said Danny.

"That would just be Eileen O'Malley," said Aunt Anne. "She promised to bring me some good essence of juniper, the day."

The house blocked the rider out of view, so Daniel Kinsale leaned out the window in time to see Eileen O'Malley pull up at the back of the place. The gray horse wanted to go on, but between a buck and a plunge, big Kerry Kinsale took the girl under the armpits and swung her to the ground. He kissed her.

"There's no sense in your hands, Kerry," she said. "You've half broken my ribs." And she kissed him again.

"You shouldn't be riding this beast till I've gentled him for you," said Kerry.

"After you've gentled a horse, darling," said Eileen O'Malley, "it's no more mouth than a stone post."

First, Daniel Kinsale looked at the girl and then he squinted at her. But what's the use of talking about her? It's enough to say that she was a Clonmel woman.

Daniel said over his shoulder, "What's the age for a man's woman to be married?"

"Half your own age plus seven," said Aunt Anne.

Daniel turned from the window, for the two had passed from sight entering the house.

"Aye, or minus seven," said he.

"What are you mumbling about, Danny?" she asked.

"I was only saying what a long time I've been away from home."

"Hello, Eileen!" said Anne. "Did you remember the juniper, sweetheart? . . . This is The Kinsale."

"Is that The Kinsale?" asked Eileen. "I never saw one so young!"

Like a Clonmel girl that knew her manners, she went up to Daniel and kissed him without any haste whatever in the leaving.

"It's a lovely thing to have The Kinsale in the Valley," she said. . . . "What are you standing around for, Kerry? Or is there no whisky in the house?"

He brought in the huge jug and the glasses again.

"Can you drink it at this time of day?" asked Daniel, looking the girl in the eyes.

"A drop in time saves nine," said Eileen. "And the pure dew of Clonmel never did a good woman harm, drinking to The Kinsale."

II

That was all the welcome Daniel had in the Valley. He had thought, when he locked up his desk in New York, that the women and the old men of Clonmel would stand at gaze for the sake of one who had gone so far from home and filled so many headlines in the course of thirty years, but after a week he said to Aunt Anne: "What's the matter with it all? They treat me as though there were no eyes in my face to see them and no ears in my head to hear them. I talked to The O'Donnel and some others Wednesday about building a golf course and a race track and a new church for them all, and they asked me why should I spoil the Valley with fences and could a man pray better inside of stone walls than wood? In seven days there's not one that's called me The Kinsale! Only you and Eileen O'Malley know that I'm in the Valley."

"Now, Danny dear," said Aunt Anne, "it's you they want, and not your money."

"But, confound them, they have me, haven't they?" asked Daniel. "Anyway, I'll be building a new part on the house for all of us."

"Ah, but, Danny, so long as there's the one good fire to warm the legs of us, why should we have two to be wasting good wood?" asked Anne.

"There, d'you mind?" shouted Daniel. "You're like the

rest of them, thwarting every turn of my hand! I'll be up and away from this place!"

Yet he stayed on, though he found himself a stranger in his home country, and the hurt of it every day walked deeper and deeper into his heart. He took to watching young Kerry, for who else would be his heir in the end?

Daniel said to him, "What would you have of the world?"

And Kerry answered, "Eileen O'Malley and the bay mare of Michael O'Reilly."

Daniel replied: "What a man wants with his eyes he must get with his hands. . . . How long are you in the plowing of that field?"

"Two weeks come Saturday," said Kerry.

"It's not a four-day job, with two such horses as you work in the plow," remarked Daniel.

"No, sir," said Kerry, "but there was two dances and a wake in between."

"You've been out of the Valley, Kerry?"

"Yes, sir. I've been out to school."

"What did you get from your school?"

"I got this scar over my eye," said Kerry.

"How many of them were there?" asked Daniel.

"There was only one of them," answered Kerry sadly. "But he had a good left hand and a fist that was like a stone in my face, till I broke his ribs for him."

"I never see you at work in the field in the mornings," said Daniel.

"No, sir. I must give the morning to Rourke."

"And who is Rourke, if you please?"

"He's the five-year-old that makes the off horse at the plow. He jumps all but timber very well, even now."

"No good Irish horse will abide timber," agreed Daniel. "They know that the dirty English gibbets and scaffolds were built of wood. . . . But the five-year-old is not the horse for you. The other one in your team could gallop him down in a day's running."

"Are you meaning Barnaby?" asked Kerry.

"Aye. The brown that's the near horse of the team."

"He will never blow out your eye with his speed," said Kerry. "He's a good old man's horse."

"After five mile," said Daniel, "the Rourke would never look him in the eye."

Kerry laughed. Then he spat.

"Barnaby is weak in the quarters," he said.

"Rourke is a weed," said Daniel.

"I wish the ground was covered with weeds like him," said Kerry.

"Rourke is gone in the knees," said Daniel.

"If he's the least over in the knees," said Kerry, "he's not in at the hocks, like Barnaby."

"There's no fool like a young fool!" said Daniel.

"I've heard that put the other way around," said Kerry.

"I'll try Barnaby against you and Rourke any day."

"I wouldn't have the boys laughing at an old man," said Kerry.

"And mind you," said Daniel, "though blood may make you heir to The Kinsale, the name is not yet the money."

"Who asks for it?"

"Let me see you doing a man's work and not a boy's

play," said Daniel, and walked away.

Kerry went that evening to Eileen O'Malley.

Her father sat mending a bridle in the front room where the table was laid for the seven O'Malleys.

"Hai, Tim!" he called. "Tell Eileen to put another plate on the table and another potato in the stew."

"I'm not staying to eat," said Kerry.

"The whisky jug is behind the door," said Mr. O'Malley, "and I wouldn't be minding a wee spot of it myself. . . . D'you mind O'Sullivan's wall-eyed bay colt with the four good legs under him?"

"I mind him. Aye," said Kerry.

"He's gone," said O'Malley.

"In the feet?" asked Kerry.

"Spavined," said O'Malley. "Where are you bound to?"

"I'll have a word with Eileen."

"Mind, the last word you had with her, the steak was burned black."

Kerry went into the kitchen where three hungry young O'Malleys watched Eileen at the stove through the smoke of frying and the steam of boiling. The kitchen fog had set her hair glistening.

"It's over between me and the money, Eileen," he said. "The Kinsale and I cannot see eye to eye."

"What would I care about the money?" asked Eileen.

"Do you mean it?" he said.

"I do mean it—but let me breathe, Kerry."

"One more thing would make me happier than any man in the world," said Kerry.

"What would it be, darling?"

"At the next dance don't be wasting yourself on The Kinsale so much. It makes people talk."

"Does it? Then they have little to do!"

"Not that I care, myself. For a man of sixty—"

"He's only fifty-five," said Eileen.

"It's the same thing."

"It is not. He might be the father of four or five, by sixty."

"Eileen, what would you be talking about?"

"A girl with a brain in her head must think about her children, and all."

"Is it The Kinsale that you're thinking about?"

"Would you be putting my thoughts on a halter?"

"I won't have you playing fool with him," said Kerry.

"You'll have what you get, and no more," said she. "And what right have you to throw away the fortune that God made for you, anyway?"

"D'you want me to be a slave and kiss the foot that kicks me?"

"You'd rather have me for your slave, I take it. Moiling and toiling and mopping the floor of a hut, and the life pulled out of me by your brats while you drink whisky by the stove and win the Kentucky Derby with every pipeful you smoke—"

"No, Eileen!"

"—and put the savings into a new horse—"

"Eileen!"

"—and walk before me all through life, so that others won't see my rags so well."

"Eileen, will you listen once?"

III

So the iron entered the soul of Kerry Kinsale. For if Eileen willed that The Kinsale must be suited, and if only labor could please Uncle Daniel, then labor it had to be, and no more mornings of schooling Rourke. He rose in the morning with the dawn and made the blacksmith shop ring as he sharpened the plowshares. All morning he ran the furrows, and all afternoon, with the cry of the Clonmel hounds weaving in and out of the horizon and sometimes the horns and the shouts of the hunt leaving a sweet sad echo all through his brain. Aunt Anne wondered over him with a troubled eye and The Kinsale studied him from time to time with an increasing approval.

"I see that you've taken my word to your heart, after all," he said on a day. "I thought it was wasted, but there's many a good horse will kick at the whip before it gallops."

Kerry smiled and tasted the pain to the core of his soul because the words in his throat were unuttered. Yet the worst of all was to have to follow the plow while The Kinsale walked up and down beyond the hedge with his feet on the firm smooth ground.

So it was on that last morning of mornings. The horses had barely begun to steam and the birds were flying down into the black furrow; blue mist filled the hollows, blown clouds filled the sky, when the cry of the pack came over the hills and down toward the farm like a thought from the mind into utterance.

He drove the plow straight on, while his heart trembled.

Automatically, his hands tooled the plowshare around the danger of the rocks; and a cold sweat of desire stood out on the back of his neck, yet he would not look up, for he felt the grim and watchful eye of The Kinsale upon him. "Was the man never young? Did he never follow the hounds?" said Kerry to his heart. But at last the horses turned the corner of the field and there was the hunt just before him, sweeping up the hollow. It was cold enough for the breath of the horses to stain the air, so that they seemed to be breathing out the mist of the Valley.

He saw Mary O'More on her new colt, and Samus O'Connell with his hat gone, flying the wall, and Dinny O'Hanlon on the bald-faced bay, and sweet Maggie O'Sullivan laughing, and Dick McCarthy shouting, and then five Flahertys driving like five devils all in a flock, and more, and more from the edge of the O'Banion Wood to the wall of Shaughnessey's meadow where the hounds were streaming over in full cry. Their heads went up. The note changed. Yes, on the rim of the hill the fox ran in view with his tail still up, a true fox of Clonmel!

The Kinsale, as he walked up and down in a green sweater with green house slippers on his feet, stopped at the kitchen window to speak a word with Aunt Anne. She leaned over the sink to see the hunt streaming through the Valley.

"There goes the Clonmel, Aunt Anne," said The Kinsale. "And why have I never even been asked to join the hunt?"

"Because God loves your bones and wants to keep them whole," said Aunt Anne. "Will you notice our Kerry walking straight and true behind the plow, whatever?"

"He needed a steadying hand, and he got it in time," said Daniel Kinsale.

"I'm proud of the big boy," said Anne.

"I'm proud of the work I did on him," said The Kinsale.

The plow team at this moment halted, and Kerry, running forward, worked a moment on the straps of Rourke; then he flung the harness to the ground and vaulted onto the bare back.

The Kinsale shouted: "Kerry, come back! By the eternal, almighty, thundering—"

"Mind your talk, Danny!" called Anne.

Kerry, at the call, turned his head for one wild look toward his uncle; then he loosed Rourke after the hunt.

The Kinsale began to shout, "You blathering—"

"Mind your tongue! It's God that's hearing you, Danny!" cried Anne.

"I'll have the worthless, ungrateful fool of a boy hearing me too!" yelled The Kinsale. "He's thrown down his fortune with that same harness, and he'll never be able to pick it up again; and that's what I'll tell him."

"Oh, Danny, darling!" cried Anne Kinsale. "Will you wait a wee bit of a minute? Think twice! The first thought is the pagan, and the second thought is his good Christian brother! Will you—"

She stopped her outcry, since Daniel Kinsale already had cleared the hedge and was running through the plowed ground toward Barnaby, who had turned his head after the roaring hunt and was sounding a long horn of regret. In the sticky, deep ground, one slipper left the foot of The

Kinsale; its fellow tossed in the air immediately after, and he stepped on a sharp stone.

Being a man of Clonmel, he hopped the rest of the way on one foot and said nothing whatever as he snatched the harness from the back of Barnaby. He gathered the reins in his left hand, with the same fingers clutched the wisp of mane closest to the withers, turned his back to the neck of the gelding, made a step forward and leaped. His right heel caught over the ridge of the back. He stuck there, the left dangling down to the ground.

"And the infernal woman is seeing me!" said The Kinsale to his heart. At once strength came to his arms and he pulled himself onto the back of the horse.

"Be the bright Barnaby for me," said The Kinsale. "Don't let me fall at the first jump."

The wall came at them, bigger with every stride. He dug in his knees. He clung with leg and heel, putting weight forward on his hands. Big Barnaby rose and winged over that wall like a bird.

"Half my age minus seven!" said The Kinsale, and laughed.

The invisible hunt on the other side of Cloyne Hill now was turning to the seat in a drowsy stream of noise, so he followed the chord of the arc over the low flank of the hill. Through a hedge, Barnaby jumped low, trailing his clever heels, and they came out in the rearward of the hunt with the song of the hounds flowing cheerfully down the slope toward Clonmel River. There is a tale of a stranger who referred to the "river" as a "trout stream" and the ending of that story is not a pleasant thing; for, if you're asking, what is a valley that has no river to it whatever?

The Kinsale passed through the skirts of the field where old, old men and old, old women cantered their horses, for after seventy or seventy-five the people of Clonmel took their hunting more easily, unless something happened that stirred their blood. They looked at Daniel without a greeting and his heart ached in him. He was a stranger who never could come in Clonmel, but if once he could get near enough to Kerry to give him the rough side of his tongue, he would leave the Valley forever and go back to the city like the roar of a lonely sea.

Daniel, looking forward, marked in the middle ranks of the field a redhead on a horse without a saddle.

"The fool has lost his hat already," said Daniel, and pulled his own hat farther down on his head. He had a feeling in that moment that in a stride or two his horse could devour all the misty beauty of the landscape to the Clonmel River and over Waterford Hill beyond, but for all that, he rode with care, knowing that downhill work is hard on the shoulders of a horse; and Barnaby was no longer a five-year-old; not by the half of it. So they went down the slope without picking up much ground; they waded the shallows of the Clonmel with the gravel bottom golden bright beneath them, and up the easy side of Waterford Hill Barnaby cantered, fighting for his head. When they got to the top, the music of the hounds went dim in the Tuam Woods beyond. In those naked woods he saw a spot of sunshine. That was Eileen O'Malley on her gray.

"Ah, hai! The Kinsale!" she cried. And a ringing sweet

chorus of voices around her called, "The Kinsale!"

"Half my age minus seven," said The Kinsale, and rode up beside her to find out.

"Where's that blathering boy of a Kerry?" he asked her.

"How should I know at all?" she asked. "Except that if you follow close to the hounds you'll usually find him there."

"He's needed home at the plow," said The Kinsale, looking her deep in the eyes.

"And what better place is there for him to be?" she answered.

The Kinsale laughed and went on at a good round gallop as the hunt swept out of Tuam Woods and straight on through the village of Aghadoe, which once was a flourishing town, but gradually all the people left it, and what a pity that was! Through streets of roofless houses the hunt sent roaring echoes, and out into the open again, for it was a Clonmel fox and he thought shame to dodge away among the thousand holes and alleys of that man-made covert. Instead, he chose to bear to the right under the flank of the Ossory Hills and so straight on for the Bog of Ross.

No horse was ever foaled with a foot light enough to run over the Bog of Ross, so, while the hounds swept into the marshland, the hunt veered left and right far around the margin of the wet ground. The Kinsale watched the water, here and there dash to silver over the Clonmel hounds, and far across he could see Kerry and Rourke, who had taken the wrong way around. Wrong way or not, Kerry passed the bog a good bit in front of his uncle, but at the

very next jump he and Rourke went down together and
flourished their heels in the air while they rolled their
faces in the mud. The Kinsale bore down on them and
slowed Barnaby, with all the words of his anger curdling in
his heart, but when he came closer to them and saw them
get up, sticky-black and dripping, it came to him that there
was a better thing to do than to pour his wrath out at that
moment. And as he sailed Barnaby over the fence, he
laughed as he shouted, "Keep his head straight at the
fences!" He shouted it so loudly that he made sure sweet
Eileen O'Malley heard the words as she came winging up
on her gray; and the whole heart of The Kinsale laughed
and laughed inside him. At this moment also the clouds
split apart, the sun rushed through, and all the country
laughed with beauty far before him to the Lismore Hills;
and all the hounds gave tongue with a sweeter music; and
all the right Clonmel horses pricked their sharp ears for a
little jump of a hedge and a ditch that a five-year-old child
could take on its first pony.

But the black devil lies in wait for our most secure moments. He it was that nudged the left forefoot of Barnaby
as that honest horse landed on the other side and caused
him to roll over and over with The Kinsale himself rolling
over and over before him. When he got up, he had to spit
twice and rub his eyes once before he either could breathe
or see. He said: "The devil fly off with the man that dug
the ditch and the spade he dug it with and the rain that
filled it."

Then he got on Barnaby with the main body of the hunt
roaring past him like a Christmas wind down an empty

chimney. He got into the skirts of the crowd and charged furiously through Rathkeal Wood, but a check beyond it, with the hounds casting right and left for the line, let him come up again. He made straight for Kerry. It was in his mind now that the devil had nothing to do with that fall at the ditch and hedge, but it was all the folly of Kerry, who had led his elder away on this mad ride. The words to speak were warming the very cockles of his heart when someone shouted and the whole hunt streaked away like quicksilver for Emly Hill.

The way was steep and the fiend had lightened the pads of the fox that fled up it. Even Clonmel horses and Clonmel men could not hold to that pace. Back they fell, laboring; and now Clonmel voices were heard blistering the wind, but only the Clonmel hounds could keep in sight of the quarry. It was now that The Kinsale saw a strange thing. For he saw Kerry Kinsale, all black from the bog, turn slantwise down the flank of Emly Hill toward the right. Once he looked and twice he wondered; then he cried out and followed his nephew as fast as Barnaby could leg it.

He was far around the lower hill when he saw that Kerry had guessed it right. The fox ran on beyond Dunlin Creek, a weary creature with a dragging brush, and the terrible hounds of Clonmel poured up the farther bank of the stream and closed in for the kill. At that moment the field broke over the crest of the hill far behind, and Daniel blessed the wit of a Kinsale before he was aware of what he did. But the gorge of the creek lay in between, a horrible gaping mouth with a sheen of teeth clear down the throat of it.

The Kinsale cupped a hand to his mouth and yelled: "Kerry! Oh, Kerry! Come back! Don't try it! Kerry, has the red of your hair burned the brain out of you? You numskull, Kerry, come back!"

He cried other words, also, that made a screaming down the wind, so that Kerry looked back once, and then leaned again over the neck of Rourke as though he were the hunted instead of the hunter. Down he rushed at the widening mouth of the creek. The Kinsale, watching like a savage eagle, saw the head of Rourke fling up a bit, and the gallop of Rourke changed lead as he faltered, but then Kerry took hold of him and straightened him out with a horseman's hands and flung him like a stone at the gap. He rose with his heels tucked up as though for a high wall. He struck on the farther side, on the very verge, and began to dig and clamber like a dog on a ledge.

The Kinsale looked round him and the weight of his years laid a burden on his heart that even Barnaby must feel, he knew. He looked at the green flash of Clonmel Valley under the sun and wished a deep wish that all his days had been spent on its hunting fields. If only five years could be taken away from the legs of Barnaby and twenty-five from himself. But all the Kinsale was rising in him and never once did he dream of drawing rein, for, since the thing must happen, it was well for it to be while he was riding with only one before him in the field, and that one a Kinsale.

He saw Rourke still fighting over the ledge as he rushed Barnaby down the slope.

Hoofbeats pounded up from the rear and the gray mare with Eileen O'Malley shot past him. Her frightened cry rang in his ear: "Go back! Go back! Barnaby can't make it!"

She had come up under such a head that there was no turning on the brink of the stream. Up went the gray, arching low and swift over the gap, and landed a safe length beyond the farther bank.

"Go on, Kerry!" yelled Daniel. "For Kinsale! Kinsale! Will you let a scrawny imp of a baby girl outride you? Kinsale!"

But now he was close to Dunlin Brook. He felt the poor horse shudder under him. He saw the maw of Dunlin Creek opening wider. Then all the world went soundless as he threw his heart into the leap. Water flashed like a sword under them. They were in the heart of the cloudy sky. Then, dropping, Barnaby struck the edge of the gorge and sent The Kinsale slithering before him over the grass like a flat stone over still water.

Daniel Kinsale, as he felt himself gone, had time for one thought only, swift and deep as the thrust of a knife: Disgrace and a fall at the end of a hunt; a fall where even women and children jumped safely! Then the ground struck him into darkness.

Consciousness opened before him again like the brittle rays of candlelight in a great black room. He tasted the salt of blood in his mouth and heard Kerry Kinsale groaning: "Will he live, Doctor O'Neill? Will he live, for God's sake?"

"You should be asking!" said the weeping voice of Eileen O'Malley. "You that led him on to the murder of that jump!"

"Peace and be still the pair of you," said a man, "and everyone else back up to give him air. . . . Without a saddle . . . at his years . . . and an old horse . . ."

A deep voice spoke out of the distance, and the words it uttered opened a blue heaven for Daniel; for it said, "When he talked, I thought it was a bag of money clinking; but now we can see that the true Kinsale has come home to us, with a great heart and all."

The words got Daniel to his knees, and then to his feet, with Clonmel Valley reeling about him and such a shout roared into his ears as only the men of Clonmel can voice.

"Where's Barnaby?" he asked.

"Here, Uncle Daniel. Right here before you," said Kerry, "and he's hanging his head for the fall he gave you."

"Never blame him, for he has a great heart," said Daniel, rubbing the nose of Barnaby.

"It's his horse he asks after and not his own bones. God bless him," said a woman in the crowd.

By the light of her words, Daniel saw all the faces that ringed him round, and nothing but a smiling kindness in every one.

"We'll rig a litter for you," said the doctor.

"Litter is it?" said Daniel. "I'll ride home the way I came. Scatter about your business and don't be wasting the time on me."

Afterward he sat on a stone to let the ringing die out of his ears, and all were gone except, on the one side of him, Kerry, and on the other, Eileen. He looked at the swollen nose of Kerry.

He said, "Kerry, is your nose broke entirely?"

"It's no matter for my nose," said Kerry, "but there's blood on your face, Uncle Daniel."

"It's some of the old fool leaking out of me," said Daniel.

"God forgive me for leading you off," said Kerry. "But how would I know at your years the Kinsale was so hot in you? You would have beat us all if Barnaby had only a pair of hocks under him."

"You would have skimmed over like a bird if Rourke wasn't gone at the knees," said The Kinsale.

"God love you, Uncle Daniel, it was a grand jump that you made with the old horse," said Kerry.

"It was the years on his back that beat him," said Daniel.

"Shall we go back to the stream and wash the mud from your faces?" asked Eileen O'Malley. "I can't tell one from the other Kinsale just now."

"What will you name your first child, Eileen?" asked The Kinsale.

"I'll call it Daniel," said Eileen.

"The devil and all you will!" shouted Kerry.

"In honor of his granduncle," said Eileen.

"Ah, Eileen, darling!" said Kerry. "I never doubted you once—in my heart!"

But The Kinsale, being nearer, was the first to blacken her cheek with his kiss.

A Life for a Life

"When a man is backed into a corner, he can be as much as ninety per cent efficient," Faust said once. Here he is backed into a corner with young Dr. Kildare, in a scene from the first of the now historic Kildare novels, *Calling Dr. Kildare*, 1940.

HE WENT out into the rain, hurrying. The wind had come up. It gathered the dust of the falling rain and blew the thin spray into Kildare's face. He felt that he was taking his last walk through the world as he had known it. Tomorrow might bring a new existence. He wondered what life would be like without test tubes and microscopes and the faces of the sick.

When he came to the vacant house, he found a small, skulking figure under the porch. Red said: "He looks terrible bad."

Kildare said nothing. He lighted his way down the stairs with his torch. When he came to the door, he shone the light inside, the ray cutting sharply through the yellow glow of the lantern, showing him Rosalie's terrified face. She had her hands up as though she were trying to turn the force of an impending blow.

Then she cried out: "Nick! Nick! It's not the police.

He's come alone."

He leaned over Nick. The boy was far gone. He was ashen-gray. He looked like a death mask of the face Kildare had first seen.

He got his eyes open, one wider than the other. "Hi, doc," he said faintly.

"Hi, Nick."

Looking down at what might be his last case, he had a queer feeling that he was giving a life for a life. The law would strike him down for it, but the law was a fool.

"You didn't tell them?" asked Nick.

"Be still."

"Okay," Nick whispered.

The girl was smiling a little, also, but always with the look of one asking permission.

Kildare turned to Red. "Would you give some of your blood to this fellow, Red?" he asked.

"Wouldn't I just!" said Red, and came a step out of his corner.

"You've got to have a blood transfusion," said Kildare to Nick. "There are four types of blood. If one of us has the right type, we can put the life back inside of you. Your sister is the best bet, so we'll begin with her."

He had in his bag a physiological solution of salt and water, a teaspoonful to a pint. Into each of three tubes he put a measured bit of this; from the girl, from Red, and from his own finger he took drops of blood and placed them in the test tubes with the solution. He took more blood from Nick and watched the straw-colored serum of it form in the bottom of another test tube.

There was needed endless time for this. Now and then he took Nick's pulse, but the boy's look as life ebbed in him was enough. No one tried to be cheerful, but Rosalie sat down beside Nick and put a hand on his forehead.

His eyes kept following Kildare around the room, but he said to his sister: "Sing something, will you?"

She sang. She seemed unable to remember the words, so she filled in by chanting: *"Ta da-ta da—ta dum."* She tried snatches of jazz; she got down to Mother Goose, but somehow she managed to keep a song in the air.

"You got a rotten memory," said Nick, once.

"I'm sorry. I know I'm no good," said Rosalie. "I'm *so* sorry, honey."

"No, you're okay," murmured Nick. "You keep me from thinking about myself."

She sang and sang, and her singing drew them all together.

Kildare was ready for the next step. He needed a shallow, clear dish. The crystal from his watch would serve. He put the girl's blood cells from the salt solution with the drops of mixed blood serum in the crystal and held the light of the electric flash under the tiny dish while he watched for signs of grouping. Gradually minute yellowish drops appeared in the solution.

He shook the drops of serum out on the floor and said to the three intent faces: "She's no good for Nick."

"But I've got to be right for him!" cried Rosalie.

"Shut up, Rosalie!" Red snapped, keeping his eyes on Kildare as though he were reading marvels from a strange book.

The same agglutination formed when Red's blood was tried. Again Kildare emptied the tiny dish and used his own serum. When he shook the drops together, they mixed perfectly. The strong light from the electric torch showed not the slightest agglutination. He looked up with a smile at Nick.

"It's all right, Nick," he said, nodding. "My blood will fit like nobody's business."

"But wait a minute," protested Nick. "You can't do that—I mean, you can't give me—it's not right!"

"Hush, Nick," said the girl, strangely breathless.

"I mean," said Nick through his teeth to her, as she leaned over him, "suppose that something happened to him *after* he'd put his own blood inside me. D'you see now?"

It was as though a mystic importance, a sort of blood-brotherhood, must underlie the transfusion. Kildare had started boiling the instruments over a fire. It was a full dish so that the boiling had taken longer. The Erlenmeyer flask, rubber and glass tubing, cork, needles, and the big syringe all simmered together.

He cut another length of the rubber tubing and applied it as a tourniquet about his left arm after he had set up the flask and put into it the contents of some small ampules of citrate solution.

When the tourniquet had taken a good grip and the veins were standing out close to the bend of the arm, he thrust in a big needle and let the blood flow down the tubing into the flask. Nick, who had endured seeing whole oceans of his own blood, could not quite go that needle-dig. He had to put a shaky hand over his eyes; but Rosalie, bright as a bird, watched everything.

Kildare said: "Take the bottle and keep shaking it, Red, will you? We can't let the blood coagulate."

"I can't do it," said Red, his hand shrinking away from the filling bottle. "I'm sorry, doc, but it makes me kind of sick."

"I'll do it," said the girl, and picking up the bottle she kept it in steady motion. She did not change color. She only said: "Does it make you a little dizzy to lose so much? Will it be all right for you, doc?"

"To lose a pint? Of course it will," smiled Kildare, yet he was feeling a small, insistent pull on his strength.

He heard Nick whispering to Red: "But takin' the life right out of his body into mine . . ."

"Yeah, I know," said Red.

"It'll change me, maybe," said Nick.

It was a quart bottle and Kildare filled it more than half full. Then he removed the needle, stopped the bleeding, and took off the tourniquet. After that he took a sterile needle and jabbed it into a vein on the arm of Nick.

Nick moved his head and looked at the wall, refusing to watch as Kildare held up the bottle and let the blood slowly seep down into Nick's body.

It was different with the girl. She sat against the wall and kept her eyes fixed not on Kildare, but on the operation. While the blood ran, her eyes widened and fixed. Her lips parted; her head bent back a little; and as the color drained out of her face, it seemed that she was giving Nick life out of her own body. Kildare had watched a thousand transfusions, but now it was as though the operation were being performed for the first time, following it with Rosalie's eyes.

He removed the needle from Nick and cleaned the apparatus with alcohol.

Red came back from his corner stealthily to whisper: "Nick, are you okay now? You got a color back in your face. You look swell, Nick."

"Sure, I'm okay, now."

The girl was still sitting back against the wall holding her brother's free hand. She was pale and her lowered eyes showed a blue stain across the lids.

"How you feeling, Nick?" asked Kildare.

The boy looked up at the ceiling, not at the doctor. Gradually he forced his glance to meet Kildare's. "I could eat a horse," he said, "and drink a whole keg of beer."

"You're going to sleep, first," smiled Kildare.

"Okay, doc," agreed Nick. "Anything you say."

"I'm jabbing another needle into you," said Kildare. "It'll bring that sleep along a little faster."

"Go as far as you like." Nick grinned and held out his arm. He smiled at the twinge of the injection.

"Is the pain in your breast getting bad?" asked Kildare.

"It's sinking a tooth in me, but it's all right. Everything's all right," said Nick.

"How about *you?* You look knocked out," said Kildare to the girl.

She reacted to his voice as though she were awakening from a profound sleep. Her eyes opened wide like the eyes of a child; and with a child's immense seriousness she looked at him.

"I'm all right," she whispered, and gradually her smile commenced. Kildare watched it grow.

Later, with his instruments repacked, Kildare stood by Nick and watched him in fast sleep with one arm thrown up above his head.

Red twitched his coatsleeve. "Go on, doc," he advised. "Get out of here before the cops know you've been in on this deal and hang a rap on you."

"I'm going," agreed Kildare. "So long, Red. Good-bye, Rosalie."

"I'm coming out," she said, and she walked silently with him from the cellar to the entrance beneath the porch of the house.

The rain was coming down crash; the pavement shone with the bright dust of it under the streetlamps.

"I've got a car around the corner," said Rosalie. "I'll drive you back to the hospital."

"It's only two or three blocks," protested Kildare.

"I know, but I'm taking you," she insisted.

There was no strength in him for argument. He was so done in that his knees were uncertain beneath his weight. So he climbed after her into a small coupé. He could not help thinking that it was a little odd that she should have a car of her own; it went with something expensively modish about the cut of her clothes.

He was glad she did not talk. Presently the car stopped and he saw her getting out. She ran through the rain into a little corner café. He wondered after her, vaguely and pleasantly, and then she was out again and beside him with a big cup of coffee.

"Why—thanks a lot," said Kildare, a little amazed.

"Hush! You don't have to talk."

It was not the finest coffee in the world, but into the aroma of it passed a slight breath of that perfume which Rosalie was wearing. The bitterness and the heat comforted his very heart. She lighted a cigarette and passed it to him.

He took the smoke in deep breaths. It was almost gone before he had finished the coffee; and now as he pushed the door open to return the cup, he found it taken firmly from his hand. She was running through the rain again into the café, and out and into the car. Her tweed coat was moist enough to give a pleasant, outdoor odor and the fur-piece ruffed up around her throat a thousand glittering little jewelpoints. He took lazy note of her and closed his eyes again.

Presently the car was making speed and on either side he heard tires ripping and whirling over wet pavement. He opened his eyes and found that they were curving up through Central Park.

"But wait a minute, Rosalie," he said. "I ought to get back to the dispensary. I'm late."

There was something different about her. Perhaps it was because she had taken off her hat and tossed it into the space behind the seat. It gave her head a new and softer outline, and perhaps it was this that seemed to lend her a different meaning.

"You'll be back before long," she said, and leaning across him she twisted open the small ventilator at his side.

"Get some of that in your face."

He put back his head again. A foolish weakness in his face kept him smiling a little no matter what he did to stop it. The world of serious care remained far behind them, and every spin of the wheels carried them farther and farther away from it.

"There's a quiet place ahead where we can sit and talk," said Rosalie. "I have to say something, and Nick will be all right, won't he? Red won't leave him."

Kildare nodded. He kept his eyes half open. Through the coursing water on the windshield, he looked out at a drowned world, an infinitely involved pattern of crimson and gold and purple which took on, in the distance and in the night, a general tone of bronze.

Presently the car pulled up near the edge of a pond. The headlights showed an open boat with the rain beating ceaselessly down upon it. She switched them off. The lake remained visible in the light of the myriad rain-splashes on its surface. A tree, which held its branches over them, kept the downpour from rattling like stones on the roof of the car.

"Now," said the girl, "we can talk about Nick. I want to tell you everything I know about it, so that you'll see what you've done. But now that the job is finished, the law will never be able to touch you. You'll be all right, won't you?"

"He still needs a doctor's care," said Kildare.

"I won't let you go near him again!" cried Rosalie.

"Won't let me?" he repeated. He laughed a little weakly. "She won't let me!" he murmured, and he closed his eyes. "Tell me how you'll keep me away."

He waited for an answer until the pause troubled him and he cast about in his mind for a way of reopening the conversation. Sleepiness dimmed the world and thrust away the illumined fairyland of Central Park South.

It seemed to him that he was saying something about them, and then he wakened with knowledge, like a shadowy handstroke past his face, that much time had passed. Even that alarm did not rouse him to complete consciousness at a stroke, but by degrees he passed out of the world of his sleep. And every wind that blew in that other universe carried the fragrance of that perfume of Rosalie's.

His face was pillowed in fur. He had side-slipped in the seat and Rosalie had given his head a place on her shoulder.

"I'm sorry," said Kildare, starting up. "I'm terribly sorry."

"Are you?" asked Rosalie.

"I mean you wanted to talk . . ." said Kildare.

"It was better than talk," said Rosalie. "It was lovely."

She had a dreaming softness of voice and Kildare, peering with clouded eyes, saw that she was smiling to herself. Her head lay back against the top of the seat and her half-opened eyes regarded the lights over the lake.

Something was lacking from the world as it had been before he fell asleep. He could not tell what the change had been; he was puzzled and confused, trying to find it.

He leaned forward a little, trying to understand her smile, which troubled him. The girl, staring, seemed unaware of his gaze. Suddenly he realized that she was seeing him with her mind's eye. He spoke her name, quietly, and gradually her eyes turned to include him in her dream.

He lifted her hand, palm up, and kissed it. The soft tips of her fingers touched his face and held to it lightly.

The Luck of Pringle

Faust believed that the battlefield was the most honorable place to die, and he died on one, to complete the peculiar symbolism of his life. This story reflects his personal thinking about war and the values and choices that confront men in battle.

Pringle fell in the mud and lay still. Everybody else had fallen in the same way, for the sound of the shell as it dropped passed from a roar to a shrill staccato, a long bright needle of sound that drove through the brain. Pringle did not hear the explosion but he felt the earth tremble and knew the mud was being bucketed up in tons. A few drops of it struck him. They were warm, which put a horrible thought into his head.

Then everyone was getting up and going forward again, but Pringle remained in the mud; because, when he looked up, he saw through the mist by the flare of the Very light the bomb thrown by a trench mortar coming down like a little whale, sharp-nosed, with steering flanges at the tail. When one of those things burst, it did not dig a proper hole for itself and then chuck ruin up into the air. Instead, it squattered down against the earth, smashing flat and blowing out straight to the side chunks of steel as big as your arm.

On his first day in the trenches Second Lieutenant Walter Pringle saw a man cut in two by one of those flying fragments. This was his second day, and now fear cut his throat and let the courage out of him like hot blood. Nothing but a cold ichor remained stagnating in his arteries. He kept his lips fast shut, but a rapid pulse was beating against them from the inside and the pulse consisted of words, saying: "Walter Pringle is a coward; Pringle is a coward; Pringle of the Class of 'eighteen, shot for cowardice on the field of battle; Second Lieutenant Pringle, for conduct not becoming an officer and a gentleman . . ."

He got himself up on his elbow. Legs were going by him, sagging at the knees with labor in the mud. The feet were soundless in the uproar. Soundlessly they were going to their death—thousands, tens of thousands, millions to die in the war as insects die in hosts with the first frost.

A queer sound began to saw into his brain. It came from all around him like the song of bullfrogs in a marsh, but he knew that bullfrogs were not making the music.

He tried to keep remembering that when you hear the noise of a shell you are safe; it already is past you, traveling faster than sound. The big shells overhead left pulsations in the torn air behind them, strange rhythms like the self-starters of motors beginning, ending.

That was almost a comfort to Pringle compared with the rifle bullets singing high and thin, little flashes of wasplike sound flickering past the ears and always close, close, close, whispering intimately. A kiss from one of them, anywhere between the shoulders and the hips, and you're gone.

The hole a bullet goes in by is small; it tears hell out of you when it comes through, however. Remember when you've pricked your finger with a pin or jammed a splinter under a fingernail, and then consider what the pain must be, Pringle kept considering. Most men after they first hear the whine of the bullets lose the panic ecstasy of their terror, but he knew that his own agony never would abate. Yet he had to get up; he had to go on because his father was the colonel of his regiment.

Perhaps that was where the roots of the trouble ran. A strange surgeon is better than a friend when a vital operation must be performed, and the cold eye of discipline with a stranger behind it might have cut through to the fear that was in him and let it out, like a chilly poison. Instead, the near presence of his father sustained him in a mental gesture of reaching out for comfort, for help. Cannot we learn courage like other lessons? But he had not studied long enough. He was not sufficiently prepared when he was rushed into this examination on the battlefield.

A hand caught him under the armpit and lifted. He got to his knees, to his feet. It was Lieutenant Jim Gaffney, so thin that it was no wonder he felt at ease in the midst of battle. As well shoot at the edge of a knife as at Gaffney.

"It's Big Pringle," said Gaffney. "Have they got you, Walter? Where?"

It seemed to Pringle that he was being held up by the scruff of the neck for the world to see by Very light a poor dangling scarecrow, a shameful mud-dripping rag of humanity.

"I'm all right," said Pringle. "I just—"

"You're all right!" shouted Gaffney. Then scorn twisted his face. "Ah, hell!" he said, and went suddenly on with that wave of the attack.

Pringle tried to go after him but his feet would not stir. He made out the nature of that noise which had been sawing into his brain like the croaking of bullfrogs. Now he realized that it came from the wounded. They were all around, and some of them were screaming. Something dragged itself toward him on two arms. It had no legs.

Pringle ran forward, bogging his feet, sagging his knees at every step. He wanted to overtake Gaffney and explain; yet he knew that he never would be able to confront that face of scorn again.

Where it wasn't mud, it was up and down of trenches. The place was crazy with trenches. The ground was a junk heap, a garbage pile. There were cans everywhere, most of them untrampled. Barbed wire grew up out of the mud like horrible, thorny weeds.

There were old shoes underfoot, heels or toes sticking up, or else stamped flat on the side. All the old shoes in the world were there; and all the torn-up letters and tattered newspapers were soaking into the wet earth. In the spring a harvest of words ought to grow, loving words, and songs of international hate.

The fog was in his face, in his soul; he breathed of it, and it was like breathing smoke; and through the dreadful confusion the rifle bullets kept kissing the air close to his ear. If he could see death coming—if it would only come at him like a straight left in the boxing ring—if it were a clean, visible thing, he could stand it, but to smother in the dark of a garbage heap, a junk pile . . .

They had gone on forever. There were no Germans to shoot at. There was no Company K. A counter-flood of noise flowed toward them, split to both sides, washed back toward the river. It was that barrier of water to their rear, he felt, which killed his heart in him. To cross a river and then plunge right ahead into German trenches, with that little river like a knife cutting off retreat—that wasn't generalship. It was madness. He listened with dread to the pouring sounds of battle that moved past them on both sides.

"It's the counterattack, isn't it?" he yelled at a face.

"We've caught hell," yelled back Lieutenant Mays. "They've got us blocked off on both sides and in the rear."

At least there was no more marching through the mud. The men sank down into the bog. They dropped on their backs. They were all mud, anyway, so it didn't matter. Rifle bullets flickered in the air all around them, but they didn't care for that, either.

Pringle lay a little flatter than the rest, trying not to think. If every man of them were killed, still the rumor would be alive in the world to tell people at home that Walter Pringle was yellow; that Jim Gaffney had seen him turn yellow right on the battlefield. A yellow dog who lay down in the mud and let the charge go past him. Perhaps a bullet had reached the colonel. It could not kill him more surely than this news about his son.

Then the men began to drag themselves out of the mud. There was a German dugout right under them, and they were crawling down into it.

By the time Pringle got into it, the dugout seemed already full, but more men were still streaming into the long tunnel with its bunks on each side. It was all concrete. The Germans knew how to make things permanent, and safe, safe, safe. He began to breathe again; his heart commenced to beat.

The air turned incredibly foul with the steam from wet, dirty bodies, but that didn't matter because there was warmth, and Pringle realized that he had been horribly cold for hours, for eternities. He began to do what others were doing, raking off mud, but all the while he was waiting, waiting, waiting for the news of his cowardice to spread until faces should turn toward him, sick with disgust. An American, but yellow; a big American, but yellow; and his father was the colonel of the regiment.

He lay down on a bunk. The autumn cold still kept touching him with fingers of ice, but by degrees the heat of his body warmed his wet clothes, and the clothes then warmed his body.

In the dugout, the fuming cigarettes had thickened the air to a whiter smoke than the land mist which hung over Mézigny. Some were heating cans of bully beef over smokeless fires; some passed round a stock of Rhine-wine bottles that had been uncovered; a phonograph played German songs. Some worked over the wounded, particularly the German wounded. Some wandered about gaping at the pictures of girls over the bunks and reading aloud the strange German words of endearment that went with the signatures.

Ah, God, how kind and comfortable the Germans could be, with their beer and their music and their family devotions; and what an honest, hard-working people they were; and how could they want to turn butchery loose upon the world? Pringle would not hate them for it. Hatred was immoral. Shorty Waters was holding up the head of a wounded German, tilting a bottle of wine at his lips. The wine spilled over the fellow's throat. Waters took the bottle away. He laughed, and the German laughed.

They made a nice picture together; Pringle wanted the whole world to be filled with brothers and brotherhood. Was there not one Bach for all the world? Was there not one Shakespeare? Had not the Germans put up a statue to *"Unser* Shakespeare"? These tokens of a common humanity of mind and spirit deepened the ache in Pringle's sick heart, as he waited and waited.

Then, suddenly, the colonel was upon him. He was there with Major Carlton and Captain Reeves. Pringle got up. His father laid a hand on his shoulder and bristled his short gray mustache with a smile. The major and the captain moved away from this family scene.

"Muddy business, Walter, wasn't it?" asked the colonel. Then: "What's the matter? Have you been nicked somewhere? Are you sick?"

The lieutenant smiled a little. He could feel the smile crinkle the drying mud on his face. "I'm sick," he said, and waited again. The whole thing had to come out, one time or another. Then he saw truth strike like a shadow across the eyes of the colonel.

It was not until then that he saw his father's left arm was

tied up in a sling. The colonel's eyes tried to hold to the face of his son, but they slipped and dodged away, staring into far corners of this wretched world.

"I'll try to see you later," he said. "I'll try . . ." Then he was off through the stifling mist.

Pringle's knees gave way beneath him, and he had to lie down on the bunk again. Without looking about him, he could learn from random words the history of their attack and their present situation. The attack had proceeded so swiftly because the colonel had seized on the best possible moment. But by a devil of bad luck under the fog the Germans had an unreported reserve close the point of attack. It was that reserve which had smashed both wings of the attack.

The whole ground on both sides and behind what was left of the regiment was occupied by German troops. Now, in the thick of the land mist, for the moment contact was lost with the enemy. Colonel Pringle had some four hundred men lodged in the throat of the salient, and when they were found, the Germans would swallow them. It was time to surrender; but to those stupid brutes canned beef seemed more important than the sweetness of life. They went on cooking, eating, endlessly.

Pringle tried to keep them out of his mind but one sound continually tore open his heart, It came from a man who had been shot through the hand. Sometimes he endured for whole minutes, with grinding teeth; then the groans came, and last the horrible noise of sobbing.

The colonel's voice brought Pringle to his feet again. His father said: "I've found a way out for you—you're going to go back to our lines. You can find the beginning of the communication trench just outside. You follow the general line of it, zigzags and all, and never leave it, because it winds up right at the edge of the Mézigny—and once in the water you're as good as home. You can swim."

"But if they see me on the way down the trench?"

"You'll have a German uniform on. We'll take one out of the dugout."

"So that I'll be shot as a spy if they catch—"

"Don't you see that they won't catch you?" said the colonel. "You can speak a little German. You know how to swear in it, at least. If you're challenged, start cursing and swagger your way through. Only one of all these men can live; I choose that it should be my son."

Pringle felt himself choking.

"You'll go back to our lines," said the colonel. "The river twists back into them. You'll report to General Bailey that we're established here in the throat of the salient and that if he counterattacks, we'll take them with our fire from behind. Tell him that I am rigging whole lines of machine guns. As a matter of fact, I'm starting to entrench now. Tell him that, if he attacks, he's to send up a cluster of five Very lights; if I don't see the signal, at dawn I attack the Germans anyway. You understand?"

"Can you pick me out like this?" asked Pringle, trembling with hope. "Can you give me my life like this? Won't it be held against you?"

The colonel paused. Then he said: "I'm going to put the proposition to the regiment in very stark terms. When I ask for a volunteer to carry the message, you can be sure

there'll be no sudden answer. I want you to shout at once.
Do you see, Walter? I'll put it in such a way that you'll
seem a hero."

Pringle discovered suddenly that he was alone, for two
steps through the mist had turned the colonel into a distant, wavering figure of black through the white, foul
smother of the dugout. Now some loudly shouted orders
brought the soldiers to attention. The colonel's deep voice
seemed to Pringle as big as drum and bugle combined.

"We are stuck here like a fishbone in the throat of the
Germans. If our friends across the Mézigny knew we
were here, they'd make the Germans try to swallow—and
choke in the process. Our job, now, is to let General Bailey
know where we're located. If we get one man across the
trenches and over the river, I think another attack would
be launched, to help us and to use us. Otherwise, when the
day comes, we'll be found and stamped out by the heavy
artillery.

"The only way to get a messenger through the lines and
across the river is to put a German uniform on him. He
ought to be able to speak a little German, to help him
through a pinch. We don't want a man who's depressed by
the knowledge that he's carrying the lives of four hundred
men with him; we want a fellow who'll be inspired by the
thought."

It seemed to Pringle that all the days of his American
life had been spent in sunshine, with green grass underfoot
and drowsy summer hummings of contentment in the air.
It seemed to him that all the rest must be thinking of their
country in the same way, and that every man in the dugout

must realize that the colonel was opening a door to safety out of this hell of mud and fog.

Then he heard the colonel saying: "Of course a man caught in a German uniform will be shot out of hand as a spy. I don't want to minimize the other dangers, but I'm asking for volunteers."

He stopped. And Pringle's heart stopped at the same time. He wanted to shout out, but his own eagerness filled his throat like a gag. A second or two went by.

Then Pringle's voice came to him and he sang out. Many heads turned. A space opened before him. He heard voices saying, "Who is it?" and then the unmistakable nasal whine of Jim Gaffney exclaiming, "It's Pringle! Pringle, by *God!*"

They were making a hero of him. They didn't understand—because the colonel had not explained to them how easily the thing could be done. Shame roused up suddenly in Pringle as he confronted his father. Major Burnet was saying: "We can't allow this. You can't let your boy go, sir."

He heard that, but he was hardly aware of words or of anything about him as he was helped out of his uniform and into German clothes. The dying life which fear had been gnawing at the roots was returning to him. A mighty river of hope was beginning, a current which seemed already to be bearing him home.

Then he was shaking hands. He saw eyes widened with admiration and fear of what lay before him. Then his father was holding both his hands, and now he was at the entrance of the dugout.

And then there was the mist, the fluttering nightmare battle lights, and the uncertain footing where he began to stumble the moment he took a step. He was remembering his father's face and eyes which in the moment of parting had seemed to shine with pity, with grief, and in farewell.

He found the zigzag communication trench and followed it. The voices of the battle came and went in great flooding pulses, with moments when the uproar of the great guns trampled all thought from his mind, and again pauses of emptiness during which he was aware of the smaller noises. In those pauses he heard the thin whining of airplanes as they drew little patterns of complaint in the air.

It seemed strange that those tribes of the air should be divided against one another instead of combining in a splendid fury against all the earth dwellers. He knew the song of the three-inch shells and the handstroke of air when they passed. But always the incredibly swift, short whistlings of the rifle bullets ran through his consciousness like the dots and dashes of a telegraphic code, spelling in a thousand ways a single word. But behind and around all these sounds he was conscious of one constant utterance, like the mournful lowing of cattle far off. He refused to put his mind on that sound, because he knew it was the lament of the wounded.

Something flowed through the mist along the ground. It poured like water. He made out the helmets of a thick column of Germans pouring up the communication trench toward the front. Their feet made no sound. They were a column of ghosts already walking to death.

The full sickness of fear returned upon Pringle. He sank into the mud and remained there, hardly breathing. Rain came down with a crash. It washed the manhood out of him. It beat him like a sodden rag into the mud.

When he pulled himself to his feet again, his brain was spinning. He had forgotten in what direction he should be going. Along the communication trench—but which way?

The horizon all around offered a circle of smoky glares. There is no up or down, no north or south in hell.

He almost lurched against a tree trunk. It turned into a solid figure with a rifle at the ready, nearly touching his breast. A German voice was saying something angrily, blurred in the rain.

The prepared words came yelling out of the throat of Pringle. *"Verdammter—Schwarzkopf!"* he shouted, and knocked the rifle aside.

He strode on. Fear pierced his side like a thrusting bayonet, but at the edge of his consciousness, he seemed to be aware of the German standing at attention by way of apology. Then he was alone again except for what he was stumbling over. Sometimes the earth grew teeth that tore and cut at his boots. Sometimes it was sloshing mud. Sometimes it was lumped with soft forms.

The battle noise, all at once, drew far away and became dim, so that Pringle felt he must be fainting. But it was only one of those pauses in the racing heartbeats of a fight.

Out of the fog he heard a voice scream: "Put me out of it! I can't stand it any more! Kill me, will you? Put me out of the pain—oh, my God!"

And a deep German voice full of a father's gentleness

said, *"Sei ruhig, sei ruhig, mein Kind!"*

Pringle fled from the voices.

Here the mud underfoot turned into something knee-deep and cold. He found that he was standing in running water and knew that he had reached the Mézigny. He was on the verge of safety.

He pulled off clothes and shoes, lunged forward, and the water received him with dark, cold arms. He needed only to float. The current was floating him toward his country. Thereafter, he never would look at a stream, he never would hear the music of running water without a sense of gigantic deliverance.

Then a white eye opened in the sky above him. A magnesium light was dropping slowly down under its parachute. Its glare turned the river and its bank to silver, obscurely marked by tangles of ink-black shadows.

Pringle saw this as he dived. Under the water he kept swimming slowly, holding his breath until his lungs burned and were bursting. When he rose to the surface, the brightness of the magnesium light was intensified. Then something pierced his leg; a needle-thrust, a hammer-blow, and after that numbness from the hip down.

He swam on, the left leg a senseless weight to drag.

The glaring face of the river was cut with dark whip-strokes. Little wasp sounds flocked about his head. That was a machine gun feeling its way to find him.

He dived again, endowed with extra strength, for the ghost which had haunted him now dissolved into a silly little man-made scarecrow. This was the whole terror of the battlefield, and the bullet-stroke was hardly more, actually, than the ache of a bad tooth.

The thought was like fresh air in his lungs. It had been, after all, mere excess of expectation, like that brief moment of coldheartedness which comes just before a boxing bout commences; and as the first blow dissolves that nervous apprehension, so the bullet had killed the fear in Pringle.

Darkness came over the river like a mercy. He swam confidently on. He wanted to shout his good news. He wanted to print it in great red letters across the sky—to tell everyone that fear is only a fake giant.

The current was swinging him toward the left bank, so that he realized he was rounding the bend of the Mézigny. He was, in fact, already at the verge of the American lines when his reaching hand found sharp teeth submerged just under the surface of the water. He had struck a barbed-wire obstacle in the stream.

Well, it would cost him merely another kind of pain to cross it. He laid out his body with the left side down and so turned himself slowly across the uppermost edge of the wire. Twenty of its teeth entered him, cut, tore, and then he was across on the far side with his whole body on fire with the new pain.

But what was the pain of the body compared with the wounding of a man's pride? Now he knew that his spirit would be complete to the end of his days.

He had not even thought of the loss of blood until he tried to drag himself from the water with arms that refused to bear his weight. Then sudden hands were on him.

"Look at his damned Boche tryin' to sneak through," said a voice.

"Get me to an officer," said Pringle. "Get me to him fast before I faint."

For life, now, narrowed to a single bright thread to which he had to cling with desperate craft. Too strong an effort would break the thread, and the message that might save his father never would be spoken. He understood perfectly, now, the pity, the grief and the farewell in the eyes of Colonel Pringle. He had lied with a good, manly roundness to his son, sending him out to be shot down, certainly, but in such a way that his memory would live for his family and his friends like that of a hero.

But heroism isn't a question of brute courage. It's merely a matter of knowledge. What we know, we don't fear, and Pringle had looked into the whole mystery, face to face.

He was lying on a board in a trench, now. Consciousness widened and showed him the face, the shoulder-markings of the young captain who leaned over him.

"Get word to General Bailey." Pringle struggled to make each word firm and clear. "Lieutenant Pringle reporting from Colonel Pringle—the colonel has four hundred men entrenched, over there. If the general hits out and starts the Germans backing up, they'll back into a wall of fire. They'll be cleaned up. If the general doesn't attack, Colonel Pringle reports that he'll attack on his own, at dawn. If the general attacks, will he please fire five Very lights in a cluster . . ."

He could not remember, afterward, whether he had

spoken those last words or only thought them.

Out of a hazy dream, burning pain brought him back to consciousness, and he heard a voice yelling: "Look out how you handle him. Can't you see he's shot to hell?"

But the pain of the body merely warmed his inner soul.

"Five Very lights in a cluster, if there is to be an attack," he said emphatically.

Something shouted in Pringle's ear, afterward. Something of "Very lights" touched the inward nerve of his being and opened his eyes, and he saw, high above him in the night, lights opening like phosphorescent flowers in a sea of black. He counted one, two, three, four, five in that shining cluster.

"Ah, that's good!"

He fought to cling to consciousness. It came and went, however, like cloud shadows across lovely daylight hills.

He was in a dressing station. The uproar of a thundering sea had withdrawn to a distance; no, it was battle, not the crashing of breakers. Two men in blood-splashed white were doing things to him, and every touch of their hands burned him with agony.

"What do you think?" he asked them.

"You're going to have your chance. What in hell did the bastards do to you?"

"They're not bastards," said Pringle. He spoke softly, saving his breath, for one great exhalation would sweep away his soul and make it a part of that dark wind which blows between the stars. "They're like us—just the same. The way I see it, war is a game. It's a sport. We shouldn't fight Germans because we hate them, but because in the game we're on the other side. Germans. Music, singing, black radishes and beer—you can't hate all that." Then he said, "Can I give a message?"

The doctor was leaving him. "Garner!" he called. "Come here, Garner!"

A little man stood by the cot with a pencil ready above a notebook.

"To Colonel Pringle, if he lives through the attack, from Lieutenant Pringle. Walter Pringle. Tell him, if I die, that I understood."

"Understood what?"

"He'll know what I mean."

"All right. Good luck, Lieutenant," said Garner, turning away.

"I've had my luck," said Pringle, as the shadow poured over him again.

When he came to consciousness again, breathing was hard.

A voice was saying: "Nobody knows how. Left leg useless. Body cut to hell. But he got through. How? Nobody knows how a hero does his stuff. Anyway, he's the reason that salient was smashed flat this morning. They got to Colonel Pringle in the throat of it. He still had two hundred men with him; they'll get decorations. One of the damnedest things in the whole war."

"Is this poor devil going to die?" asked a second voice.

"I don't know. He's got the blue in his face."

It doesn't matter thought Pringle.

The cloud came over him again, with the softness of perfect sleep.

A Special Occasion

To please his literary agent, Carl Brandt, who thought he should achieve publication in the so-called highbrow magazines, Faust wrote this story and Brandt sold it to *Harper's.* He published another story in *Harper's,* but he had little interest in so-called serious fiction. He preferred to devote what he considered his best effort to poetry, while earning a living producing "entertainment," as he called his prose work. Ironically, the prose in final analysis proved more significant than the poetry.

CAMPBELL SAT in the locker room after squash and watched the loose flesh over his heart quivering like a jelly. Richards had beaten him. Richards always beat him now, and Cullen would no longer play with him because he was fifty-five and his backhand was no damned good. It never was more than a sort of poke, but it used to connect. He crossed his feet to take the shudder out of his knees and looked down at the folds in his stomach and the delicate rills of sweat in the wrinkles. His windpipe burned down the middle of him. One of these days he would cut out the cigarettes.

Richards, already back from the showers, was at his locker, putting on a pair of glasses with a thin black ribbon hanging down from them. The spectacles dressed up Richards almost more than a suit of clothes and kept one's attention on his tight-lipped mouth. Richards was sixty, but he still played squash because he had a pair of legs under him. He had been a footballer back there in the nineties, and a big fold of muscle hung above each knee.

"I'm giving you a drink tonight," said Richards.

"Thanks," said Campbell. "I'm not drinking. It's a special occasion. My girl comes home. The wife has been up watching her graduate from school."

Richards took out a bottle.

"I'm giving you a drink," he said. "This *is* a special occasion. It's always a special occasion when you get a chance at Bushmill's Black Label."

"I've heard of the stuff," said Campbell, "but I'm not taking it. Nothing tonight. In a house full of women, you know how it is. They hate to see the father with an edge. That's the trouble with women. They don't understand."

He made a backhanded gesture and looked round the room at the lounging naked men. He breathed the thick smell of sweat and told himself he liked it. How many tons of flesh, in the course of the year, dissolved here in fumes and sweating? Sensible men kept their bodies in a state of flux, building, dissolving. That was nature's plan. Look at the universe of stars, melting into radiation; and somewhere the radiation was regathered to form matter. The astronomers would find that out one day.

Richards uncorked the bottle and gave it to him.

"Give your nose a chance anyway," said Richards.

Campbell inhaled the fragrance. The alcohol thirst took

him hard, just beneath the Adam's apple. He thought of a big trundling automobile like his own, of night, and lights, and a woman. He could always turn off other thoughts and conceive the sort of a woman he wanted, smiling at him.

"It smells weak and too sweet," he said.

"There's no tick of bathtub gin in it, and it's not your Jamaica rum," said Richards.

"Rum is all right," declared Campbell. He frowned, expounding his doctrine: "There's something honest about rum. Made out of good molasses. It puts it on you gradually. Like putting varnish on a car, all over, coat by coat."

"Oh, all right," said Richards. "I know why you drink rum. We all know why." He laughed and poured two fingers and a half into two tall glasses. "You melt some of this in your mouth and try to form good habits. Virtue can be learned."

When a man is sixty, you have to be polite to him. Campbell was at least silent, but he sneered as he breathed of the whisky. He tasted it. "It's too sweet," he said. He tasted it again and his anger and his words loosened in his throat. "It's like a good cognac," he said. "It's like a hundred-year-old brandy, by God! It's like Napoleon. Where did you get it?"

"I told you about that case of the Cuban up for murder? You ought to read the papers, Campbell, and you'd find out a lot of good things about me. I took that case to the jury, let in all their damned evidence, and then made a speech about justifiable homicide."

"You justified murder?" said Campbell dreamily.

"It went over," said Richards. "The Cuban paid my fee

and felt he owed me something more, so he dug up a case of this Bushmill's. There's a white label too, but this black label spends twenty years in the wood getting older and wiser. You can't buy it unless you know where. It's the finest thing that comes out of Ireland."

"Barring Irish hunters," said Campbell. "I ran into a streak of bad luck three or four years ago and started falling all the time. So I gave it up."

Richards put back his head and looked at him through half-closed eyes. "So you gave up—the horses, eh?" said he. "Have some ice and soda in that."

"Don't bother me," said Campbell.

He began to drink slowly, steadily, in small swallows. He kept on drinking until the last of the whisky was down. Then he lighted a cigarette and considered. The whisky was somewhere in the top of his brain, in his heart, pumping out inexhaustible joy through his arteries. "You don't understand," said Campbell.

He went over to the bottle and poured a stiff slug into his glass again. Richards lifted a hand and turned a little, hastily, but then he settled back in his chair. Campbell pretended not to notice. "What don't I understand? About whisky straight?" asked Richards.

"I'm going to tell you something," said Campbell. "It's a kind of religion with me. You go back to Rabelais to get the start of the idea. About hearty people. That's the first thing. A man ought to be hearty. A woman too—"

Afterward he knew that he had been talking a good deal. His lips were a little stiff, his eyes felt larger. Richards had the tight face of a judge, and there was not much whisky left in the bottle. Richards had been dressing; he was ready for the street and now he rose.

"Wait a minute," said Campbell. "What's the matter? I finished most of that stuff. Look here. I want to pay you for the bottle. What I mean is, it's damn good stuff."

Richards jerked round quickly. He checked the first words that parted his lips. "Well, good night," he said, and went out suddenly.

Campbell brooded while he was taking his shower and dressing, but the familiar happiness began to grow up and brighten that world which a man sees best when his eyes are fixed on nothingness. Going down in the elevator, a number of younger members of the club were pressed about him, and he heard a low voice say, "The old boy's already on his way." A soft chuckle answered that remark. Campbell turned with a smile. "You've had a drink yourself, my lad," he said. "Whisky is the staff of the truth-teller!"

He saw the eyes of the boy widen a little. "I beg your pardon, Mr. Campbell," said the lad. And Campbell said, "My dear fellow, not at all!"

He looked at his watch when he got into his car, and was shocked. His wife had said that it was a special occasion. Two days before, when she left, she had taken him by the lapels of his coat. Her hands were tight and strong. "It's going to be a special occasion, Jerry," she had said. "You will remember, dear, won't you?"

"Drive like hell," he said to his chauffeur.

They drove like hell, as soon as the slow, regular pulsation of the downtown traffic let them go. The steady flicker of cars going past him wearied his eyes, so he closed them. Later he discovered with a start that he had been asleep. As he opened his eyes, he had a feeling that they were shooting downhill, through flame, but he found that they were merely wheeling softly past the intersection of highways at White Forest. They would soon be home. It was sunset.

This uptilt of the world to the flat once more irritated him as though he had wakened from a happy dream. Fingertips pressed steadily against his head above the ears, it seemed; the unfamiliar taste on the back of his tongue he presently located as Bushmill's Black Label. That made him remember the way Richards had left him at the club, and he reached under the flap of the side pocket of the car to the flask of Jamaica. People hate the truth, he decided. That was why Richards had been hating him with all the color pressed out of his tight lips. But the truth is that men ought to be heartier; women ought to be heartier too. You find the truth back in old Rabelais. "Drink." That was what the voice of the oracle of the holy bottle had meant. Be yourself, even the nakedness that alcohol exposes; and if the world doesn't approve, that's because the world doesn't understand—Rabelais, and a lot of other important things.

He took a short pull at the flask, then he took a long one. He took another drink in the way he had learned only a short three years ago, little swallows, rapidly taken, holding the breath. He kept the flask in his hand for comfort and felt the rum work as rum always will, honestly, steadily—no casual flicker but a good strong blaze that warms the farthest corners of the heart.

Then he saw the triangle of lights that announced the house of Cerise Mayberry, over there on the edge of the hills. He tapped automatically on the glass. "The Mayberry house," he said, and Jordan turned and looked at him a tenth of a second longer than he should have dared. Jordan knew too much; but all chauffeurs know too much. That's the way they are.

They left the sticky black of the highway and the big, soft tires went crunching over the gravel of the drive. The dark trees were kindly forms on either side, sweeping him on. A man's home is where his heart is, he felt.

Cerise Mayberry. He called her "Cherry." Cerise is a silly name. Cherry Mayberry was a nice name; there was really something nice about it because it fitted her. It had a sort of rhyme to it. More than a rhyme. Some men have poetry in them. Some haven't. That's all there is to it.

The car stopped in front of the wooden low veranda, with its three steps up. He got out. He remembered that the flask was in his hand and put it back into the side pocket.

Jordan was being chauffeurish. Considering all that Jordan knew, it was foolish for Jordan to step so far back into his manners and look at vacancy as he said, "We're not being late for home—and Miss Louise?"

"I'm only staying a minute," said Campbell. Jordan was crazy about Louise. The cook was crazy about Louise. The wife was crazy about Louise. She was all right. She might even turn out to be hearty if the wife would keep her hands off now and then. What a girl needs is the molding influence of a man, the impress of the wider, the bigger life.

Campbell went up the steps and rang the bell. He got out a cigarette and lighted it. Cerise opened the door and backed up before him into the safe obscurity of the hall before she kissed him. She came right into his arms, bending back her head while she lay there for a moment, with her lips still half-formed after the kiss. Her eyes were loving him.

"Papa, are you blotto?" said Cerise.

He shook himself free. A man ought never to permit flapperisms. The trouble with Cerise was not that she had been married a couple of times but that she had grown up to womanhood in the postwar period, and one could still find in her vocabulary tokens of the days when nothing mattered.

"Don't be cross," said Cerise, and went hastily before him through the door into the living room, slinking a little, looking back over her shoulder, pretending fright.

He followed her with a firm step. "I want to talk to you, Cherry," he said.

"About Rabelais?" she asked.

He realized that she had only been pretending fear. But one of these days she would know him better.

"One of these days you're gunna know me better, Cherry," he said.

"Better Cherry?" said the girl. "There aren't any better cherries. You know that, papa."

"I don't like it," said Campbell.

"Of course you don't like it straight," said Cerise. "You

ought to have lemon juice and things with it. Shall I make you a cocktail?"

"Aw, well. Shake one up," said Campbell.

He sank into a soft chair and tapped his cigarette ashes on the floor. The great thing about Cherry was that she understood. The worst thing about her was that she didn't understand enough. But you can't ask for the world with a fence round it. Everything has to have a beginning. After a while he would be able to teach her. For one thing, a woman ought not to be so damned expensive. A lot of the clothes they buy are name and nothing else.

Cerise came in again with the cocktail shaker. She went at her work heartily; her whole body shook with the vibration; there was even a tremor in her cheeks, and her fluffy sleeves spread into a pink cloud. Pink was her color. She could not use rouge because of the baby tint of her skin; therefore, except for the eyes and the smiling, her face was rather dim, and one had to look into it closely to see faults. Campbell preferred not to see the faults.

She brought two little base-shaped cups of silver filled with cracked ice so that the cups would frost like the shaker. Then she emptied the ice and poured the drink. It was pink—her color. That was the stain of orange juice in the rum cocktail. He tasted the first one and then he drank three, quickly. If cocktails are to be taken, they ought to be drunk before the melting ice has qualified the liquor too much. Cerise had only one; he had taught her never to take more than one because liquor makes the eyes of a woman more unclean than sleep. She sat on the arm of a chair at a little distance because she knew just how to lend herself enchantment. The platinum chain about her throat was merely a line of light; the big emerald of the pendant gleamed like an eye looking this way and that. Her head was tilted back to just the right angle. He liked the consciousness of an art that so perfectly expressed Cerise.

He had been enjoying her silently, like thought, when a football pounced on the little side porch, a door jerked open with force that sent a vibration through the old house and made the two silver cups chime softly together.

"Cerise!" called the voice of young Bob Wilson. "Oh, Cerise, darling!"

She had got to the door almost in time to stop the last words, but not quite. She opened the door a bit and called over her shoulder: "Wait a minute, Bob." Then she faced Campbell.

All he could see was the quick, high lifting of her breast and the green of the emerald, with a price mark tagged on it in his mind. He wanted to kill her, but a man has to take things in his stride, and a good actor improvises to fill a blank.

"I'm sorry I came in so late and stayed so long," he said. "Good night, Cherry. And good-by."

He could see the malice cheapen and tighten her face. What she had to say stiffened her lips. "Maybe I ought to tell you that a *lady* rang up a while ago and asked if you were here. I think it was your wife."

He turned slowly from a room he would never see again though he would keep its corners of laughter and breathless silence always in his mind. He knew bitterly that he

could never wash himself clean of this yesterday. There
was a shadowy half of his thought that told him the un-
cleanness had spread over others; and if Margaret really
had telephoned to inquire for him it meant that she had
known about this affair long enough to lose her most vital
strength, which was her pride.

He was at the door of the hall before the girl said, "Ah,
to hell with you!"

Campbell got out into his car as quickly as possible and
sat back into the cushions with his nostrils widening to
take bigger breaths of the cool evening air. As the car
turned out cautiously into the highway, he had a feeling
that thousands of doors were shutting behind him; but in
spite of that he knew that he would have to find another
road to town so that he might never again see the white,
pointed forehead of that house by day or its triangle of
lights at night.

The automobile, gathering speed, lurched long and high
over a swell in the road; a wave of nausea came up through
Campbell and left a cold tingling in his lips. He settled his
troubled stomach with another pull at the rum flask. The
familiar burn of it put his body at ease before the car
turned into his driveway; the trouble in his mind would
have to be put at rest in another way.

As for Cerise, he thought, a man can't get something for
nothing, and he had been a fool to think that he could go
to Cerise and relax like a tired body in a hot bath. She had
made a fool of him because he had chosen to be off guard.
Merely to be known, merely to be understood is what most
of us desire, as though a divine ray will surely dazzle every

true observer, as though, in fact, clear understanding would not bring a harvest of sneers and laughter. But the end of all is that one must work and never let the mind be still. He had dodged that truth and lost his happiness with his wife by the evasion. He had wished for gaiety and forgotten that the serious souls are apt to be the gentle ones also; and, though he had known that there was gold to be found in her, he had shrunk from the labor. Now he had come home to her "special occasion" drunk or half drunk. He spoke the words softly and then tried to rub the thick numbness out of his upper lip. What he would say to Margaret began to enter his throat and his hands.

The car stopped. He got out and looked at the face of his house, all obscured with vines in which the wind kept up a gently rushing sound, like that of water. He looked higher still to where the brow of the building should have risen according to those old plans which he and Margaret had dreamed out together; but through the ghost of the lost idea he saw now the dark tips of trees and the stars.

In the old days, before he had learned how much money can be made out of large contracts and two-family houses, as a young fool of an architect his thoughts had dealt with marble and with noble space. Perhaps he had been young, but not such a fool. Something in the past was worth taking up where he had left it if only he could find the lost way.

When he entered the house, he bumped his shoulders on each side of the doorway. That was a bad sign. In the still air his face began to burn. Well, Margaret would give him one of her long, quiet looks.

On a chair he saw the shapeless round of a hat and a blue coat with a collar of soft gray fur. He could remember when Louise had first appeared in it and how it had covered the tall stalk of her body and made him see only her face, like a flower.

He went on down the hall until he saw his wife in the dining room doing something with the flowers on the table. The sight of the glasses, each with its thin high light, and the frosty white of the silver made him feel that his hands were huge, witless things. He would sit silently through dinner, breathing hard; the food would have no taste; it would be something difficult, like pigeons; the women would never look at him; they would keep talking lightly.

He frowned and walked boldly into the room. "I'm sorry I'm late, Margaret," he said. He walked up to the table and dropped the knuckles of one hand on the cold, sleek wood. "Were you telephoning for me?" He had made up his mind to unmask the guns and face them.

She straightened from the flowers, without haste. It was always as if one sound or a glance had told her everything. Now she stood through a long moment considering him. She was in the rosy shadow of the center lamp, and it made her so young and so lovely that he was moved. He had to start peering before he could reassure himself about the wrinkles round her eyes.

"Yes, I telephoned," she said. "Was my voice recognized? I'm sorry for that but I thought that I had to risk something. It's a special occasion in a way, and Louise is still quite fond of you."

"All right," said Campbell, nodding as he took it. "All right. But leaving the girl out of it for a minute" —he moved the thought of her away with a slow sweep of his hand—"leaving her out, what about you? You've known a good many things for a long time, I suppose?"

She made one of those indirect answers of which she was a master, and he felt she was troubled not by what had been happening in the past but about the way he would accept her knowledge.

"You know that I'm not a radical, my dear," she said. "I'm a conservative and I believe that we should carry on with the old things—like households, I mean," she added quickly.

"All right," he said. "I know what you mean, and that the rest is a bust." But when he had finished saying this, she merely continued watching him in an anxious way, and he knew that she was hoping that he also would want to be a "conservative." Something was going out of him—the old years—like the swift, dear breath from his body. "Well, where's Louise?" he asked. He would carry on for the moment and afterward he would confront that blank night, the future.

"Louise took a lantern out to the pasture," she said. "She wanted to see Bachelor and Steadfast."

"I'll go out and find her," said Campbell, turning gladly.

"Wait a moment. Don't you want a cup of strong coffee?" she asked.

He saw the sense of that. "Yes," he said, facing about. "Some strong coffee. And put something in it, will you?"

That meant morphine. At least he could thank God that
Margaret had enough brains not to be horrified by the
thought of the drug. She had known, during these last
years, that he used morphine after he had been drinking;
it helped to take the jitters out of the nerves. But now she
kept on in one of her silences for quite a time. He had not
been very sure of his "S" in that last sentence, and perhaps
she was going to be disgusted. He could not be sure, because he could not see her face very clearly. Nothing was
very clear. He wanted another drink. The silence went on
for two or three great seconds.

"Now, look here," he said, "I'm not going to have you
upstage with me." He gripped his hands. The tips of his
fingers slipped on the wet of the palms. Anger rushed and
thundered in him. "None of this damn' pale martyr stuff. I
won't have it. A man takes a drink—why, hell, I won't have
you being the offended saint and all that damn' business.
Get—get me that coffee!"

She actually waited for another moment.

"All right," she said. "I'll bring it to you."

She went through the swing-door to the pantry, opening
it slowly, letting it close so slowly behind her that it made
no swishing back and forth. This deliberation made him
catch in a deep breath of anger and stir a little so that he
saw himself suddenly in the wide mirror above the side-
board, his face deeply set behind the big bright images of
the silver. His hand went up quickly to the bald spot to
cover the sheen of it. He pulled his fingers down over the
soft puffing of his cheeks. He turned his head until he saw
the hanging fold of flesh beneath the chin. Even if he got

rid of his belly, there was nothing to be done about the face; if he thinned it, there would be more repulsive flabbiness of skin to hang about the eyes and the smile.

Margaret came in with her eyes down on the coffee cup. She had a way of giving a religious solemnity, a processional beauty to her smallest movements.

He took the cup. The phial lay on the saucer beside it.

The little bottle was still sealed, and that meant there was a lot of power within the pinch of a thumb and forefinger, a lot of sleep. He kept on looking at Margaret and stealing toward the truth through darkness until he came into the light of full comprehension. She was watching him as a doctor might watch a patient whose chances are doubtful. Of course she had no real hope, but she would fight to the end to keep the home intact to all appearance. That would be for the sake of the girl. He also had once been very near Louise, but that was back in the old days, at the time when he had won the point-to-point on gray Crucible and little Louise had wept with happiness and pride.

"What's the matter?" asked Margaret, with a gasp in her breathing. "What are you thinking of?" And she came quickly up to him.

He put out his hand to keep her away, but his hand patted her shoulder. The drink was beginning to go out of him in clouds. It left the familiar weakness in his knees. The chill that came up through the center of him might be fear or exhaustion. An idea began to flicker into his consciousness, dimly and from far away. When he was alone it would be clear. His wife was coming across years of distance to him. Her eyes begged as though she feared a judgment.

"Smile for me, Meg," he said. "Then go out and keep Louise occupied for fifteen minutes. I'll be in the library, pulling myself together."

She left him hesitantly, forcing herself away. As she reached the door, she tried to smile. "It's going to be all right," said Campbell. Then she passed into the dimness of the hall. Now that she was turned, seeing her slenderness like that of a girl, the sweetness of the past came over him and the vain desire to return to it. It was a sort of homesickness for which the Germans have a better word—home-woe.

He felt sick; he was weak, and yet his mind worked so clearly that he knew this was an end, not a beginning.

As he had promised, he went into the library, carrying with him the cup of coffee, like the bitter conscience that would have to temper his thinking. As soon as he entered it, he regretted having chosen the library because it could never be a place of peace; in those days to which he could make no return he had spent too many hours of struggle and high hope in this room. The big drawing board was still in the corner; he knew every stroke of the unfinished design on it.

He sat down in a deep, soft chair, putting the cup on the little side table. There was no other light than that from the floor lamp beside him. He would have to make up his mind; he would have to finish grappling with that idea which was approaching him from the distance before the coffee was cold.

He was alone. When he looked about, he could recognize only a few of his books which were in light-colored bindings. The Rabelais, for instance, was distinguishable because it was done in unstained levant morocco, and the polished vellum of a photographic reprint of Caxton's Chaucer shone like a lighted candle; but he could not find Thucydides, the clear thinker. The dark red of that leather was lost among sober shadows. But even Thucydides, calm and great, would be little help to him. He had forgotten almost everything except the seventh book, and that was an empire's ruin. He had forgotten too much. In his youth he had done his reading; afterward he had bound the volumes and put them away on shelves.

However, a man should not shrink from being alone. As the panic grew, he wanted to throw open a window and call for Meg, but she could not help; she could not follow where he had to go with his thoughts. It was easier to send the mind back into the past, discovering half-remembered moments of delight, until he arrived, finally, at that picture of the clean-jawed young fighter which stood on the table in Margaret's room. That was the fellow, also, who rode Crucible in the point-to-point. He shrank from that and found himself launched into the future, while his heart sickened. He was not even making money; there, too, he was only a parasite that lived on the past. As for the time to come—well, already he wanted another drink.

So he opened the little bottle and poured it in, to the last crystal.

Then he raised the cup with a strong temptation to pour it all down his throat at a single gulp, covering the irrevocable distance at a stride; but then it came to him that he, who had posed as a connoisseur, ought to proceed with a more civilized deliberation now that he was tasting death. So he only took a good swallow and then lowered the cup gently into its saucer.

The taste was very strong, the bitterness working into the roots of his tongue. The beauty of the thing was that only Meg would know the truth. As for the family doctor, he had understood for a long time that Campbell took morphine and had warned him repeatedly about an overdose.

A soft, warm rushing began in his head, which was proof that even in the single swallow he had taken as much of the drug as made up his ordinary dose. When he took the rest, the end would come quickly. He had expected a last-moment panic which might make him break off with the act unaccomplished, but there was no fear at all. He wanted to run to the window and call in Margaret and Louise. He wanted to tell them that he was about to die but that he was unafraid. This, however, would spoil everything; the best was that Louise should find him smiling. As for Margaret, he ought to leave her a note to tell her what a happiness this was; but still the nature of a woman can be sweetened by some regret.

The telephone rang across the hall, not loudly. Coming at this moment, the call made him smile, for in a little time he would have outstepped even the reach of electricity, and even light leaping forward through millions of years could never overtake him.

The bell was ringing, fading, pausing, ringing, fading,

pausing, ringing. In this modern world we supply ourselves with mechanical bodies, with electric nerves that
reach round the earth, and it is for that reason that we
never can be alone. Someone was calling up to ask them
for bridge or a cocktail party, someone inert, unexpectant
of anything beyond roast chicken and ice cream and high-
balls through the evening, someone who could not dream
that his telephone call was tapping insistently at the door
of death. This fancy charmed Campbell; suppose that he
could open the door wide enough, suddenly, to draw that
unknown with him into the empty darkness!

Then it occurred to him that the noise of the bell might
bring Margaret or Louise suddenly back to the house before the coffee was finished, or at least before the morphine
had done its work. So he put the cup aside and went out to
the telephone.

When he spoke into the receiver, the voice of Cherry
Mayberry sprang out to answer him, like music and a light
pouring into his brain.

"I prayed that you'd be the one to answer. Otherwise I
couldn't have talked. I would have had to ring off."

He said, "I'm busy, Cherry." Yet he wanted to stand
there and listen.

"I know you're busy, but I'll only take thirty seconds.
Will you listen, darling? Will you please listen?"

Does one say of a Stradivarius, "This is a good or an evil
instrument"? Well, concerning women also many a wise
man has cast away the standards of moral judgment and let
the beauty, good or evil, flow into the soul. She was lying;
she was panting from the fullness of her lie, never to un-

derstand how all-knowing death was now helping him to smile. The sweetness and the breaking of her voice plucked at strings near his heart and made them answer.

"Why, I'm listening," he had said.

"I sent him away," cried Cherry. "I couldn't stand his silly young face. It just made the house more empty. I sent him away. I'm not trying to tell you anything. I'm only saying something. Darling, darling, I'm bad. I've always been bad. Maybe I always *will* be bad. Just tell me that you'll see me once more. I don't care why—just come and damn me—just—"

"Steady!" said Campbell. "I'm an old man, Cherry. I'm a soft, flabby pulp of an old man, and you know it."

"I *do* know it," said Cherry. "I know you're soggy with booze a lot of the time too. I don't know why I love you. I don't want to love you. But, oh, God, the house is so empty, and I'm so empty and lonely."

"Hush," said Campbell. "Don't be excited."

"Do you mean it?" she pleaded. "Do you mean I'm not to be excited?"

"Come, come," said Campbell. "This is all nonsense. We'll see about things later on. I have to ring off."

"Don't ring off. Give me ten seconds more to tell you that—"

Firmly, like one delivering a blow with an edged weapon, he struck the receiver back on the hook and stood a moment half smiling and half frowning. Of course she had been lying and yet not altogether lying either. For if you think of a girl like Cherry Mayberry for a moment, you understand that you are considering a tiger that easily will be urged to strike, as she had struck at him this evening. As for young Bob, well, it was true that there was a certain emptiness about his face, and a girl of experience might prefer more maturity. She cost a lot of money, but then there was a lot of Cherry. She had said she knew he was old and soft; she had said that he was soggy with drink a lot of the time too. That was honesty. Between thieves also there is honesty. And perhaps he had become a habit, insidious and surprising to her, an obsession whose force she could not realize until he had walked out of her house quietly without reviling her, in the calmness of strength. Well, he had her back, and after a break the knot is the strongest place in the cord.

The door of the library, dimly lighted, opened before him the straight road to the end of things. Suddenly he clicked his teeth and turned his shoulder to it. The voice of Louise was coming in laughter toward the front door. It was a young voice as thin and clean as rays of starlight and there was an upward springing in it, as life should be at the beginning.

The Sun Stood Still

In the end we come to the beginning. As a boy, Faust
worked on just such a hay-baling crew as the one de-
scribed here. Such experiences shaped his basic notions
of what constitutes manhood and reality. This largely
true story appeared in *The American Magazine* for De-
cember 1934.

THEY SPENT Monday morning moving the hay press
down to the Cooley place and setting it up against the
stack nearest the house. It was a good thing to have an easy
Monday morning because everyone except Bill Turner
went to town on Saturday night and got drunk. Sam
Wiley, the boss, drove to Stockton on Sunday evening and
at the cheaper beer saloons picked up his crew. Some of
them had to be loaded in like sacks of wheat; the others sat
up and finished their drunk with whisky on the way home;
and the whole gang went about with sick faces and com-
pressed lips on Monday morning.

But the evening before, Wiley had failed to pick up the
most important of his men. That was Big George, the best
bale-roller in central California, and his absence was a serious loss.

After lunch, they lay around under the fig trees near the

Cooley house and smoked cigarettes and talked about what they might do when one o'clock came. But Bill Turner did not smoke; neither did he join in the discussion. He was only eighteen, and his long, skinny body oppressed him continually with a sense of youth. His position was that of roustabout, at twelve dollars a week, and, since his bed was a shock of hay and his food came from the cookhouse, the money was clear profit. He would need it in the autumn when he returned to school to work again toward that higher destiny which was his pride; but all summer that sense of superiority had to be stifled when he was the least member of a hay-press crew.

"We might get Cooley to roll the bales for one afternoon," suggested Lacey, the power-driver.

Bill Turner moved his head so that he could see the sleek, repulsively self-conscious face of Lacey. The forelock of his long, pale hair was always plastered down with water whenever he washed for a meal. According to his anecdotes, Lacey was an irresistible beau. He had carried his conquests as far as San Francisco and could name the mysterious and expensive places of the Tenderloin.

"Cooley!" said Portuguese Pete, one of the feeders.

"Yeah, Cooley's no good," said Jumbo, the other feeder.

Bill Turner got himself to one elbow and looked toward the pock-marked face of Jumbo. Except for smallpox he would have been an eminently fine-looking fellow, but that disease had ruined his face as a ten-year sentence had ruined his life.

"Why's Cooley no good?" asked Bill.

Jumbo turned his head slowly, after a manner of his

own, and looked at the speaker with his pale eyes.

"Don't you know why Cooley's no good?" asked Jumbo.

Bill thought it over. Cooley had 1,100 acres in wheat and wild-oats hay which ran ten tons to the acre, this year, and it was said that he was going to get $12 a ton. That might mean $20,000 profit, though it was hard to believe that such a flood of money would pour into the pockets of a single farmer. In person, Cooley was sleek and down-headed, and his jowls quivered a little when he talked or chewed tobacco.

"Maybe he's kind of funny," said Bill thoughtfully, "but I don't see why Cooley's no good."

"You've been going to school, ain't you?" asked Jumbo.

"Yes," said Bill.

"Well, keep right on going," said Jumbo.

Great, bawling laughter came from the entire crew, with the piping voice of Sam Wiley, the boss, sounding through the rest like a flute through the roar of a band.

Bill Turner gripped his hands hard and slowly rolled over on his back again. His face was hot. Perhaps he ought to spring up and throw an insult at Jumbo; but he knew that he dared not face the terrible pale eye of the feeder. It was not so much the fear of Jumbo that unnerved him as it was a renewed realization that he was not a man. Others—yes, far younger lads than he—could take an intimate and understanding part in the conversation of grown-ups, but in some necessary mystery he was not an initiate.

As he lay on his back, he felt his shoulder and hip bones pressing painfully against the hard ground and he told himself that one day, by dint of tremendous training, he would be robed in great muscles; he would be shaggy with strength.

The thin half-face of Sam Wiley came between him and his upward thoughts.

"Listen, kid. You roll bales for this afternoon. Big George, he's showed you how to tie and everything."

"My jiminy!" said Bill, laughing weakly. "I'm not strong enough. Why, I only weigh about a hundred and sixty. I couldn't last it out. Those wheat-hay bales will run up to two hundred and forty."

Sam Wiley drew back.

There was a silence, and someone cursed softly. Then Jumbo said, "Yeah, he's *big* enough. He just ain't got it."

The implied insult was too great to be stomached. Bill sat up suddenly and cried, "What haven't I got?" He heard his voice shrilling, and he was ashamed of it.

Portuguese Pete chuckled. "He wants to know what he ain't got!"

"Ah, hell," said Jumbo, and wearily started rolling another cigarette.

Sam Wiley's face, narrow from chin to brow like the head of a Russian wolfhound, turned again to Bill. He was sun-blackened, except about the eyes, where the wrinkles fanned out in lines of gray. The only thing that was loose was his mouth, which seemed too big for the skull behind it, and that showed all its extra sizes when Wiley spoke.

"You can do it, and I'm gonna give you a shot at rolling bales."

The outfit could average around 40 tons a day; at 18 cents a ton, that made $7.20 a day for the bale-roller—

against the $2 which Bill made as roustabout! Then you subtracted a cent a ton for wear on gloves.

Wiley said, "I'll pay you your regular two bucks and another dollar thrown in—"

"What!" cried Bill, outraged.

"But if you don't stop the power-driver too much, you get the full rate, kid," finished Wiley. "Better go out to the dog-house and look things over. You been in there before."

Being active and willing, Bill had been favored with a turn at all the important jobs, now and then. He had flogged the power horses around their dusty circle; he had handled the big fork on the stacks or out of the shocks which were run up on bucks; he had stood on the table and built feeds under the instruction of Portuguese Pete or Jumbo; and he had even been in the dog-house of the bale-roller, taught by Big George how to knot the wire in a figure eight with one cunning grasp of the left hand. He looked down at that left hand, now, and wondered if it would betray him in his time of need.

"You get away with it, and I'll keep you on the job," said Wiley. "You're a pretty good kid, and Big George is too much on the booze."

Bill left the shade of the trees. The sun fell on him with a hot weight; his shadow walked before him with short legs. As he crossed the corral, he saw the pigs wallowing in the muddy overflow from the watering troughs. They were growling and complaining; some of them had lain still so long that the sun had caked the mud to white on their half-naked hides. They luxuriated half in heat and half in muddy coolness.

Beyond the barns, Bill crossed the summer-whitened field toward the nearest stack against which the press had been set. The stack burned with a pale, golden flame. Other great mounds rose among the acres of Cooley, some of them filmed over by the blue of distance. Every stack was heavy wheat and oats and when you lift a 240-pound bale three-high you've done something.

The shadow under the feed table promised coolness in the dog-house, but that was all illusion; it was merely dark instead of flaming heat. The wide shoulders of the stack shut away the wind. The big hay hooks of George lay on the scales, to the top of which was tied the box of redwood tags for the recording of weights. The iron rod for knocking over the locking bar leaned against the door. These were the tools for the labor. Bill was weak with fear. He had no shoulders. His arms hung from his skinny neck. He remembered the gorilla chest and arms of Big George, but even Big George had to groan in the hot middle of the afternoon. And this would be a scorcher. In the cool beneath the trees around the house the thermometer stood now at a hundred; it was better not to guess at the temperature in the dog-house or to imagine the middle afternoon.

Sam Wiley in person appeared, leading the power horses. The boss as roustabout made Bill smile a little. The other men came out. Jumbo and Portuguese Pete paused beside the ladder that climbed the stack.

"When you get the bale out, slam that door and lock it fast, because I'm gunna have the first feed pouring into the box," said Jumbo.

"Aw, the kid'll do all right," said Portuguese Pete. "Look at him. He's all white."

Pete opened his mouth for laughter but made no sound. He looked like a pig gaping in the heat; he had the same fat smile.

Old Buck could be heard off to the left cursing the black derrick-horse, Cap. The power team was being hitched.

"Five minutes to one!" called Wiley.

"Whatcha want, Pete? The stack or the table?"

"I'll start on the stack. But leave the kid alone, Jumbo."

"Yeah. Maybe," said Jumbo.

They disappeared upward. The boards of the feeding table sagged above the head of Bill. Jumbo let down the apron of the press with a slam. Hay rustled as he built the first feed. So Bill got on his gloves. He left one hook on the scales. The other he slipped over the bent nail which projected from a beam at his right. Sam Wiley was marking an angle with his heel, kicking into the short stubble.

"Put your first bale here, kid!" he called. "Build her twenty long."

It was a terrible distance, Bill thought. If he had to build the stack as big as that, it would mean taking the bales out on the trot and then coming back on the run.

He licked his lips and found salt on them.

"All *right!*" called Jumbo.

Lacey called to his power team. There was a jangling of chains. One of the horses grunted as it hit the collar. The press trembled as the beater rose. It reached the top, the apron above rose with the familiar squeak. The derrick pulleys were groaning in three keys. From far above there was a sound of downward rushing, and the first load from the great fork crunched on the table. It was a big load; a bit of it spilled over the edge and dropped to the ground by the dog-house.

Bill kicked the hay aside because it made slippery footing. He felt sicker than ever.

The beater came down, crushing the first feed to the bottom of the box and pressing thin exhalations of dust through invisible cracks.

Jumbo was yelling, "What you mean tryin' to bury me, you damn' Portugee Dago?"

The apron slammed down on the feed table again.

Bill looked at his left hand. It would have to be his brains. As for the weighing, the tagging, the rolling, the piling, he would somehow find strength in his back and belly for these things; but if he could not tie fast enough, everything else was in vain. The left hand must be the master of that art.

A word struck into his brain: "Bale!" How long ago had it sounded in his dreaming ears? Were they already cursing his slowness?

He leaped at the heavy iron, snatched it up, fitted it in, knocked the locking bar loose. As he cast the iron down, the door swung slowly open. He pushed it wide with a sweep of his left arm. Already Tom had the first wire through. Now the second one slithered through the notch on the long needle that gleamed like a thrusting sword.

A good bale-roller ought to tie so fast that he waits for the last strand and insults the wire-puncher by shouting, "Wire! Wire!" Bill grasped the lower and upper ends of the first one. He jerked it tight, shot the lower tip through the eye, jerked again, caught the protruding tip with his left thumb, pushed it over, cunningly snagged it with the fingers of his left hand, and as they gripped it with his right thumb gave the last twist to the wire. The knot was tied in that single complicated gesture.

The three middle wires were bigger, stiffer. But they were tied in the same quick frenzy—and now he saw with incredulous delight that the fifth wire was not yet through.

"Wire!" he screamed.

It darted through the notch at the same instant and he snatched it off the forked needle.

"Tied!" he yelled, and caught the hook from its nail. He sank it into the top of the bale at the center, and leaned back with his left foot braced against the lower edge of the box. The beater trembled, rose with a sighing sound, slid rapidly upward.

His strong pull jerked the bale out. He broke it across his right knee, swerving it straight toward the scales. With his left hand he caught the edge of the door, thrust the heavy, unbalanced weight of it home, at the same time disengaging the hook from the bale and with it pulling the locking bar in place. He had had a glimpse, as he shut the door, of the down-showering of the first feed, and knew that Jumbo was giving no mercy but was rushing his work even as he would have done if Big George were in the dog-house.

Bill turned the bale end-up on the scales, slid the balance, found 195. The fingers of his right hand, witless behind the thick of the glove, refused to pick up a redwood tag from the box. At last he had it. The pencil scraped on the wood in a clumsy stagger. Who could read this writing, this imbecile scrawl? His teeth gritted as he shoved the tag under the central wire.

Then he rolled the bale out. He had to go faster. He had to make it trot the way Big George made a bale step out on legs of its own, so to speak. He put on extra pressure. The bale swerved. It staggered like a wheel that is losing momentum, wavering before it drops. Then, in spite of him, it flopped flat on its side, jerking him over with the fall.

Somewhere in the air was laughter.

He leaped that bale to its side again, hurrying it toward the angle which Wiley had marked on the ground.

"Bale!" shouted Lacey.

Well, that was the finish. He was simply too slow. With his first attempt he was disgraced, ruined, made a laughingstock. And all of those hardy fellows, relaxed in the profound consciousness of a sufficient manhood, were half smiling, half sneering.

He put the bale on the mark and raced back. All was at a standstill. The power horses were hanging their heads and taking breath. Old Buck leaned against the hip of Cap. Jumbo was a statue on the feed table; Portuguese Pete stood on top of the stack, folding his arms in the blue middle of the sky.

The yell of Jumbo rang down at him: "If you can't use your head, try to use your *feet!* We wanta bale some *hay!*"

But the voice of Jumbo and the words meant less than the sneering smile of Tom, the wire-puncher. He was one of the fastest wire-punchers in the world. Once he had been a bale-roller himself, but now his body was rotten with disease and he walked with a limp.

Bill had the second bale beside the first and was on his way back, running as hard as he could sprint, before that terrible cry of "Bale!" crashed into his mind again.

"Don't go to sleep at the damned scales," shouted Jumbo. "Get them tags in and walk them bales! Here's a whole crew waiting on a thick-headed kid. Are we ever gunna bale any *hay?*"

In the dog-house there was a continual cloud of dust, partly trampled down from the feeding table, partly drifted from the circling of the power team as its hoofs cut through the light hay-stubble and worked into the dobe. Hay dust is a pungency that works deep through the bronchial tubes and lungs; the dobe dust is sheer strangulation.

Life is a hell but real men can live through it. He remembered that. His own concern was to labor through that stifling fog and get the bales out of the way of the feeders. He was doing that now. Sometimes he was clear back to the press and waiting with the iron rod, prepared to spring the locking bar the instant he heard the word "Bale!" The sun was leaning into the west, slanting its fire through the dog-house. He had laid the whole back row of the bale-stack; now he was bucking them up two-high, remembering to keep his legs well spread so that the knees would make a lower fulcrum, always avoiding a sheer lift but making his body roll with the weight.

He laid the row of two-high; the three-high followed. For each of these he had to allow himself a full extra second of lifting time. Big George, when in haste, could toss them up with a gesture, but Bill knew that one such effort was apt to snap his back or knock his brain into a dizziness as though he had rammed his head against a wall. The thing was to rock the bale up over his well-bent knees until the edge of it lodged against his body, then to straighten, lifting hard on the baling hooks, bucking up with the belly muscles and hips and freeing the hooks while the incubus was in full motion. He gave it the final slide into place with his forearms and elbows.

Every one of those three-high bales was a bitter cost. They weighed 200, 220, 240, as the big fork bit into the undried heart of the stack. Bill, himself, a loose stringing-together of 160 pounds. He had not the strength; he had to borrow it from someplace under his ribs—the stomach, say.

Sometimes when he whirled from the stack the world whirled with him. Once he saw two power teams circling, one on the ground and one in the air just above, both knocking out clouds of dust.

When the teams were changed, he caught the big five-gallon water canteen up in his arms, drank, let a quart of the delicious coldness gush out across his throat and breast.

They were baling well over three tons to the hour. That meant a bale a minute tied, taken from the press, weighed, tagged, rolled, piled, and then the run back to the dog-house with the dreadful expectation of "Bale!" hanging over his head.

It was three hours and a half to four-thirty. He piled three and a half full tiers in that time and then found himself in the dog-house with the great iron bar in place, waiting, waiting—and no signal came.

Tom, the wire-puncher, called the others with gestures. They stood for a moment in a cluster and grinned at Bill.

"You poor fool!" said Jumbo. "Don't you know it's lunchtime?"

The mouth of Bill dropped open in something between a smile and a laugh. No sound came. Of course, at four-thirty there was a lunch of stewed fruit, hot black coffee, bread, and twenty great, endless minutes for the eating. The men went out and sat in the shadow of the stack of bales—his stack. He followed them. As he came closer to the dark of the shadow, he bent forward, his arms hanging loosely, and spilled himself on the ground.

Half a dozen men were putting shakes on the top of the barn, somewhere, he thought; then he realized that the rapid hammering was in his body, in his brain, as his heart went wild. Out here the air stirred, faintly; it was hot on the eyes and yet it cooled the skin; and every moment breathing became a little easier.

A heavy shoe bumped against his ribs. He looked up and saw Jumbo.

"Why don't you sit up and try to eat your snack, like a man?" asked Jumbo.

"Yeah—sure," said Bill.

He got the heels of his hands on the ground and pushed himself up against the bale. The rest of the crew were at a distance; their voices came from a distance, also; and the only thing that was near and clear was Mrs. Peterson, their cook, carrying a steaming bucket of coffee.

"Are you all right, Billy?" she asked.

"Yeah," he said. "Why, sure. Thanks a lot. I was just

taking it easy."

"Leave the kid alone!" called the harsh voice of Jumbo.
She shrank away. "Women are always horning in!" he
added loudly.

Bill was still sipping the coffee when Sam Wiley sang
out like a rooster, "Come on, boys. There's a lot of hay
waiting."

Bill swallowed the rest of the coffee and got up to one
knee, gripped the edge of a bale, pushed himself to his feet.
The dizziness, he was surprised to find, had ended. He was
all right, except that his feet burned and his legs seemed
too long.

And then in a moment, with what seemed a frantic hurrying to make up for lost time, the press had started. He
finished the fourth tier, built the fifth, and at the end of it
found himself teetering a heavy bale on his knees, unable
to make the three-high lift. The terrible voice of Jumbo
yelled from the stack, "Hurry it up! Are we gunna bale
any *hay?*"

A rage came up in him; he swung the weight lightly into
place as Lacey sang out, "Bale!"

The sun was declining in the west and he remembered
suddenly that the day would end, after all. He was not
thinking of seven dollars; he was thinking only of the
sacred face of night when at last he could stretch out and
really breathe.

But the sun stuck there. It would not move. Somewhere
in the Bible the fellow had prayed and the sun stood still—
Joshua, wasn't it?—while the Jews slew their enemies. Now
the sun stood still again so that Bill Turner might be slain.

He still could tie the wires and take the last of the five off the needle. He could get the bale out and roll it. But even the two-high lift was an agony that threw a tremor of darkness across his brain. That place from which the extra strength came, that something under the ribs, was draining dry.

Then, as he came sprinting to the cry of "Bale!" he heard Jumbo say, "He *could* do it, Pete, but the kid's yellow. There ain't any man in him!"

Bill Turner forgot himself and the work he was doing with his hands. He forgot the watery weakness of his knees, also, remembering that somehow he had to kill Jumbo. He would devise a way in fair fight.

And suddenly the sun was bulging its red-gold cheeks at the edge of the sky.

"That's all, boys!" Sam Wiley sang out.

And here were the feeders coming down from the stack; and yonder was the familiar cookhouse streaming smoke on the slant of the evening breeze. Someone strode toward him from the stack of bales.

"Look out, kid," said Tom. "There comes Big George, drunk and huntin' trouble. That means you. Better run."

He could not run. He saw Big George coming, black against the west, but he could not run because his legs were composed of cork and water. He got to the scales and leaned a hand on them, waiting. Lacey, wiping black dust from his face, said, "You poor fool, he'll murder you."

Big George came straight up and took Bill by the loose of his shirt; he held him out there at the stiffness of arm's length, breathing whisky fumes. It was not the size of

George that killed the heart of Bill; it was the horrible contraction of his face and the crazy rolling of his eyes.

"It's you, eh?" said Big George. "You're the dirty scab that tries to get my place?"

"He ain't got your place, George!" shouted Sam Wiley, running up. "He only filled in while—"

"I'll fix *you* later on," said Big George. "I'm gunna finish this job first or—"

"You can't finish a job," said the voice of Jumbo.

"I can't do what?" shouted Big George.

"Take off your hat when you talk to me," said Jumbo. Big George loosed his grasp on Bill.

"Hey, what's the matter?" he demanded. The magnificence and the fury had gone out from him as he confronted the pale eye of Jumbo. "Hey, Jumbo, there's never been no trouble between you and me—"

"Back up and keep on backing," said Jumbo. "Get your blankets and move. The kid wouldn't run from you, but you'll run from me or I'll—"

It was quite a soft voice, with a snarling that pulsed in and out with the breathing, and Big George winced from it. He shrank, turned, and in a sudden panic began to run, shouting, with his head turned over his shoulder to see if the tiger followed at his heels.

"The kid didn't stop the press today, and he won't stop it tomorrow, Wiley," said Jumbo. "If he ain't good enough to roll your bales, I ain't good enough to work on your stacks."

"Why, sure, Jumbo," said Sam Wiley. "Why, sure. Why not give the kid a chance? Come on, boys. I got a heap of fine steaks over there in the cookhouse for you."

They were all starting on when Bill touched the big arm of Jumbo.

"Look, Jumbo," he said. "All afternoon I didn't understand. Thanks!"

The eye of Jumbo, too pale, too steady, dwelt on him.

"Aw, try to grow up," said Jumbo.

Supper went with a strange ease for Bill. No one seemed to notice the shuddering of his hands even when it caused him to spill coffee on the oilcloth; eyes courteously refused to see this, and the heart of Bill commenced to swell with a strength which, he felt, would never leave him in all the days of his life.

Toward the end Lacey said, "About three o'clock I said you were finished, Bill. I waited for you to flop. Well, you didn't flop."

"No," said Portuguese Pete, "you didn't flop, Bill." He grinned at the boy.

"Ah, you'd think nobody ever did a half-day's work before!" said Jumbo.

That stopped the talk but Bill had to struggle to keep from smiling. He was so weak that the happiness glanced through him like light through water.

Afterward he got a bucket of cold water and a chunk of yellow soap. He was the only one of the crew that bothered about bathing at night. Now, as he scrubbed the ingrained dirt and salt and distilled grease from his body, Sam Wiley went past to feed the horses, and the rays from his lantern struck the nakedness of Bill.

"And look at him," said the voice of Lacey out of nothingness. "Skinny as a plucked crow, ain't he?"

Bill got to the place where he had built his bed of hay, under an oak tree away from the circle of the other beds, because the snoring of Portuguese Pete had a whistle in it that always kept him awake. Half in the blankets, he sat up for a time with his back to the tree and watched the moon rise in the east beneath a pyramid of fire. He made a cigarette with tobacco and a wheat-straw paper. The sweetness of the smoke commenced to breathe in his nostrils.

Now the blanched hay stubble was silvered with moonlight as though with dew and, as the moon rode higher, turning white, a big yellow star climbed upward beneath it. That must be Jupiter, he thought. When he turned to the west, the horizon was clean, but in the east the Sierra Nevadas rolled in soft clouds. This great sweep of the heavens made him feel it was easy to understand why some people loved the flats of central California. It had its beauty, and the breath of it was the strange fragrance of the tarweed which later on would darken the fields with a false verdure.

He had never been so calm. He had never felt such peace. All the ache of his muscles assured him that at last he was a man, almost.

Then a horrible brazen trumpeting rolled on his ears, seeming to pour in on him from every point of the horizon; but he knew that it was the jackass braying in the corral. Before the sound ended, he put out his smoke and slid down into his bed, inert, sick at heart again. Somehow it seemed that even the beasts of the field had power to mock him.

Through his lashes, he saw the lumbering form of Portuguese Pete approaching with a bottle in his hand. Pete was stopped by another figure that stepped from behind a tree.

"What you gunna do with that?" asked the hushed voice of Jumbo.

"It's good stuff," said Pete, "and I'm gunna give the kid a shot."

"No, you ain't," said Jumbo.

"Yeah, but I mean the skinny runt lifting those bales—this'll do him good."

"Leave him sleep," said Jumbo. "Whisky ain't any short cut for him. Come along with me and I'll finish that bottle with you. Tomorrow we'll see if the kid can take it, really."

"You kind of taken a fancy to the kid, ain't you?" asked Pete as they moved away.

"Me? Why, I just been kind of remembering, is all," said Jumbo.